SAVING GRACE

SAVING GRACE

BY

CELIA GITTELSON

ALFRED A. KNOPF

NEW YORK

1981

THIS IS A BORZOI BOOK
PUBLISHED BY ALFRED A. KNOPF, INC.

Copyright © 1981 by Celia Gittelson
Copyright Conventions. Published in the United States
by Alfred A. Knopf, Inc., New York, and simultaneously
in Canada by Random House of Canada Limited, To-
ronto. Distributed by Random House, Inc., New York.

Library of Congress Cataloging in Publication Data
Gittelson, Celia. Saving grace.
I. Title.
PS3557.183S2 1981   813'.54   81-47520
ISBN 0-394-51776-8   AACR2

Manufactured in the United States of America
First Edition

FOR MOM AND MOKE AND EVE AND TONY,
WITH GREAT LOVE

"As long as I lived in my cell in the monastery I felt safe for my salvation. When I was appointed Bishop, my certainty began to fade, and, as Pope, I am not safe at all about my salvation."

POPE ST. PIUS V

SAVING GRACE

I

LEO HAD SLEPT FITFULLY. It was not unusual; the Supreme Pontiff was more and more the victim of restless nights. Now he awoke with a start; his legs shot out as if to break a fall. At five o'clock, a pale crescent moon grew paler in the morning sky; soon it would be invisible. Outside near the fountains, the pigeons were already alert. They cooed loudly, wrangling among themselves for the crumbs left behind on the piazza by tourists. *Il Papa* could hear their angry cries.

The first early morning traffic was careening up and down the Via della Conciliazione, the wide avenue that ends in the awesome embrace of St. Peter's Square. Through the heavy drapes and musty, thick old walls of the Apostolic Palace, the bleat of automobile horns and the squeal of brakes mingled with the voices of the pigeons. A truck rattled by, shifting gears rhythmically.

Leo XIV lay on his side, his eyes open, drenched in sweat that had been warm during the night but now turned icy. His right hand was curled in a fist below his chin. His mouth hung open, the tongue coated in a gluey film, the pillow damp beneath his cheek. He could not clearly reconstruct what had happened in his sleep, although he was certain that it had not been dreamless.

What he did remember frightened him. Lately his nighttime world quaked with monsters: headless angels, hunchbacks, hermaphrodites. Sometimes *il Papa* saw himself among them. Old and enfeebled, he was leaning upon the altar with crabbed hands, clinging to it for dear life.

He dreamed of his recent election to the Chair of St. Peter and, on the ceiling of the Sistine Chapel, the hair of God turned black, green, brown and writhed with snakes. Then he found himself pinioned in a cage in which the yellow walls were smeared with excrement and an elephant lumbered about, watching him with censure in its tiny, wrinkled eyes. Other dreams consisted only of a repetition of words and phrases from the Scriptures; but even these were distorted, absurd, or outrageous, as if based on an infantile misunderstanding of the text.

Weeks passed when every night Leo dreamed of celebrating the Mass. The lights were bright in the basilica as nonsense spilled from his lips and the whole world watched his performance, aghast. The liturgical order was disrupted. At one moment he intoned *Sanctus, sanctus, sanctus, Dominus Deus,* and at the next he was borne aloft over the heads of an outdoor throng on his *sedia gestatoria,* wearing three bowler hats, one on top of another. Then he sat before the great altar about to deliver a Christmas sermon. The gigantic bronze columns of Bernini's *baldacchino* revolved like barber's poles. But in his dream, Leo looked up to discover that the canopy and the double dome of St. Peter's had disappeared, replaced by a clear, star-filled night. And when he looked down, the Vicar of Christ saw that the pages on which the sermon should have been written were blank! Panic jolted his heart.

Il Papa pulled the blanket over his head. The room in which he slept was chilly. A window had been left open. He knew he would

I

LEO HAD SLEPT FITFULLY. It was not unusual; the Supreme Pontiff was more and more the victim of restless nights. Now he awoke with a start; his legs shot out as if to break a fall. At five o'clock, a pale crescent moon grew paler in the morning sky; soon it would be invisible. Outside near the fountains, the pigeons were already alert. They cooed loudly, wrangling among themselves for the crumbs left behind on the piazza by tourists. *Il Papa* could hear their angry cries.

The first early morning traffic was careening up and down the Via della Conciliazione, the wide avenue that ends in the awesome embrace of St. Peter's Square. Through the heavy drapes and musty, thick old walls of the Apostolic Palace, the bleat of automobile horns and the squeal of brakes mingled with the voices of the pigeons. A truck rattled by, shifting gears rhythmically.

Leo XIV lay on his side, his eyes open, drenched in sweat that had been warm during the night but now turned icy. His right hand was curled in a fist below his chin. His mouth hung open, the tongue coated in a gluey film, the pillow damp beneath his cheek. He could not clearly reconstruct what had happened in his sleep, although he was certain that it had not been dreamless.

What he did remember frightened him. Lately his nighttime world quaked with monsters: headless angels, hunchbacks, hermaphrodites. Sometimes *il Papa* saw himself among them. Old and enfeebled, he was leaning upon the altar with crabbed hands, clinging to it for dear life.

He dreamed of his recent election to the Chair of St. Peter and, on the ceiling of the Sistine Chapel, the hair of God turned black, green, brown and writhed with snakes. Then he found himself pinioned in a cage in which the yellow walls were smeared with excrement and an elephant lumbered about, watching him with censure in its tiny, wrinkled eyes. Other dreams consisted only of a repetition of words and phrases from the Scriptures; but even these were distorted, absurd, or outrageous, as if based on an infantile misunderstanding of the text.

Weeks passed when every night Leo dreamed of celebrating the Mass. The lights were bright in the basilica as nonsense spilled from his lips and the whole world watched his performance, aghast. The liturgical order was disrupted. At one moment he intoned *Sanctus, sanctus, sanctus, Dominus Deus,* and at the next he was borne aloft over the heads of an outdoor throng on his *sedia gestatoria,* wearing three bowler hats, one on top of another. Then he sat before the great altar about to deliver a Christmas sermon. The gigantic bronze columns of Bernini's *baldacchino* revolved like barber's poles. But in his dream, Leo looked up to discover that the canopy and the double dome of St. Peter's had disappeared, replaced by a clear, star-filled night. And when he looked down, the Vicar of Christ saw that the pages on which the sermon should have been written were blank! Panic jolted his heart.

Il Papa pulled the blanket over his head. The room in which he slept was chilly. A window had been left open. He knew he would not fall asleep again, but fatigue wracked his brain. There was a light, reverent tapping at the door. *"Grazie,"* he whispered. The tapping came again, this time more insistent: three sharp knocks. Leo pushed aside the blanket. *"Grazie, mille grazie,"* he called, irritable, sitting up and throwing his legs over the edge of the high, narrow iron bed. In one motion, he descended to the floor, knelt, and began his prayers. His lips moved rapidly, as if reciting from a worn lesson book, then were still as he passed several minutes in silent meditation. Gathering up the long skirt of his nightdress, he hastened to the door.

A childhood injury caused Leo to walk with a slight list; on bad days, when the weather was damp or his mood was low, it became almost a limp. Although usually imperceptible to others, it was nevertheless of sufficient magnitude to produce within him a lifelong feeling of being off balance, his internal scales faultily weighted. Sometimes moving forward could seem to him not so much a natural thing as an action he had consciously to will. Outside his door, Leo picked up, as he did every morning, a tray holding an earthenware mug and two small pitchers, one of steaming milk and one of strong coffee. Placing the tray on his bedside table, he retired to the bathroom.

As simple as the Papal bedroom was—bed, bureau, plain chair, wooden crucifix—the decor of the Papal bathroom (over which *il Papa* exercised less control) was ornate. Its opulence distressed him. The four walls were of the finest marble, and on the one facing the door, over the toilet, hung a gold crucifix from the seventeenth century. It was not that he liked this room too little, he thought, but that he liked it too much. There were mornings when he spent nearly a quarter of an hour dawdling in the bathtub, preparing to face the day.

Long enough and deep enough for two grown persons, the tub—riding on immense brass claws—appeared ready to pounce. White towels drooped like luxuriant jungle flowers from metal bars beside the sink, behind the door.

Three elderly nuns cared for *il Papa*'s private apartment. Each time he washed his hands they changed the towels; every time he slept in his bed they put on fresh sheets; in the morning after he shaved they furnished his razor with a new blade. When his knobby big toes poked holes into his socks, they insisted on buying new ones at once. "No, sew them up. The slippers cover everything," he said. They could not do enough for the Servant of the Servants of God, and he, in turn, was fond of the sisters. In their gentleness, they reminded him of his mother, who had died when he was only seven. As often as he could, Leo invited the inseparable old women to have coffee with him; on official occasions he saw to it that they were provided with good seats, three in a row, and he tried, by a nod or a smile and a wave, to acknowledge their presence in the midst of thousands.

Now he stood before the mirror over the sink, trying to calm his sleep-tossed hair, using the same stiff pig-bristle brush he had used as a cardinal and, before that, as a bishop—a few things never changed. Leo's hand trembled as he lay down the brush, regarding himself in the glass. The reflection showed a handsome man: His black hair was thinning on top and flecked with silver. He had a long, slender nose, intelligent hazel eyes, and a high, smooth forehead that seemed almost to radiate light. His complexion was quite fair, uncommon for someone born south of Rome; a fine network of veins was visible just under the skin. His lips were full and sensual. He was six feet tall. His physical attributes, and the fact that he was only fifty-four years old, had occupied not a little space in the world press since his election eighteen months before. Speaking one day to a reporter from *L'Osservatore Romano*, the Vatican daily newspaper, he remarked sadly, "I sometimes fear that people remember me more for the way I look and for the way I behave than for any of the ideas that I try to express."

The choice of the then Cardinal Giuseppe Bellini as Holy Father had not been without its detractors. Indeed, the campaign of persuasion both for and against proved to be intense. Some maintained that he was too young to be named spiritual leader of the Church. Others found him guarded in his dealings, contentious at ecclesiastical gatherings, too political, not political enough, excessively devoted to the Blessed Virgin and likely to lead the Church into Mariolatry. Still others complained that Bellini, unwilling or unable to retreat from positions he took, would stay up all night hotly debating some trifling point of canon or civil law. One cardinal called his colleague "an angel-and-pin man." Yet in normal, everyday conversation, someone else pointed out, he seemed to ask at least as many questions as he answered, and to enjoy listening to the stories of strangers as well as friends. "A good quality for any Pope," as one of his compatriots grudgingly admitted, "but, let us be candid about it, not determining."

Bellini's wartime issuance of hundreds of false baptismal certificates to Jews and gypsies—he had worked in the chancery in Naples at the time—pleased and reassured certain factions and dismayed others. His decision was the cause of controversy, but under such extraordinary and extenuating circumstances he had resolved that, humanly, he could not do less.

Two days before his election, Cardinal Bellini paced the floor of the cell he had been assigned at the Vatican. Wringing his hands, close to despair, he gasped: "A few more days and the axe may fall on me!" He had spent many hours upon his knees, until his flesh felt soldered to the wood of the prie-dieu—until it was almost more painful to rise than to remain kneeling—praying fervently, in anguish, for some sign from God. But He kept His silence, unyielding to Bellini's persistent pleas. "Perhaps I do not yet know how to pray," he said, finally, getting to his feet. "Then I must be content with the darkness and trust that He is by me, merciful God." Bellini drank a little red wine poured from a bottle he kept in his traveling bag, and opened up a quarterly journal of socialist thought. The words frolicked before his eyes, mocking him. The door creaked and a fellow cardinal entered, uninvited.

"*Buona sera.*"

"*Buona sera,*" Cardinal Bellini said, closing the magazine on his thumb.

His colleague looked disapproving. "Don't you think it's somewhat, ah, sacrilegious to carry that sort of stuff in here?"

"I am extremely curious. I read all that I can in order to keep informed. On this point at least," Bellini replied, opening the journal again, forcing the encounter to a conclusion, "my conscience is clear. It is on a deeper level that I feel unrest."

The next morning, the Sacred College of Cardinals convened for the first time in the Sistine Chapel. The cardinals' thrones ranged along the walls with tables set in rows before them. Outside a storm raged, and thunder could be heard, along with the faint blasts of police whistles and the noise of cars. Giuseppe Bellini sat near the front of the chapel, studying a graphic, life-size wooden crucifix positioned over the altar: Christ's chest pierced, blood flowing freely, ribs straining against their pitiful container of flesh. The face of Jesus mirrored resignation, patience, grief, exhaustion.

Six tall candles, each as thick as a man's forearm, stood on the altar. The cardinals, dwarfed by the vaulted ceiling, eyed one another furtively across the room. The air—still and warm, smelling of something sweet—turned Bellini's stomach. Cologne? he wondered. Hair oil?

Several minutes passed. One of their number could have risen spontaneously to propose a candidate, thereby moving for election by way of inspiration; then the others, also moved by divine inspiration, might have signaled their approval by calling out *"Eligio!"* That way, a Pontiff would have been quickly elected. But this was not to be: the hall was silent, no man stirred.

So the election would be "by scrutiny," and at last the process began. With the others, Bellini inscribed his choice on a card under the words *Eligio in Summum Pontificem.* On the first vote the results were widely scattered among ten candidates. Then, threaded on a silk cord, the ballots were placed in an iron stove that rested at the far end of the chapel and burned on a bed of damp straw.

At the luncheon recess, the members of the Sacred College ate from round tables set up in the Borgia Apartments, in the room known as the Sala dei Pontifici; then each man went to his individual cell for what was prescribed as a period of meditation. Instead, many took the time to consolidate strength for a particular *papabile.* Smoking cigars, sipping expensive cognac brought in from outside, they met in their rooms, and in the corridors, whispering tensely in small knots.

Cardinal Bellini stayed in his cell. But during the afternoon, several of his brothers came with the news that the field was so broad, with factions pulling in so many directions, that sentiment was steadily mounting in his favor. It began to seem that, in the end, he would be the compromise candidate. Bellini sat on his pallet, his hands in his lap, listening quietly, confining his comments to innocuous pleasantries. He kept his own counsel, in part because he had not yet sorted out what he felt: dread, terror, hope, gratitude, the call of destiny?

At three o'clock the men returned to the chapel, depositing one more ballot. This time, Bellini had the edge. After supper they went back to cast yet another vote. No final decision was reached, but now it appeared certain that by the next day Cardinal Giuseppe Bellini would be elected. The time had arrived for him to speak. He rose in his throne. The eyes of all in the room were hard upon him.

"My conscience compels me to address you this evening. What I have to say is simple, and I say it humbly. I have reviewed my feelings over many sleepless nights: I, among all of you, am unworthy and incapable of the papacy. I have none of the qualities it demands. I am neither a diplomat, a politician, a tactician, nor an administrator. In these last days I have come to realize that I am, in my heart, a country fellow, that is all, with no fervent wish to become involved in a world larger than the one I now administer. I ask you to allow me to return to my former life. In your wisdom," he continued, his voice quavering, "I beg you to forget me and to give your votes to a more zealous candidate. . . . For the love of God, forget me, please!"

That night, lights burned late. The other cardinals debated among themselves, holding their hushed conferences in the hall directly outside Bellini's cell. He heard muffled voices raised in argument, then lowered in assent; he listened to the rustle of cassocks, and the gentle scuffing of slippered feet on the hard floor. Doors opened and shut as the cardinals canvassed their elite and tiny neighborhood.

At midnight, the Italian Cardinals Lisi and De Giolio and the French Cardinal Never confronted the candidate in his cell. On his knees on the floor, Bellini held his head in his hands, his elbows resting on a low wooden bench. As he prayed, he pondered all he knew of papal history, aware that, through the course of centuries, those who had tried to turn away in fear, agitation, or uncertainty had been obliged to turn back.

Precious few Popes had ever actively desired the office, after all. St. Gregory the Great, upon learning of his election to the Chair of St. Peter, persuaded some merchants to carry him out of the Vatican in a basket meant for transporting vegetables to market. For three days and nights he wandered, taking his rest in the caves and forests outside Rome. Eventually a search party discovered him, led to the place, it was said, by a towering pillar of fire. Gregory agreed to return, submitting to the will of God, but no less dismayed than before by the responsibility of his spiritual primacy.

To John, Patriarch of Constantinople, Pope Gregory later wrote: ". . . I know how steadily and anxiously you tried to escape the burden of the episcopate, yet you have done nothing to prevent the same burden from falling on me." (Bellini knew the words by heart.) "It is clear you do not love me as yourself, for you wish me to bear the burden which you were unwilling yourself to carry. Worthless and weak I have taken charge of an old ship very much battered; the waters break in everywhere, the rotten timbers creaking in the daily storm threaten shipwreck; hence I ask you for Almighty God's sake to give me by your prayers a helping hand in this danger."

To another friend, Gregory wrote, "When you so beautifully picture the sweets of contemplation, you renew my lamentations at my ruin, for I recall what I have lost when I was raised without merit to the highest dignity of government." (Bellini dwelled on the long-dead Pontiff's letters.) "Know that I am so stricken with grief that I can scarcely speak, a cloud of sorrow dims the eyes of my soul, everything looks gloomy, and what others think pleasant seems cheerless to my heart. . . ."

Cardinal Lisi coughed raucously in the quiet of Bellini's cell to gain his attention.

"Remove these chains," Bellini pleaded, getting to his feet, approaching him. "Tell them to do me this act of charity."

"*Sua Eminenza, si faccia coraggio, il Signore L'aiuterà,*" Lisi replied. Tears clung to Bellini's lower lashes. "*Grazie, molte grazie.*"

"The Church throughout the world is in great difficulty," the other Italian, Cardinal De Giolio said, softly. "The strength will come to make all the decisions you are called upon to make."

Bellini bowed his head.

"There is no longer any doubt," Cardinal Never declared, speaking in French, "that you will be obliged to accept . . . and soon. The balloting now goes in your favor."

"Has everyone closed his ears to my wishes?" Bellini asked, addressing the paunchy Frenchman in his own language.

"Rather than lowering the esteem of the Eminences, you have raised it by your excellent modesty." Never held his round hands under his belly, as if to keep it from sagging.

Bellini nodded.

"A man of your humility, learning, and wisdom must not turn away from Rome."

"Humility perhaps, but neither the learning nor by any means the wisdom you imagine." His voice was raw.

"Your learning is above reproach . . ."

"Not really. I fear that my emotions may be more profound than my intellect." Bellini saw himself tossed like a chip on the high winds of events beyond his command (or over which he had somehow relinquished command). He gazed silently upon his earthly achievements and perceived them as so much wreckage, heaving their splinters in all directions. One of them had caught him in the heart and lodged there.

". . . As to your qualifications for the papacy," Cardinal Never was saying. "Well, only the Lord can finally judge that. You would be well advised to leave it to Him."

"Tell me," Bellini asked, "simply because a cross is a cross, does it necessarily follow that it is the cross God means for you?" Silence prevailed. "May I not decline both the burden and the honor?"

"Decline, if that is your wish," De Giolio said harshly, the conversation reverting to Italian. "But it is cowardice, not modesty. And you will be haunted by it for the rest of your life."

This time Bellini did not flinch. "I am no coward," he said. "However, I must confess—I feel ill-equipped for earthly cares. I fear that I shall lose sight of heavenly ends."

"It is just that fear which recommends you to us."

His tormentors knew no mercy. Perhaps somewhere in his depths, Bellini was prepared to run, but they would not permit his escape. They persuaded him to sit on his bed and arrayed themselves around his stooped frame. A single dull table lamp caused the figures of the men to cast long, ill-defined shadows across the floor.

"Accept it. The Lord requires it. The Sacred College is doing His will! It is inconceivable that you should refuse," Never insisted.

Lisi, a tall, diffident man, adjusted his red skullcap. "Any man who disobeys the unmistakable word of God takes his mortal life into his hands."

"As I have been trying to communicate since our arrival here, it is the fate of my immortal soul that worries me," Bellini replied, a new edge in his tone. Then he looked up at them, vanquished at last, and said, as they knew he would: "But may His will be done."

"Be strong, *Eminenza*."

The Sacred College came together again in the morning. As the second balloting commenced in the afternoon, Giuseppe Bellini knew that he would be Pope. The cardinal closed his eyes, sinking into deep prayer.

At six in the evening, as the bells of St. Peter's rang the Angelus, the ballots burned clean. A puff of white smoke, rising pure as a cloud, announced to the crowd—both anxious and convivial on the piazza surrounded by the colonnades—that there was a new Vicar of Christ.

Four cardinals, old men with skin as thin and white as tissue, got up from their thrones and came toward Bellini. They held on to each other for support: One man licked his chalky, cracked lips as if savoring an experience he would never live to enjoy again. Bellini listened to their raspy breathing.

"Reverend Lord, the Sacred College has elected thee to be the Successor of St. Peter. Wilt thou accept pontifically?" they asked in unison, in Latin.

He did not answer immediately—at the moment of decision, still unreconciled. "If it is not possible that this shall pass away, then may the will of God be done."

The cardinals scowled. This was not the proper response.

"Reverend Lord, the Sacred College has elected thee to be the Successor of St. Peter. Wilt thou accept pontifically?" Bellini was asked a second time, more loudly.

Once again, he pondered before speaking.

"I accept it as a cross, in obedience to our Lord, and in total confidence in His mother, the most Holy Madonna." He paused, and proceeded so softly that only those men nearest him could hear. "I pray only that the cross is meant for me to carry. *Miserere mei Deus* . . . *Miserere mei Deus!*"

The canopies on all the thrones, save for the throne of the new Pope, billowed down. The members of the Sacred College struggled to their feet as quickly as age and weak legs would allow. Soon Bellini left the chapel, passing through a small door behind the altar that led into the sacristy, the *camera del pianto,* the room of tears.

Under the supervision of the secretary of the conclave, the sacristan—a bird-faced, effeminate man with shaking hands—looked over the new Pontiff like a tailor. Both men assisted Bellini to dress. Although he was six feet tall, and towered over them, such was their fluster that they presented small, medium, and large white silk soutanes for fitting. The small garment did not close across his chest. The medium, too short at the wrists and ankles, "failed to make a statement one way or the other," according to the secretary of the conclave. The large was settled upon, although this too needed alteration. Pricking himself several times with safety pins, the sacristan's nerves got the better of him; he began to sniffle while tacking up the new Pope's drooping hem.

"Hush!" the secretary of the conclave muttered.

"One more Successor to St. Peter has been elected," said Bellini gently, reaching for something to set the beet-colored gentleman at ease. "Such things have happened before. It's not the end of the world."

Finally, Bellini had assumed all the garments of his office: white soutane, white hose, sash, the pectoral cross, red slippers embroidered with gold crosses, the red cape trimmed in ermine, the pallium, and the gold-embroidered red stole. Turning to the sacristan, he asked for a glass of water.

"*Ha sete?*" the man said, alarmed, as if he could not imagine for the life of him where fresh water might be found.

"*Sì,*" Bellini replied. "*Il Papa* gets thirsty too."

The water was brought. After drinking most of it, Bellini wet three fingers, applying them to his throbbing eyes. Then the secretary of the conclave kneeled and offered him a white *zucchetto,* the papal skullcap.

"By what name shall you be known?" the cardinals requested, when he returned to the chapel. He hesitated. By what name? . . . It was not a question to which he had given thought.

Then he knew. "I will be called Leo." Leo XIV. His predecessor—in name—Leo XIII, known as "The Workers' Pope," had cried upon his election, "They want to kill me, not make me Pontiff!" A noble tradition.

Each morning, in winter and summer, at exactly six-thirty, Leo celebrated Mass in a chapel adjoining his bedroom. His private secretary and confidential aide, Monsignor Francesco Ghezzi, served the Mass from the very first day. Sixty years old, with thin, bluish lips and skin, and heavy circles beneath his cool, inward-gazing green eyes, Monsignor Ghezzi looked like someone from whom the blood had been recently drained. Two pairs of thick-lensed glasses hung from silver chains around his neck, and his severely pointed Adam's apple was visible over the collar of his cassock. Ghezzi's movements, somber and precise, were those of a man who carried the book of regulations in his head. His posture was so rigid that his spine might have been an iron rod rather than made of human bone. It announced to all in his presence that he knew better than anyone—including *il Papa—the way things went.*

The monsignor was never separated from his small tablecloth of a handkerchief with which he constantly poked and prodded his hooked nose. "Perhaps he keeps his brains in his nostrils, and he wants to be sure they are still there," *il Papa* said to himself one day, not long after making Ghezzi's acquaintance. A strain of wry humor, which until then he did not know he possessed, helped him survive those early months.

Leo experienced some remorse because, even as time passed, he could not summon more love for the glutinous, adhesive little man. His secretary was always by his side, directing Rome's swiftly moving traffic around and away from this national monument, this international treasure—his sole responsibility—*il Papa.* But neither could Leo find it in his heart to have Ghezzi transferred elsewhere. Most of the priest's life had passed inside the walls of the Vatican, much of it within the bosom of the pontifical family. It was home to him.

Every morning, after Mass, the two men sat reading the breviary. It did not take *il Papa* long to notice that Ghezzi always licked his index finger to turn the pages, as though browsing in a popular magazine. This habit made him unreasonably cross, and he cringed inside, eager for the monsignor to go away and leave him in peace. Leo liked to spend a few quiet moments alone in the chapel following Mass—the only time that his mind rested, and his imagination cooled.

Time passed slowly. The days varied so little that sometimes *il Papa* felt entombed. At seven-thirty, he ate a light breakfast with Monsignor Ghezzi and the *Maestro di Camera,* Monsignor Alfredo Rocca, a golden blond man in his early forties. A pink scar ran down Rocca's forehead, across his cheek, and under his chin, disappearing behind the collar of his black cassock. Otherwise his face was smooth, unlined and immature, as if trapped forever in puberty. Leo wondered from time to time if the scar itself might have caused this odd effect, stitching the skin over his face so tightly that he would never seem to age. No one knew where or how he had been so disfigured, and Rocca never spoke of it. Vatican gossips put it out that, as a youth, the monsignor had been the leader of a street gang at the port of Ostia, and that his cut was the result of a scuffle over a woman's handbag. It was said that during his convalescence at a hospital staffed by nuns, he experienced a miraculous conversion at the hands of a young sister, and upon his release, joined the seminary. But who ever knew the real truth of things?

Antonio di Paolis, *aiutante di camera,* Leo's valet, always acted as waiter at the morning meal. A servant of Pontiffs for over thirty years, Antonio was convinced that, like a woman, he menstruated every month. Although he did not bleed, in his own mind he experienced all the symptoms: lassitude, abdominal cramps, weeping, swelling of the chest. Now in his later years he endured change of life, complaining of flushes and profuse sweating. Today, Antonio stood several paces behind his master's chair. The few wisps of white hair left on his head wreathed his skull like smoke. He wore a short white jacket, too tight for him, and held a silver tray in one gloved hand.

Monsignor Rocca, drawing a finger absent-mindedly across his scar, scribbled a note to himself on a piece of paper. He opened a leather-bound folder on his lap.

"Grace please, Father," Ghezzi reproached his colleague.

"Ah, sì, scusi."

Rocca closed the folder that contained a list of the Holy Father's appointments for the day, clasped his hands, and repeated the customary thanks for the gifts they were about to receive. Leo glanced at the younger priest out of the corner of his eye: He crossed himself sloppily—a bored, limp-wristed gesture, executed somewhere in the vicinity of his left eye.

He watched Monsignor Ghezzi take a dainty bite of roll, remove his handkerchief and snort gustily. It amused *il Papa* to fancy that his secretary must have ordered pockets sewn into the arms of his cassocks for the express purpose of storing this linen. Then he berated himself for his disrespect. Glancing back and forth between the two priests, it came into his mind that Pius IX was only one of many popes to see himself as a "prisoner of the Vatican."

Light played on the long oak table from a great crystal chandelier that blazed day and night. The table was set with heavy silver, fragile pale blue china, and white napkins. Leo leafed through a morning newspaper drawn from a stack of them at his elbow, running his eyes quickly up and down the crowded columns of type. A yellow canary he now kept as a pet perched on the table. Every so often he reached over with one hand and offered the bird a crumb or two of bread, sometimes dipped in jam.

"You think Edoardo's putting on weight?" *il Papa* asked. Edoardo paraded in a neat circle around Leo's coffee cup.

"Well, you are exceedingly good to him, Holiness," Rocca replied.

"Perhaps a little less bread at breakfast," Ghezzi agreed.

The bird paused beside Leo's cup on a sheaf of documents, the daily news summary, that demanded *il Papa*'s attention.

"Anything of particular interest to you, Holiness?" Ghezzi asked, thrusting Edoardo away with the back of his hand.

"Much of it is of interest, but none of it is good," Leo replied, lifting his head. "I grieve for the mortal, not to say the spiritual, life of the planet. What, I often wonder, what can be my role in such a world?" The Monsignori Ghezzi and Rocca exchanged looks.

Leo closed the paper. "Antonio, would you come here for a moment? I have something to ask you."

The valet shuffled to the Pope's chair. "*Sì*, Holy Father?"

"Did you remember to tell the kitchen that my sister will take lunch with me this afternoon?"

Antonio shook his head. Leo restrained a grimace. Why should the men of the Vatican be more efficient than men elsewhere? "If I tell you again now, do you think you will remember, or shall I myself let the kitchen know?" he asked, speaking to the old man not without affection.

"I will."

"You will tell them, my friend? You won't forget?"

"I will. *Non si preoccupi.*"

"What will you tell them then?"

Antonio thought. His lower lip trembled. "*Non lo so.* Tell me once more, Holiness, what I will tell them." His eyes watered, but it was hard to tell whether the man was perspiring or crying.

Leo took the napkin from his lap and handed it to Antonio. "Here, wipe your face. There's no need to become upset, no need at all. Just say that my sister, Signora Cavagna, will be joining me for luncheon today. We shall eat alone. Can you remember that?"

Nodding, Antonio repeated his instructions: "Your sister. *Sì.* For lunch. *Sì.* Alone! This I can remember!"

Monsignor Ghezzi and Monsignor Rocca sat in Ghezzi's office on the floor below *il Papa's* study. The walls were hung with paintings: a portrait of St. Francis of Assisi, a Madonna and Child with Saints, and a monochrome of St. Jerome, all by anonymous Tuscan masters. On the far wall, a tall glass case displayed, among other religious articles, a monstrance with a golden cherubim as its pedestal, and a collection of seventeenth-century glass pitchers, their spouts in the form of birds' heads, which once held holy oil and water. When Ghezzi received his appointment to the pontifical family, he had ordered certain works and artifacts from the Vatican museum moved to the Apostolic Palace. Many had wound up in his private study.

"Never tell him!" he had admonished the other members of the household staff when Leo first assumed office. "Or he'll insist that I give it all back. He's that sort of fellow—but he doesn't need to know everything. It's better that these treasures come to live with us. We can appreciate their beauty. Why should they hang in those drafty halls where stupid tourists roam who ask only 'Where is the cafeteria?' 'Where are the bathrooms?' 'Where is the Pope?' "

The two priests sat across from each other in deep armchairs upholstered in rosy velvet. Rocca lit a pipe with a gold lighter that flamed like a torch.

In this hour before lunch, Leo was alone in his study, reading, thinking, writing. Earlier in the morning—meeting with cardinals, bishops, and the heads of congregations—he had received reports from missions all over the world. The cardinal prefect of the Congregation for the Propagation of the Faith appeared a few times a week, as did the president of the Vatican Council, and the pro-secretaries of state. Vatican finances were vast and complicated. The chief of the Special Administration was educating Leo in the magnitude of the Church's holdings. *Il Papa's* afternoons were as busy as his mornings, with private audiences extended to important diplomats, heads of business and industry, and the leaders of foreign countries visiting Rome. Leo worried that he never had enough time to spend with those he believed needed him most—the sick, the dying, the defenseless, the forgotten. As he said to Alfredo Rocca one day in the middle of a pastoral visit to a hospital, "The favors of the powerful are meted out only to the powerful; and we continue to neglect the neglected of the earth."

Although accountable to no human authority in affairs either spiritual or temporal, Leo felt responsible to everyone at once. Church politics was difficult and complex. Men's wishes, needs, and desires came into conflict. Consensus was never finally reached in matters of faith. Bitterness could be left in the wake of the slightest reinterpretation in a point of doctrine. Even the canonization of a saint provided an occasion for violent disputes to erupt: What constituted miraculous intervention to one camp was mere coincidence, simply accident, to another. In worldly affairs, *il Papa* was seen by some as an anachronism, constrained by the very nature of the Church's enterprise, unable to adapt himself fully to rapidly changing times. Indeed, his office was deemed by many critics as a mere scrim for the bureaucratic, often Byzantine, workings of an oppressive empire.

The telephone rang often in Leo's study, and he enjoyed taking certain of the calls himself. Visitors, as well as those on his staff, were struck by his informality. When absorbed in paperwork, he would sometimes absently wipe his pen on his soutane; or, during the blistering Roman summer, dispense with his robes altogether and attend to business in his shirtsleeves and a pair of cotton trousers.

Il Papa had, too, a natural and irrepressible appetite for "getting about," as Monsignor Ghezzi referred to it with some dismay. One late afternoon in the middle of the first winter of his Pontificate, a frantic call went out: "The Pope is missing!" For an hour and a half, the staff—led by Ghezzi—searched the Vatican from top to bottom in a desperate attempt to locate the Primate of Italy. Monsignor Rocca received a casual telephone message near dinnertime: Leo and his driver had taken the car and gone to visit a convalescent home some miles outside Rome. A few weeks later, Leo was discovered in one of the basement offices of the Vatican, having a cup of tea and trading stories with the janitors. "It is quiet down there, I like the conversation, and they brew better tea than Antonio serves me," he explained when reprimanded.

Not long after these events, Monsignor Ghezzi instructed the Roman police to station two motorcycle *carabinieri* at the exit of the Apostolic Palace. They were to follow the Holy Father whenever his personal limousine pulled away from the gate, whether Leo waved them off or not.

"He is entirely too restless, if you ask me," Ghezzi said to Rocca, gesturing toward the ceiling with the penknife he was using to pare an apple. Over the heads of the monsignori, the floorboards creaked. "Listen to him—like a caged animal—up and down, up and down, all day long. Not a good sign, Alfredo," Ghezzi warned. "But of course it has been coming . . . from the beginning, I suppose."

"Sometimes I meet him in the corridor, in the evening, on his way to the kitchens for a glass of milk. He nods and goes on as if he hardly recognizes me," Rocca said. "How many times have we told him that if he wants something, anything at all, he must ring for

it? Still, he persists. The Holy Father will not accept that his life has changed; he is no longer a parish priest, and hasn't been one for twenty years or more!"

"It's true." Monsignor Ghezzi popped a piece of apple in his mouth. "Well, at least he has not got through the gates again lately and disappeared, the way he used to. But just yesterday the shoemaker, Faccialorda, came by to fit him for a new pair of slippers. When it was over, I found him walking with the man down the Scala Regia to the courtyard. To the courtyard! If I had not stopped them, I believe he would have escorted the shoemaker all the way to the Piazza del Risorgimento. As soon as Faccialorda was on his way, I said, 'Pardon me, Holiness, but I think I have suggested more than once that taking a *stroll* is absolutely out of the question. It is not done.' "

"And what did he say?" Rocca asked, leaning forward.

" 'This is my home. I was showing a guest to the door.' "

"That's it?" Rocca said, chewing up a mouthful of rich cherry smoke.

"That's all. Oh, yes. Later he admitted he had been rude to me. 'I have not yet adjusted to my status as Supreme Prisoner,' he said; then promised that he would try to keep the regulations in mind. Of course I need not tell you that I do not believe him for a moment. His Holiness is always experimenting, always testing in strange ways this thing or that thing. All the time, he seems to be exploring the limits of every situation. Some would say that this is an appealing quality. But I don't find it to my liking."

"Just today," Rocca chimed in, his voice growing high and querulous, "he invites his sister to lunch. But instead of telling me about it, he takes it into his head to pass the word through Antonio—that senile old man who does not know the time of day or the day of the month!" Suddenly Rocca chuckled. "He used to know the day of month, when his . . . *woman's* calendar was in, ah, order. Still, I quite dislike . . ."

"It worries me, Alfredo, that Signora Cavagna is descending upon us again," Ghezzi interrupted the younger man. "She's been here too much lately."

"D'accordo," Rocca said, drumming his fingers over the crevice in his face, which, when it itched, was a torment. "She's no good for him. She's worse than he is. They both behave as though to become the Successor of the Prince of Apostles may be the worst tragedy that can befall a man. His sister reminds him of another time, of his dead past—before he came here, no doubt even before he took his orders."

"The past is never dead. It is only the past."

"Yes. Therefore the less we see of Cecilia Cavagna, the better."

Ghezzi consumed the last slice of his apple, closing the penknife with a snap. "And that is your duty, Alfredo. We should not arouse his suspicions, but in the future let us have no more of these solitary luncheon hours into which he can simply slip his sister. Since he does not follow tradition, and hates to take his meals alone—I believe he would invite a gorilla to sit with him to avoid that—please make certain that he has official visitors scheduled. Or else you and I must join him. I don't much care whom you invite, as long as it's not that woman. Besides, solitude brings introspection and, in him, introspection gives rise to doubts."

II

THE CLOCK STRUCK ONE as *il Papa* sat alone at the long dining table. His guest was late for lunch. Sunlight glanced off the crystal goblets casting a rainbow of refractions on the walls. From St. Peter's Square came the far-off sounds of afternoon: the shouts of children, the ringing of bicycle bells, the cries of hawkers who sold postcards, souvenir keychains, maps of the Holy City, plastic replicas of the *Pietà* lit from within, and large paper sheets bearing portraits of the present and former Popes.

Out of the tall windows at the far end of the room, Leo could see the rooftops of Rome. In the distance, on top of Janiculum Hill, he observed the long, low building that housed the Propaganda Fide College, the seminary for all nations. He recalled his days as a student, and the swirl of color that seemed always to surround him then: the scarlet soutanes of the German and Hungarian seminarists, called *gamberi cotti,* "boiled lobsters"; the Scots in purple; the Greeks in blue with red belts; the Poles in black with green belts; the Americans in black with blue piping . . . He wondered to himself if some future Vicar of Christ was at this moment studying there. Would there ever be a Pope from Nigeria? From Argentina? From Brazil? He sighed.

As Bishop of Rome for nearly two years now, Leo had already made two trips abroad. At every stop, he was greeted by exultant throngs. They cheered and sang for him, waving flags and homemade banners, all clamoring to reach *il Papa,* to catch his eye, if only for a moment. Their demands were often strongly personal, not quite transfigured by spiritual concerns. All his life, he had spurned adulation, public or private. Now, as Pontiff, it required an act of will to remind himself that it was an inevitable consequence of his exalted position. Nevertheless, he maintained a certain distance as he moved through the throngs, smiling, offering his blessing, and moving on, as parts of his person were grasped, then reluctantly released.

But no act of will could control his unsettling dreams. The monsters that had besieged him in his sleep had made way for another apparition, in its way no less alarming. The girl smiled and addressed him by his baptismal name, "Giuseppe," as if they were old friends. She had begun to haunt him, whether asleep or awake. He knew her well by now, since they met night after night and day after day: she, reclining nude on the main altar of St. Peter's at a shocking travesty of a High Pontifical Mass, her legs crossed demurely, her long hair falling like a veil over her breasts; he, in full vestments, including the cope, the mitre, and the long pastoral staff.

She called him closer and he went, putting aside the staff and lifting a heavy chalice of wine. For a moment, he held it aloft for the gaping congregation to behold, then he tipped the cup, spilling its contents over the girl. "Let us proclaim the mystery of faith!" he said, as the liquid slipped down her haunches and a purple stain spread over the pristine white of the altar cloth. He could not erase this vision of the woman, or of the wine that turned the ends of her light brown hair dark against her luminescent skin. . . .

Now a commotion in the hall outside the dining room startled Leo out of his contemplations. The door burst open. A short round woman in an unfashionable black dress and a raspberry-colored coat bolted across the threshold. Two plastic mesh shopping baskets and an armful of smaller parcels weighed her down. "Giuseppe! Peppe!" she wailed, racing toward *il Papa,* her arms outstretched. "Darling Peppe!"

Monsignor Rocca trailed the woman, the old wound on his face inflamed to pomegranate. "I asked her . . ." he said between his teeth. "I pleaded . . ."

"Ah, Peppiniello! *Bambino!* Your priest told me I must wait to be announced and I said to him, 'Since when are sisters *announced* to their brothers? Since when?' But he chased me all the way—two flights!" She paused. "Cowboys and Indians!" she cried in English. "I must sit down or I'll die!" Cecilia Cavagna's black hair, beginning to grey, was disheveled; long, sweaty tendrils escaped from a bun at the nape of her neck. Her plump face, worn but still young, shone with perspiration.

"Yes, sit down, Cecilia, and catch your breath. You must not die. I need you too much for that." Each time Leo saw his older sister, he began to miss her almost as soon as she entered the room, already anticipating the moment when she would have to leave.

"I tried to explain to her, Holy Father, about our procedures. I tried to make Signora Cavagna understand that we cannot just have *persons* . . ." Rocca glared at her, "wandering about the halls. Please excuse me, but there is proper conduct and improper conduct. Your own safety is at stake. Relax the rules for one guest—"

"*Sì, sì, Padre,*" responded Leo.

"Procedures? Rules? For the public, for *outsiders,* there are rules—but I am his closest living relative," Cecilia interrupted. "For me, we—" She looked up at Rocca. "—we throw away the book!

Capisce? This is my brother's household now. You are not the warden in a penitentiary."

Monsignor Rocca scowled wordlessly.

Leo smiled. "It seems that a streak of anarchy runs through the hearts of the Bellinis like an arrow. Either one of us is trying to break in, or the other is trying to break out," *il Papa* said softly, turning in his chair to Rocca. "I will speak to Cecilia. Forgive us for the disturbance."

Rocca made a brittle little bow, as though he might break in half at the waist. The door slammed as he left the room. The forks and knives on the table jumped.

". . . So she will get a divorce as soon as she can. The marriage is over."

Leo did not reply. His eyes betrayed him to his sister; he was only half listening.

"Giuseppe, do you hear? My best friend, Susanna, you remember her?" Leo nodded. "She is getting a divorce."

"That's unhappy news. Very unhappy."

"Her husband beats her."

"Are you sure?"

"I have seen the welts. Last week, her black eye, it looked like an eggplant riding on her face!"

Leo shook his head in sorrow. "Has Susanna talked to her priest? Has she gone to him?"

Cecilia clapped her hands to her head. "That's the trouble! Her husband refuses to go with her. He hasn't even been to Mass in over a year. She has to go alone with the children. But here's my question, Giuseppe . . ."

"*Sì?*"

"Susanna needs a special dispensation."

"I don't hand them out over lunch," Leo reminded her. "And that is not a question, but a bald request."

"Don't make fun of me. This is important. She needs a dispensation so that she can continue to receive holy communion."

"Divorced Catholics cannot receive communion. That's the law, Cecilia."

"Then perhaps you ought to change the law—and in a hurry too. Put it on your calendar. What do you *do* here all day? Anyway, in the meantime, just for Susanna, please make a little exception." Here, the sister's tone grew coaxing. "We'll keep it quiet, I promise. A secret between the three of us. All I need is, is ..." She searched her mind. "A note! A note that she can show to her parish priest saying that, after the divorce—if that happens and God knows it won't be easy!—the priest may go on giving her communion."

Leo shook his head, slowly and firmly.

Cecilia blushed, balked, and studied her brother's face. He did not look well to her. His stubborn streak had hardened into something more disturbing.

"Are they feeding you? You're thinner and meaner than I've ever seen!" Signora Cavagna put a hand on her brother's flushed forehead. "And you're warm, too, Giuseppe. Are you running a fever?" Leo felt his own forehead, then shrugged. "Do you eat at all?"

Despite her unwelcome intercession on behalf of friends, he relished the fact that she had arrived. "I eat, but I haven't much appetite."

"You were always a serious eater. Your stomach was as big as the Piazza del Popolo." She paused. "Blessed Mother of God! When I first heard the news of your election I knew that a great misfortune had befallen us. I wept tears of mourning, like when Mama and Papa died, and I said to myself, 'Why must they take my brother? He is young. I will never see him again!'"

"You see me ... from time to time."

"But it's like talking to a man who looks like you, yet inside himself is not you."

Il Papa turned away. All his life he had withheld much of his true nature and his feelings from everyone, including Cecilia, whom he believed he loved. Even as a small child, he could walk around for days weakened by fever and no one in the family knew. In those times, when Cecilia spoke to him, sometimes his answers were honest and almost complete, but more often he was evasive, hiding behind feigned irritation and unfinished thoughts. One moment he might allow intimacy, and the next grow remote, staring into the distance with glassy eyes.

Still, Cecilia's love for her brother persisted, and although she did not possess an original mind, Leo understood that his sister had a unique and tender spirit. There were some women—she was one— who loved purely, without worldly regard for what they received in return. They did not keep in their hearts ledgers of debits and credits. As a child, Leo had been soothed by Cecilia's attention, especially since their own mother had been taken from them too soon; it was only as he grew up that he had become wary of Cecilia's sentimentality.

She placed the palm of her hand on his cheek. "*Bambino!* I brought you some wonderful surprises, all your old favorites: *cannelloni, tortellini, minestrone, sfogliatelle,* cherries, eggs from our farm. They have nothing decent to eat here in the city."

"Cecilia," he said, wagging his finger and smiling, "this is God's city."

Signora Cavagna stared into the plate of *spaghetti alle vongole* that Antonio di Paolis dropped, more than set, before her. The clam sauce was loose and formed a brackish pool around the edge of the dish. "There was a time when you would have thanked me."

"Well, of course I thank you! I only mean to say that whatever I want, I need only ask for it. You are not the Red Cross. There is no disaster here." He put his hand on Cecilia's. "Tell me something: How are my nieces and nephews? And Pio?"

"They are all well, thank God. It is you who concerns me. What bothers you, Giuseppe?"

Taking a long sip of wine, her brother clutched his glass so tightly that his knuckles grew white. "Nothing," he said at last. "You worry like a hen."

"Because I am a hen."

"Then confine your anxieties to your children and your husband—your own family."

"You are my family."

"Not in the old way," he replied, a note of sadness lowering his voice. "Anyway, my troubles are mine—and are inevitable under the circumstances. They should not be yours as well." He thought what he might tell her, without telling too much.

Cecilia ran her thumb under *il Papa's* eyes. "Look, Peppiniello, you're exhausted. Such rings here . . . and here! Do you sleep?"

" 'Do you sleep? Do you eat?' Dear Cecilia, I am not your little boy, I am your brother. My position is not an easy one. Certainly sometimes my appetite is affected and my sleep is disturbed."

"Then you must insist: More time for rest, more time for simple pleasures!"

"If it were only feasible . . . but it is not feasible," Leo said. "As it is, many of my colleagues complain about me. 'Nothing is being done.' 'The Holy Father spends too much time on his knees,' they say, 'waiting for divine inspiration.' '*Il Papa* says Mass in the mountains and in the meadows. He writes and studies far more than he should, and makes too many pastoral visits to schools, hospitals, and prisons. He travels around the world as the work of the Church piles up . . .' "

Leo toyed with the glass in his hand. "Meanwhile poverty grows worse, the weak suffer more, and I am less confident than ever that God hears my prayers . . ."

He heard himself pouring out his woes, realizing, abashedly, how irascible and contentious he had become. "They want a bureaucrat or a banker, not a Pope! I often believe their final ambition is to install an accountant in the Chair of St. Peter."

Leo gulped his wine. "And so life goes on. The situation worsens steadily in every part of the globe. Meanwhile, my voice—the voice of the Church—dies away, reported everywhere but heeded practically nowhere. Perhaps this is the fate of the modern Papacy, Cecilia: to bear witness to horrors which one can do nothing to prevent."

Leo twirled the stopper on the wine decanter. "Do you know how I spend most of my time?" he asked. "This morning I met first with the director of the Special Administration. He read me a budget for a project of which I had never heard, I did not approve, and could not understand. Then, three bishops from the United States—a circus act, if ever I saw one—reported from their notebooks on the habits of American Catholics, which they said had been compiled by a computer. 'Attendance at Mass,' the first man told me, 'is down five percent in the last seven months.' 'And,' said the second, 'there has been a gross decline in the rate of confession—on the other hand, communions keep going up.' 'Baptisms,' the third chimed in, 'are climbing at a nice one-and-a-half percent a year.' 'Yes,' the first man agreed. 'But it seems that we begin to lose them quite soon after birth.' When I asked the bishops to tell me about the mood and the preoccupations of the faithful in their country, they were not friendly to my questions. I suppose it irked them that I did not attach enough honor to their statistics.

"These men meant well, I know. And this study of theirs undoubtedly cost thousands of American dollars to prepare . . . But that makes it all the worse. The rest of the morning was taken up with reading official documents. Monsignor Ghezzi put them under my nose one after the other—enough to kill a man if the pile fell on him all at once. I am ashamed to admit that I skimmed them indiscriminately. My secretary assured me it did not matter—just routine—and whisked everything away." He hesitated. "Not that it was so different when I was a bishop, even a cardinal . . . only now, it is worse. Because I am who I am."

Cecilia examined her brother's countenance, which had turned pink, both from the wine and emotion.

"An ocean of men flow about me, ceaselessly, moving in and out like the tides," he continued, dreamy now, as if carried on the tide of his own recounting. "Rocca waits, day and night, to pounce on me, to throw a shawl over my shoulders, to protect me from a chill that I myself cannot feel. If I take a walk in the gardens, security guards monitor my route, crouched behind hedges and fences, contriving accidental meetings with me between the rows of trees. Some of them carry little radios on which they communicate with their commander, when they believe I am out of earshot. But I hear the static clearly. I always hear the static."

Helping himself to another glass of wine, Leo emptied the decanter. Only a shallow ruby puddle remained at the bottom.

Cecilia gazed at *il Papa* in pity and terror. "Enough," she said, shaken. She stilled his hand as he lifted the goblet to his lips. "You don't eat, and you don't sleep, and you drink too much. That's all I know—what I can see with my own two eyes."

He put down the glass. "You have only this to say? I bare my soul to you and you tell me that I drink too much? Sometimes the evidence of your eyes is not definitive." His pink face grew red. "Besides, their Excellencies Monsignors Ghezzi and Rocca remind me often enough of my shortcomings, of my neglected obligations, of my trespasses, and my mistakes. Have you *nothing* better to do than come here and add to their list of criticisms?" He caught himself, regretful. "It's only wine. We grew up on it."

Signora Cavagna frowned. "You ought to look elsewhere for solace, Giuseppe."

"I look to God for solace, not to alcohol." He smiled. "But lately He has not looked back."

Cecilia stood abruptly, pushing her chair back with such vigor that it rocked on its legs. "Well, as you have told me many times, He is a hidden and inscrutable God! And since you refuse to help yourself, I will have to take the first step."

Leo sat back in his chair, his hand on his chin, remembering their mother as he watched her.

"You must go away," Cecilia said.

"Away? Where? To Castel Gandolfo?" His spirits rose at the thought of going anywhere.

"No. Everyone would follow you there. No! To my house, to the country. Tomorrow you tell those jailers of yours that you are going to visit your sister and her family. You will stay with us until you have . . . recovered."

Leo drew his hand across his face, as if to defend himself against her vision. "In the first place, I am no ordinary prisoner. They will bar the doors and wall up the cellar to prevent my getting out. Besides, a trip to the country cannot 'cure' this . . . malady, whatever it may be. Your hot meals will not set everything straight."

His sister rattled on as if she had not heard him. "No bishops, no budgets, no Ghezzis and Roccas. There will be nothing to disturb you—only sunshine, fresh air, prayer, and serene thought. You will find your peace and your place among living things."

"Listen to me," *il Papa* said. He stood up to confront her. "I cannot leave. There are 'living things' right here, and pressing business, too, whether it suits me—or you—or not."

Signora Cavagna's eyes flashed. "There will always be pressing business! Where does it say in canon law that the Pope cannot rest? Without some relief—and soon—mark my words, there will be another conclave before you have grown much older. As it is, you are serving no one well: neither the Church, nor yourself."

She regarded her brother quizzically. "You know, I've never really understood you, Giuseppe. All your life, I've watched you close yourself away within yourself. But if you cannot respond to simple human affection, then how can you expect to love God? And how can you expect that He will love you, and bring you under the influence of His grace?"

The Holy Father, attempting to smile at his sister, failed. But even a smile, he knew, would leave those questions unanswered.

Arranging himself at one end of the sofa, Leo spread his skirts loosely over his legs. He was nursing a headache, brought on by the wine of lunch. His conversation with Cecilia still engaged his mind. Two young priests, aides of Francesco Ghezzi, moved swiftly and silently around *il Papa,* preparing for the customary stream of afternoon business visitors. They set out bulging Manila folders, pens, writing tablets on the long marble coffee table before him. Leo gazed at the men with a combination of chagrin and envy—chagrin at the quiet complacency with which they worked; envy at the tidy containment of their chores: small tasks, neatly accomplished, completed by sundown.

Soon the door opened. Monsignor Ghezzi entered first, followed by Monsignor Benito Pecci, secretary of the Institute for Religious Works. The Institute was, in point of fact, a bank. It had been established in 1942 by Pius XII to administer the funds for religious work, and it operated much like any other bank, albeit with priestly tellers.

Pecci was a man of middle height and years who had recently been diagnosed to have a muscular disease that in time would reduce him to jelly. He wobbled a little as he walked, his arms held unnaturally close to his body. In one hand he carried a slim black attaché case. He wore gold-rimmed half glasses on his face, which was speckled with white blotches near his eyes and nose. Leo rose as the men approached, and helped Pecci to sit down beside him on the sofa. Ghezzi assumed his usual position in an armchair.

"The purpose of this visit, Holiness, is to present some financial plans that need your approval before we may proceed," Monsignor Pecci began respectfully, but without preliminaries. "The first matter I would like to bring to your attention is of deep concern to us." Pecci opened one of his folders and leafed through its contents. "Savings deposits are down—alarmingly so—in the first three quarters of this year. If you will kindly look here . . ." He pushed a sheet of ledger paper bearing columns of figures toward Leo, sidling down the couch with it as he spoke. ". . . you will read the sad tale."

Il Papa stared dumbly at the page: Gross capitalized assets. Long-term amortized liabilities. Projected fourth-quarter liquidity. His eyes resisted the numbers. He shifted on the couch. "Monsignor Pecci, you are generous indeed to assume that I can make sense of these tables," he murmured. "But where, exactly, does one find evidence of this decline in deposits which causes you to worry?"

"Here, Holiness," Pecci pointed to one column with a pen, "and here again." He ran the pen down a second column.

"As you can see, over the last three consecutive quarters, we have experienced a steady deterioration in our short-term cash position, as well as a strain on available reserves. Projecting this trend into the next quarter—assuming we divest ourselves of marginal investments—we suspect that our net fourth-quarter liquidity . . ." Pecci's voice grew faint as he realized that Leo was not paying attention. "Am I going too fast, Holiness?"

"Yes. I am afraid that I find the language of bankers somewhat
... abstruse. Perhaps it might be helpful if you just explained the
problem to me—in your own words."

Disappointed, Pecci closed the file from which he was reading.
"When deposits plummet, we worry, Holy Father."

"Ah. *Sì*. Well, I assume you have a proposal," Leo leaned back on
the sofa, "for altering this dismal state of affairs."

"That is why I am here." Pecci retrieved the page of numbers,
while at the same time he thrust into *il Papa's* hands an even
thicker set of papers. "According to a survey we conducted recently—funds for which you personally approved," Pecci added in a
nervous aside, "our bank may be available to too few depositors.
Presently only religious are permitted to open accounts with us—
also, of course, residents of the Holy City, diplomats accredited to
the Holy See . . . Therefore, it seems that this may be an opportune
time to open the Institute of Religious Works to the general public."

Leo frowned. "It seems a rather radical strategy. The Church already owns a controlling interest in the Banco di Santo Spirito.
Haven't we ventured far enough into the world of commercial
banking? Besides, who but the most devout—no, the most fanati-
cal—would care to open an account in a bank with only one
branch?"

"We have considered the inconvenience for those who do not
actually live and work in Vatican City, Holy Father. We believe we
can mitigate against it: The Institute for Religious Works will offer
. . . gifts!" Pecci glanced at *il Papa* expectantly.

"Gifts?" Leo was puzzled. "Am I to understand by this, bribes?"

Monsignor Pecci looked pained. "That is a harsh word to use. In
America, banks do this sort of thing every day."

"If we were to follow America in everything, I would have to
run for re-election every four years."

Pecci continued, undeterred. "You see, in order to attract new
depositors, banks elsewhere offer some small enticements: a toaster,
a television set, a stuffed animal wearing perhaps a little business
suit."

"What 'enticement' does the Institute for Religious Works have in mind?" Leo squinted. "Teddy bears," he said, breaking into English, "in cassocks?"

Monsignor Pecci reached inside his attaché case and withdrew yet another sheaf of papers. "We have assembled some modest proposals," he replied, casting a pained look in the Pope's direction. "For example, someone has suggested, Holiness, that we might offer—to small depositors—a Vatican calendar with twelve different four-color photographs of yourself." Pecci regarded Leo over the tops of his glasses. "As the seasons change, so would your attire and surroundings. In July and August we might feature you at Castel Gandolfo; in December at midnight Mass; for the New Year you could give us an ecumenical theme and pose with a . . . rabbi? Holy Days of Obligation could be outlined in red; feast days in blue; secular holidays in . . ." He was unable to think of a color.

Pecci continued quickly. "Depositors of more impressive amounts would receive more substantial dividends. We propose tours of those parts of the Vatican normally closed to unofficial visitors. For instance, the gardens, the offices of *L'Osservatore Romano*, the radio station . . ." Pecci paused, glancing up from the paper to gauge Leo's reaction. *Il Papa*'s lips were parted. Pecci thought he looked stricken by some gastric upset.

"Finally, for those persons who could be persuaded to deposit quite considerable sums of money—I want to emphasize here, Holy Father, the words *quite considerable*—we would offer various tokens, personally blessed by yourself."

Leo sucked in his breath. "Such as?"

The bank executive placed the papers on his lap and folded his hands over them protectively. "Um, someone suggested strands of your hair embedded in plastic. Not tufts, you understand, just single strands . . ."

Leo shook his head, in which the ache had intensified. "Monsignor Pecci, your ingenuity and that of your staff is admirable. Unfortunately, I cannot sanction a scheme which calls for the Institute to pluck the hairs from my scalp—not that I value them so highly—in exchange for deposits of a few million *lire*. In addition,

I do not wish to bless any object that will be used merely to encourage investors—even in so noble a bank as yours. I hope you will understand."

Pecci did not understand.

"Please leave your plan with me," Ghezzi suggested to the ailing monsignor. "I will discuss it further with the Holy Father at his leisure, after he has had time to consider the bank's promotion more carefully . . ." He rose and gave Pecci his hand. "I must, however, regretfully inform you that we have run out of time."

Monsignor Pecci looked crestfallen. "There is one more particularly urgent request, from the Dominican Sisters. They feel it is high time . . ."

A blue vein palpitating near the temple on the left side of Leo's head caused Ghezzi to catch his breath and guide the agitated priest toward the door.

". . . the sisters feel *strongly* that the moment is long overdue . . ." Pecci called out weakly over his shoulder as the door shut behind him.

III

A WEEK HAD PASSED since Cecilia's visit. On Saturday the sky turned a muddy green, then black, contorted with clouds. That morning, little Edoardo left Leo's shoulder and flew through an open window in the library. The heavens seemed too big for the tiny bird, and the brewing storm too frightful. Spray from the twin fountains whipped in various directions, obedient to the breezes. People hurried for shelter in the walkways between the columns and in the magenta, burnt orange, red, tan, and yellow tour buses that were parked directly on the piazza.

Il Papa remembered his first Sunday blessing on just such an ugly day—the sound of his own voice as it echoed, weirdly amplified within St. Peter's Square; and, after his blessing, the almost funereal tolling of the bells, slow and heavy, the terrible crash of history in their peals.

Leo recalled when his superiors first took notice of him, offering a post in the chancery: He would become Monsignor Bellini. . . . Even then, reluctance and dread had assailed him. A quiet country parish seemed much sweeter. At most of the crucial junctures of his life, he had deferred to wishes other than his own.

"It is commendable that you do not lobby for position, that you seem to have no higher ambition than your present pastorate," one of his inquisitors had told him, "but remember, they serve Him too, who work in the administration of His Church . . ."

"I feel closest to God when engaged in pastoral work," Bellini had said, like a child.

"Damn it, Bellini, if you want to feel close to God, join a contemplative order and spend your days staring at the stars! Here we do not view advancement as punishment. . . ." Then his interrogator laid a hand upon his shoulder. "But rest assured you will not be asked to sever connections completely with your people. We do not wish our officials to lose touch with—how shall I put it?—the man in the pew."

Il Papa roused himself from his memories. Two long sofas and some armchairs, all covered in taupe linen, gave a look of cool impersonality to his study. Three bay windows framed by drapes of the same linen faced the Square. Glass-enclosed bookcases, reflecting light, reached halfway up the walls. His quarters, Leo thought, had the chilling anonymity of a waiting room in an expensive funeral home.

He sat down behind the desk and let his eyes wander over it as if he were a stranger: crimson desk blotter, long brass scissors, a Vatican yearbook, a breviary, a Bible concordance, an encyclopedia of saints, and a telephone directory of the Vatican. There was also his plain black telephone. No family photographs or personal possessions softened its austerity.

With an almost imperceptible whirring of the gears, the Louis XV ormolu clock on the sideboard struck six times. Its high, sweet chimes consoled him. *Il Papa* folded his hands in his lap, resting his head on the back of the chair.

The room was dark. Rain pelted the windows. Sitting this way

"So if you prefer the peace of darkness, I will be delighted to extinguish the lights again." Ghezzi's voice affected a crispness to match *il Papa's*.

"No, no. I'm adjusting."

The monsignor perceived, accurately, that the Pope—who professed to abhor sentimentality—was mourning for his pet. Privately, Ghezzi admitted to himself that he was glad the messy little creature was gone. Once, when the bird had relieved himself on the breakfast table, Ghezzi had considered drowning him in a cup of hot coffee. Rocca wryly suggested that they purchase a falcon of their own who would in time, inevitably, consume Edoardo. "I am sorry about the bird, Holiness," he said, his voice not softening much.

Leo nodded. *"Grazie,"* he replied, with sudden warmth, eager to unburden himself, even to his secretary. "I should not grieve so. It's foolish, I suppose. Perhaps even wrong. You know, Francesco, there are cloistered orders where it is forbidden for the monks to keep even a turtle for fear they will form exclusive attachments . . ."

"With a *turtle*, Holiness?" Ghezzi asked, withdrawing a step or two. "I should wonder what sort of satisfying intercourse one might have with a reptile."

"Why not? A turtle—or a canary—is important to God. Why should it not be important to us?"

The monsignor eyed Leo with apprehension. Was *il Papa* becoming unstable, or was it merely that he, Ghezzi, was less spiritually attuned than the Prince of Apostles to the smaller creatures? "Well, I have alerted the groundsworkers to be on the lookout for the little fellow. He may turn up yet. I mean, how many bright yellow canaries no bigger than the bowl of a soup spoon are flying about in the Vatican . . . ?"

Leo sighed. "Let us hope, *flying*. Let us hope that he has not been blown by the wind, God forbid, into the Mediterranean . . ."

Ghezzi raised his eyes heavenward—an obligatory gesture of solicitude.

"His heart was bigger than the bowl of a soup spoon," Leo admonished his secretary.

for many minutes, he listened to the rain, the howling wind, and the beating of his heart. "O God," he said silently, "forgive me for taking from You the time that belongs to You in contemplation—"

The outer door opened, spilling dim light from the corridor over the carpet.

"Holiness? Are you in here?" It was Francesco Ghezzi.

"*Sì.*" Leo mumbled; his thoughts had returned to Edoardo as a clap of thunder rattled the windows.

"What?"

"I said, 'Yes, I am in here.' "

"May I turn on the lights? I cannot see you."

"Why do you want to see me? You see me all the time," he replied. It seemed an odd conversation, Leo mused: two disembodied voices sparring in the dark, and the absent Edoardo more tangible to him than either one.

"*Mi scusi. La disturbo?*"

"I was ... thinking," he said, by way of explanation. "Just thinking."

"I don't ... I cannot hear, Holiness."

"Turn on the lights. *Va bene. Avanti.*"

His secretary's hand thumped along the wall, groping for a switch. All of a sudden the room was flooded with light from a half dozen lamps with beige silk shades.

"Again I say, *scusi,* Holiness."

"*Non c'è di che.*"

"But isn't that just a little better?" Ghezzi went on, walking into the room.

Leo, his lips pursed to utter a remark, clipped it off roughly. What came out was not much more civil than what at first he intended. "If one wants to sit in the light, then it is certainly better, as you've observed. However, if one is at peace in the dark, as I was, then it is less good." Leo watched Ghezzi sidling about the chamber, nervously caressing whatever fell beneath his fingers. He a lowed the silence to linger for a long moment, savoring the mon gnor's discomfort.

Ghezzi whispered a hasty prayer and crossed himself, broadly, for the Pontiff's benefit. "Not to digress," he apologized, "but the evening grows short. I have come to remind you that the bishop will arrive at any moment to hear your confession."

"At this hour?" Leo straightened in his chair, pulling at the sash around his middle.

"It was at your request, Holiness. There was no other time this week. You do not remember?"

Leo shook his head, ashamed. "No ... or yes. Perhaps I do. Never mind, he is on his way."

Monsignor Ghezzi, his eyes retracted behind his thick glasses, his Adam's apple bobbing, looked, *il Papa* imagined, like a turtle himself, who had been given—by God or some other force—the power to see into the minds of men, to read their most intimate thoughts and imaginings. The notion did nothing to calm him.

"After your confession we will dine, and then you and I must sit down together. There are several details that require your attention. A small matter of installing a new toilet in your bathroom ... repainting this office, your library ... deciding the colors you want. If we might devote some concentrated time ..."

"I am at your disposal," Leo replied, waving his hand, brusque again, as if brushing off flies. "I am at your disposal, I am at the plumber's disposal, I am at the painter's disposal. But must we always account for every minute of my waking life?"

Leo rose behind his desk and Ghezzi retreated a few paces.

"Work accumulates, decisions must be made."

"What are you going to do?" Leo cried. "*Measure* me? For the seat?"

"Precious God in Heaven!" the Pope's secretary howled, his face going to magenta.

"Go on!" Leo went on, his wrath relaxing his inhibitions. "Take out your ruler! Do it now! Take it out!" Leo faced Ghezzi, who had fallen into a chair, panting for breath. "Do you know I even dream of you, Francesco?"

"You?—"

"*Sì*, I am besieged by dreams. Usually, in my dreams you shower

me with papers. Reports. Minutes. Proceedings. *Flow charts!* ...
Now I shall dream of you chasing me about my bedroom with a
tape measure! ... I know that you and your estimable associates
have spent the better part of your lives telling my predecessors what
they should do, and how, and when. But you will not tell me! You
will not destroy me!" *Il Papa* struck his own face so hard with his
hands that Ghezzi believed he might injure himself. "No seat!
That's *one* decision out of the way! I like my toilet just the way it is.
Tell the plumber to forgive me, but to please stay out of my private
quarters . . ."

A new, even louder voice boomed in the study. "Forgive you?
Starting your confession without me, Holiness? Couldn't wait?"

Bishop Pietro Biondi, the Pope's confessor, entered. He was an
enormous man, six-and-a-half-feet tall, who looked as if he had
swallowed a barrel. His face was red, his eyebrows black, his cheeks
pockmarked, his hands and feet as large as steaks. Biondi was a titu-
lar bishop, consecrated to a diocese which, because of a population
loss, no longer existed. He had been Leo's confessor for several
years, even before he became Pope.

The bishop did not so much stride into the study as totally take
it over. He approached Leo, knelt, and—in an unexpectedly sober
gesture in view of his jaunty entrance—tried to kiss his ring.

Il Papa made him rise. "Come now, Pietro. You know my policy:
Everyone in the Vatican is to kneel just twice a day—once when he
gets up in the morning, and once before he goes to sleep. But never
before me."

The air in the confessional was stale, and Biondi had eaten garlic or
onions for lunch, Leo could not tell which. He berated himself for
still preferring the small, dark, enclosed space of the booth to con-
fessing, as he might have, elsewhere in the open.

"Forgive me, Father, for I have sinned. It has been seven days
since my last confession." He stopped. "No, five days. No . . . How
long has it been? Do you recall exactly?"

"You were right the first time: seven days precisely."

"He must have his head against the grate," *il Papa* thought, moving away a little.

"Are you there? Are you prepared to make your confession?"

"Oh yes! Let me see . . . I lost my temper just now with a man quite close . . ." Silence followed.

"And so?"

Leo shifted his weight from knee to knee.

". . . some impure thoughts . . . I do not think I can make a good confession tonight. May we talk instead?" He listened to the bishop clear his throat uncomfortably.

"We may do whatever you wish. Would you prefer to leave the booth?"

"No," Leo responded. "No, not at all."

"Good."

Another lengthy silence.

"I feel that my soul is in danger."

There followed a rapt, alarmed pause.

"In danger, Holiness?"

"I often pray to return to my poor cell," Leo continued. "Has God raised me so far only to cast me further down than I was in the beginning?"

A longer hesitation. "Your faith should be of great strength to you."

"To be truly faithful, Father, is to be faithful in the darkness to what we accepted in the fullness of light."

He could hear Biondi drawing in his breath. "Well, against that, put Thomas à Kempis: 'It is good for us to encounter troubles and adversities from time to time, for trouble often compels a man to search his own heart.' " The man's tone was falsely jovial.

"*Sì,*" Leo nodded, chastened.

"Prayer, Holiness, is the road to salvation."

"But prayer may not save us, Pietro, it may only make us worthy of being saved. Either way, sometimes I fear that I no longer . . ."

"God's mercy is so great that He helps even those who have lost the gift of prayer. He helps even those who do not believe in Him."

Just then, an inconvenient image visited *il Papa.* The girl on the altar appeared before him in the dark of the booth. He saw himself spill the wine again, intoning, "Let us proclaim the mystery of faith." Her navel stared at him like an eye peeking out through the veil of her long, wine-soaked hair. . . . *"Che cosa ha detto?"*

"I said, Holy Father, that God's mercy is so great—"

"Sì, sì." Leo felt panic and sudden claustrophobia. *"Non mi sento bene."*

"Do you want the doctor?" Biondi asked, trepidation rising in his voice.

"No, but I must get out of here now!" Leo jumped to his feet in the cramped confessional. He hit his head against the wall. Lights burst before his eyes and the girl vanished, swallowed up in the confusion.

They met outside the booth, in the chapel. "Wait!" Biondi said, trying to approach *il Papa.* But the bishop frightened him off instead. Leo backed away, coming to stand before a small statue of the Virgin. His complexion was ashen.

Dampness coated Biondi's forehead. "I am thinking, Holiness, that perhaps you really ought to consult the doctors."

Leo looked at his confessor. "Doctors? Medical doctors? I am not sick, Pietro. I long for solitude, for a few moments of . . . of obscurity. All my life I have been pushed higher and higher. I submitted. I do not exonerate myself." He spoke in a whisper. His hands had tightened into fists. "I know the Church; I am versed in the law, in Scripture, on the fine points of doctrine. But of myself?—I know very little . . . of God? . . . maybe even less. Sometimes I understand why many of the saints went into self-imposed exile. A priest who is not holy, is he not harmful to the world?"

Biondi groped, his heart sickened. "You cannot be certain whether you are ill or not until you submit to an examination. This, uh, *malaise,* it could be hormonal."

"The menopause?" Leo responded, almost amused. "Me *and* Antonio?"

Biondi sighed. "Or your diet. I have read that faulty nutrition is, in many instances, to blame for what appears to be a sickness of the . . . spirit."

"I see," *il Papa* said. "You determine now to send me to a sanitarium where I shall be poked and prodded and pumped full of vitamins and lamb urine, cathartics and enemas, and Lord knows what else!" He laughed out loud. "Is this the New Church?"

The bishop grew more agitated. "There are people with severe allergies to certain foods, Holiness, who do not even know it themselves. Eating only one strawberry, or a few strands of spaghetti made with white flour, can put them immediately into . . ." Biondi tapped his temple. "Well, they become a little . . ."

Leo slumped into one of the pews. "So that is your explanation: If it is not the menopause, then I am mad. But if only I would switch to green noodles—"

"No, no Holiness. I would never call you—" He could not even pronounce the word.

"But why? Do not suppose the thought hasn't occurred to me. It would not be the first time, would it? Pius IX was clearly out of his mind."

The bishop dropped into a seat next to Leo. Biondi suffered from edema of the ankles and varicose veins; gently he massaged his left leg.

Leo moved a few inches away from his pungency. "You must recall, of course, that Pius placed his foot on the head of a cardinal and then lifted the poor man up by his ears? His savage outbursts caused the early demise of several other men as well."

"There is much evidence to suggest that Pius was physically ill. Epilepsy, or something," the bishop explained.

"Deranged, however, Pietro. Quite deranged."

Biondi placed a meaty hand on Leo's shoulder. "I believe *you* are utterly sane. But beyond that . . ." The bishop removed his hand and wiped the sweat from his face. "I am not usually at a loss for words."

Il Papa stood, looking down at his confessor. "Then answer one question. I do not need, nor do I want, a legal opinion."

"I understand."

"In this day and age, how would the world feel if a Pope were to abdicate?" Leo strained to affect an air of detached hypothesis, as if he spoke of another man.

Biondi responded quickly. "Horrified." Then he paused, reflective. "Although I would guess that if one were to present a truly superior reason for it . . ."

Leo nodded. "There is one final request I will make of you: Whatever happens, everything that has gone between us tonight must be kept secret. May I have your word?"

The bishop gazed deeply into Leo's eyes, so black now that the whites seemed hardly visible. "You need not extract an oath from me, but of course you have my word. God bless you. God help you."

The Vicar of Christ walked in the direction of the door, his lame leg dragging slightly behind him.

Later that evening, Leo left his study. Wandering, he lost himself in the labyrinth of corridors, courtyards, and hidden passageways of the Vatican. Occasionally he encountered a priest or two, still moving about on some nocturnal business. Observing them in their long black skirts, floating lightly through the halls as if on skates, it came to him, not for the first time, how he much preferred the company of women. Of all those inside the walls of the Vatican, he was most drawn to the nuns, upon some of whose faces one was able to detect the presence of a true and immediate suffering. In his former life, when he had been at liberty to go about in the world, once in a while Leo would indulge an odd habit: He visited churches in Rome, often St. Peter's, not to pray himself but to watch the sisters at prayer. In the beginning he was intrigued, then, later, moved. He observed them on their knees, their hands clasped, their faces uplifted, contemplating the Passion of Christ or, more often, the Sorrows of His Mother. In their eyes he believed he could see etched, as if with the finest pen, the fullness of their love, the extent of their ardor. Nothing mediated between them and the object of their devotions.

Back in his room, Leo tried once again to pray : "O My God! I firmly believe that You are present and see me plainly; that You observe all my actions, all my thoughts, and the most secret movements of my heart, a heart that even I do not know! I acknowledge that I am not worthy to come into Your presence, nor to lift up my eyes to You, because I have so many times sinned against You. But Your goodness and mercy invite me to come to You. Help me, I implore You, with Your holy grace. Save me from myself, from my desire to act without reason, to move only for the sake of movement, and from undoing all that You have ordained!"

IV

MONSIGNOR GHEZZI, Monsignor Rocca, and *il Papa* rode in silence in the elevator of the Apostolic Palace. The attendant, Carmen Gibilisco, was a stocky man with a bosomy chest and powerful biceps. He had inherited his position from his father, who had inherited it from his father before him. Scrubbing floors, polishing marble, guarding relics, running an elevator—indeed, performing any service for *il Papa* or his City—carried with it uncommon distinction. Most such occupations were handed down through families with pride. Gibilisco maintained his space lovingly: the gold carpet on the floor was spotless; the brass handrails gleamed with twice-daily care.

"We'll call you every day," Monsignor Ghezzi said to Leo, blowing his nose lustily.

"Two, three, *four* times a day," added Monsignor Rocca, as they stepped from the cab. Holding his leather portfolio to his breast with one hand, he reached out with the other to adjust Leo's white skullcap, which clung tenuously to the back of his head. "Are you certain you want to go through with it?"

"You can still change your mind," Ghezzi prompted.

As they walked down a shadowy underground passage illumined only by naked lightbulbs, the priests' black cassocks billowed about their legs. *Il Papa* wore his obligatory white, a red traveling cape fastened over his shoulders.

"I admit to you, Holiness, I am distressed by your wish to leave us," Francesco Ghezzi mumbled.

"D'accordo," Rocca added. *"D'accordo!"*

Leo stopped in his tracks. "Gentlemen. It will be only a short holiday—two weeks. We shall keep in touch. Believe me," he said, smiling, "things will go remarkably well in my absence. And when I return, your headaches with me—for which my conscience suffers—will just begin all over again."

"Don't speak of yourself that way," Monsignor Rocca objected.

"You are my life, Holiness," Ghezzi said.

The monsignors stepped aside to allow *il Papa* to pass through a small door that opened into the Vatican garage. The only available light filtered through rectangular green windows near the high roof. But even in the gloom one could discern the Papal automobiles and, behind them, the Papal carriages. There was a great golden coach with spoked wheels and mammoth springs that held it suspended in midair. A jet black carriage, with door handles fashioned of the crossed Papal keys, was parked beside three smaller white conveyances with gilt wheels and folding tops. In former times, all these had been employed to carry Popes on afternoon rides through the Vatican gardens.

At the entrance to the garage—under a marble arch on which were carved the words *Raedis Pontificum Servandis,* "For Storing Pontifical Coaches"—a dark blue Mercedes sedan waited, curtains drawn over its back windows, its engine running. As he saw the party approach, the driver opened the rear door.

"Arrivederci."

"Holiness, you are quite convinced that you do not prefer us to accompany you?" In the half-light of the garage, Rocca's pink scar assumed a greenish cast.

"I forbid it. I am undertaking this journey because it is imperative, and I must go alone. God will be with me. Saint Peter will be my guide."

"I don't care *who* is your guide," Ghezzi protested, desperate. "It is extraordinary and unwise of you to leave the walls of the Vatican by yourself and unguarded."

"I am not without protection. Marco is with me. He will take me safely to my sister's home and return to pick me up."

The chauffeur, Marco, as broad as he was tall, sporting a luxuriant mustache, smiled, quite pleased with himself.

"Yes," Rocca agreed brusquely, before the driver could respond. "He is well-trained, or that is what his certificate says. But what if there should be, Heaven forbid, an accident?"

Il Papa gathered his gown and slipped into the back seat. "Then there will be an accident. In the event that we both survive, Marco will go for a tow truck and I will stay with the car. I might go myself, but it would be simpler for him. He doesn't wear skirts."

"I cannot tell you how much this excursion dismays me," said Monsignor Ghezzi, bending forward to talk to Leo through the open window. "The Holy Father must never travel unescorted. *È proibito!* Reconsider: Go to Castel Gandolfo. At least there will be a staff equipped to care for your needs. Alfredo and I can join you."

"That is the point exactly: Everyone will follow me to care for these *needs,* as you say—needs I do not have. I want to take care of myself. Now, once again, good-bye to you both."

The car, with Marco proudly at the wheel, crept away from the garage. Only a Mass kit, such as those carried by missionary priests, lay on the seat beside *il Papa.* In it were chalice and paten, ciborium, a package of Hosts, a bottle of altar wine, as well as a consecrated stone—all that he would need to celebrate Mass. Later, he would set the stone—a portable altar—upon a table in his sister's house and, with his family, partake of the Eucharistic Meal.

Ghezzi and Rocca watched the automobile until it turned out of sight. "We could not stop him," Rocca said with terrible finality, looking intently at the point at which the car had disappeared.

Ghezzi raised his eyebrows, sighing like an exasperated parent. "We tried. But he is Leo XIV and, whether we like it or not, in the end answerable to no *human* authority."

"For better or worse, as with Pontiffs all through history."

"This time, for worse."

"You are very worried?"

Ghezzi stared fiercely at his companion. "I am not easy, Alfredo."

.   .   .

Cecilia Cavagna and her family lived two hours outside Rome on a small farm where they kept chickens, ducks, goats, an old horse, and a cow. Save for the horse and cow, the animals ran free. When Leo's car pulled into the dusty drive before the house, they rushed it like an invading army, evincing no fear. The chickens pecked vigorously at the ground around the hot tires; the ducks, thrusting fat breasts forward, beat their short wings; the goats, a mother and her baby, cocked their heads questioningly to one side and gazed with slitted amber eyes at the man in white robes struggling to emerge from his car.

The drive was bounded on two sides by pens, a chicken house, and a grey barn. At the end stood the Cavagnas' residence, a three-story structure with a sagging front porch and windows of varying sizes punched into the façade. The entire family of nine was standing on the porch when Leo drew up. Seven children and Cecilia ran to join the animals surrounding the automobile. Pio Cavagna, *il Papa's* brother-in-law, left alone on the steps, stood with his hands jammed into his trouser pockets.

Pio, a gaunt man with prominent cheekbones, graying hair, and heavy-lidded eyes, was a civil servant in the nearby town, in charge of issuing government documents. Citizens bought and sold land; they contracted and deeded and exchanged titles; they were born and they died; they drove cars, carried guns, got married. For everything a certificate was required, an official parchment, a seal of approval. It was Pio's job to issue such papers. But this was Satur-

day, and time for lunch, and he had discarded the despised shirt and
tie in favor of a sweater. A lukewarm grin appeared on his lips as
his children set upon Leo. He observed his self-exiled relative with
objectivity untarnished by awe.

The family, with Leo still in his papal robes, ate an elaborate
lunch: pasta, meat, *insalata mista, formaggio,* oranges, two whole
pineapples cut in rings, and *gelato.* The children—the youngest six
years, the oldest nineteen—were ranged on both sides of an oblong
table. Leo sat at one end, Cecilia at his elbow, Pio at the other end.
Everyone called the guest Uncle Giuseppe. One of the ducks wad-
dled in from the yard, perched on a high stool next to Guido, the
youngest child, and ate pieces of crusty bread from his hand.

At the conclusion of the feast, *il Papa* said the grace after meals:
"We give you thanks, O Lord, for all your gifts, which we have received from your bounty through Christ, our Lord. Amen."

Then he picked up the duck in his lap and, for a long time, sat
stroking its feathers.

The first three days at the Cavagnas passed quietly, except for persistent telephone communications from the Monsignors Ghezzi
and Rocca. Only the most intimate members of the pontifical family were aware that *il Papa* was outside the walls. A story, released as
soon as he had left, maintained that the Holy Father was confined
to bed with a bad chest cold and a high fever.

"I don't know that we're going to get away with it," Ghezzi said
on the first evening, opening the door to the Pope's bedroom and
glancing up and down the corridor before he and Rocca went inside.

"They got away with it in 1848, when Pius went into exile in
Gaeta," Rocca replied.

Ghezzi closed the door quietly. "Bravo. I never knew you were
such a student of Papal lore, Alfredo."

"Oh, *sì,*" the younger man said eagerly. "D'Harcourt, the French
ambassador, was in on the scheme. He arrived at the Quirinal for a

private audience with Pius—or so he said. But in fact, he spent two hours alone in the papal study, reading newspapers aloud to the empty room." Rocca burst out laughing.

Ghezzi gave him a sour look. "It isn't all that funny," he said. "In point of fact, it's very sad."

But Rocca was regaled. "Pius had already slipped away! He had changed from his robes into a plain black cassock and been taken, by secret passageways, to a waiting carriage. This took him to a second carriage in which," Rocca paused to catch his breath, "hidden among ordinary people, he was driven to Gaeta!

"After a while D'Harcourt came out of the room and said to everyone, 'The Holy Father is exhausted and needs rest. You must not disturb him.' Actually, it was some time before anybody discovered that Pius had escaped."

"It seems there is always a precedent," Ghezzi admitted glumly, sitting down on the edge of Leo's bed. He drew a piece of paper from his pocket, spread it on his knees, and began to compose the announcement that appeared the next morning in papers around the world.

POPE, STRICKEN WITH INFLUENZA,

CANCELS PRIVATE AUDIENCES

Rome—Pope Leo XIV has a case of influenza and has canceled private audiences scheduled for the rest of the week, the Vatican said today. A Vatican spokesman explained that the Pope, who has been hoarse and coughing during the past five days, canceled the audiences because of "a slight influenza-type indisposition."

It is the first confirmed case of illness for Leo since he was elected Pope.

Leo's meals, sent up to his quarters in the Apostolic Palace at the usual times, were consumed by Alfredo Rocca, who had the appetite of three men. The Papal physician, Doctor Silvano Grassano, visited twice a day. He drank brandy with Ghezzi and talked of world politics, about which he knew next to nothing; Ghezzi suffered his queer, windy opinions for appearances' sake.

Otherwise, life in the Vatican proceeded without undue interruption. Ghezzi was surprised to learn that Leo's prediction had been accurate: Things went remarkably well in his absence. The monsignor had just begun to enjoy his new power when the inside of his nose broke out in warts. Doctor Grassano administered an injection and prescribed a foul-smelling ointment to be applied with cotton swabs. The treatment eased the discomfort but failed to diminish the size of the growths.

When not conferring with his aides by telephone, Leo spent his time on the farm reading, writing, and praying. After hours on his knees, he returned to the temporal world weakened and often in tears.

Late in the evening of the second day, his tongue loosened by the wine they were drinking, Leo confided in Pio. "For many years," he said, "I have been living as a man in exile from himself. Now I feel compelled—consigned, even . . ." he searched for the word with the proper force, "*driven,* you know—to explore the boundaries of my faith, at whatever cost." His brother-in-law nodded, suspicious and skeptical at once.

Since Leo's arrival, the weather had been altogether pleasant. Although late autumn, the air was golden and still sweet. In the morning, he sat in a rocking chair on the porch and watched the chickens as they moved about nervously on the grass, their expressionless faces seeming somehow sly with secret intent. "They are not so innocent as other creatures," *il Papa* thought, remembering Edoardo. "These birds seem hostile, convinced that their yard is a death cell. Well, maybe I would be the same if I knew my neck was next on the chopping block."

In a pen to one side of the house was the old mare, Ada. She was blind in one eye and a little deaf. The ground in her corral was hilly and uneven; large boulders worn smooth by years of exposure protruded from the brown dirt. Leo became interested in the horse after observing her for a few days. He saw that sometimes she felt very old and tired, as if life were too great a burden. She walked in circles, her head held low, tripping over the big stones. Or she stood quietly, gnawing on a fence post. At other times, particularly after a breakfast of mash and oats, she behaved like a filly. Galloping from one end of the pen to the other Ada would suddenly halt at the low rail, planting her hooves in the earth. She stormed the fence with gusto but never once attempted to jump, to bolt from her enclosure. *Il Papa* wondered why this was so: With only a little more effort, on one of her good days, she could have cleared the railing.

It was the fourth morning of his vacation from the Vatican. Cecilia had gone to shop. Pio was at work in the government office, and the Cavagna children were also at work or in school. Leo stared down at the crimson slippers that he still liked to wear. The gold crosses on them glinted dully in the sun. He felt his toes twitch inside the soft cloth—and then it came to him, as if the idea had been there all along. Not shocked, not even quite surprised, he rose and went inside. The terror, perhaps, would come later. In the kitchen, letting the stillness of the house enfold him, he spoke to God: "I am about to go away, in search of what, I am not sure. I pray that You will guide my steps, although I do not deserve Your ..." Quickly, the terror overtook him. He was unable to complete the thought.

From Pio's closet, Leo borrowed gray woolen trousers, a dark blue flannel shirt, a sweater with some buttons missing, and a pair of high walking shoes with sturdy soles and thick laces. Pio was even taller than Leo; *il Papa* stepped on his brother-in-law's trouser cuffs. He stood in the center of the bedroom in confusion: It was many years since he had been forced to confront the vexations of ordinary life. Even conventional clothing now puzzled him. At last, recalling a trick from his childhood, he turned the waist of the pants a couple of times into a narrow roll, and secured it with a belt.

When Leo finished dressing he carried his papal attire into his own room and laid the garments on the bed. Next to the robes, the white skullcap, and the slippers, he placed the gold pectoral cross, large as an outstretched hand. It sank deep into the folds of the quilt, its short arms open expectantly. *Il Papa* snatched up the cross as soon as he had put it down and ran from the room. Back in Pio's closet he found a brown felt fedora, which he clamped on his head. He slipped the fisherman's ring from his finger and plunged it deep into his pocket.

Money!

Cecilia kept a wad of bills under the mattress of her bed. Leo thrust his hand into the warm space between the mattress and the springs. There it was, big as a fist—soft, beaten bills in several denominations. "Cecilia, dear Cecilia, always expecting catastrophe!" Withdrawing his hand, he peeled away half the pile and replaced the rest. "And now at last you have one!"

In the driveway near the horse's pen stood a small truck that Pio used on weekends. The tires were caked with mud and the license plates had fallen off years ago. Pockmarked with dents and rusting holes, the windshield cracked, the headlights hanging at awkward angles, walleyed, its appeal was almost human. Leo approached it cautiously. He stuck his head into the open window. A key dangled from the ignition. *A blessing? A curse?* he asked himself, elated and shaken at once. *Il Papa* strolled around to the other side of the truck. There was a small bed in back; a taillight, split jaggedly in half, winked at him. He came around again, opened the door, and eased himself gingerly behind the steering wheel.

The cab smelled of gasoline; the seats were torn. Leo felt a hard metal spring press against his thigh. He placed one foot on the accelerator, the other on the clutch, and cupped the palm of his right hand over the stick. Starting the engine, he tried to persuade the automobile to move. It lurched forward, and came to a stop; the engine died. Twice more he attempted and twice more he failed. The truck leaped like a gazelle, in long, fluid arcs; it hopped like a rabbit, in a series of short, rapid bumps. And each time it shut down. *Il Papa* had not driven a car since his youth. Sweat pooled in his armpits, trickling down inside his shirt. He talked to himself in a conversational tone. "So here is where it ends—before the adventure begins." His hand was wet on the wheel, making it slippery and difficult to maintain control. "I've succeeded so far in bucking around in a circle." His leg shook so furiously that he had to fight to steady his foot on the gas pedal. "I will try one more time. If I fail again, then it is Your will."

Leo let up very slowly on the clutch and pressed down as smoothly as he could on the accelerator. The truck inched forward, gaining speed quickly. He cut the wheel sharply to avoid crashing through the rail into the horse's corral. Narrowly averting a head-on collision with a goat, he left the yard, throwing dirt, dust, and gravel in his wake. Warmth spread within his chest, far beneath the skin, filling up the cavity behind his ribs, as if something had ruptured there. He felt pervaded by a sudden, ludicrous calm. His spirit soared.

V

Drive slowly. Stay away from Rome. Steer clear of cities. Remain on back roads. In public places, wear Pio's hat. Il Papa put a hand to his face. He had forgotten to take his brother-in-law's sunglasses. *I am a car thief without a decent disguise.*

The immensity of his departure had not yet taken hold. Instead, Leo seemed cloaked in a protective amnesia that allowed him to settle his attention on small things. Again and again, he checked the gas gauge and became agitated when the needle began to descend too rapidly. He dreaded having to stop at a filling station. Guiding the car with one hand, Leo drew the other to his chest and touched the four ends of the cross that hung, hidden, underneath his shirt. *North. South. East. West. Like the points of a compass.*

It was beginning to get dark. Leo had been driving for a long time. The road, winding and deeply rutted, ran between two fields planted with peas and beans. Miles ahead of him a low mountain rose, covered—from what he could see—with scrub and brush. Cool breezes blew into the window. He brought the truck to a stop at the edge of the road and sat for a while watching the colors of the sky deepen.

Stars dotted the firmament like a thousand random pinpricks. On the horizon there appeared thin bands of purple and a wide slash of bloody red.

"Why has Your hand not stopped me?" Leo wondered aloud. He was startled by his own voice, which sounded, after seven hours of silence, almost like a stranger's. "How is it that You tolerate my betrayal? What does it mean that You have brought me to this moment?" Leo peered into the darkness ahead, struck by the recognition that he had no idea of where he was and, what was worse, of where he was going. To be lost was the lot of the traveler; it occurred to him with a shudder that he was completely . . . adrift.

For the first time, Leo was overwhelmed with the urge to return quickly on the road that, even now, drew him farther away. He calculated that if he drove without stopping in the opposite direction he could return to his family's farm perhaps before daylight. Monsignors Ghezzi and Rocca need never be aware of his transgression, and to Cecilia and Pio he would simply explain . . .

But even as *il Papa* was preparing to turn the truck around, he recalled one of the lessons from his childhood: the parable of the sparrow from the Book of Matthew. There is a certain Grace even in the fall of a sparrow, Jesus had told the Apostles. ". . . Fear them not therefore: for there is nothing covered that shall not be revealed; and hid, that shall not be known . . ." Leo recited slowly, from memory. "Are not two sparrows sold for a farthing? And yet not one of them shall fall on the ground without your Father." Leo looked at the road stretched out in front of him. Although nothing had changed and the darkness remained, he released the brake and piloted the truck forward, into the night.

The silence was dense and extraordinary. All day long he had been alert to it; in fact, the farther he got from Rome the more conscious he became of the beneficent absence of the battering, ceaseless chatter of Ghezzi and Rocca and those countless others who daily besieged him.

Although Leo did not know precisely where he was, he realized he had come along the coastal route, through Anzio, Terracina, Gaeta, Capua, and then had moved a little inland. He guessed that he was farther south than Naples, but how much farther he could not be certain. It was almost full night now; there were no markers on this lonely path, and the headlights of the truck were weak. "I must still be traveling south," he said, reaching that conclusion more by intuition than by reckoning.

Il Papa strained to pierce the veil of night, half hoping to discern the lights of an oncoming car in the distance, and half fearing that he would. He saw nothing.

.   .   .

"Now let's not lose our heads! All of you, sit down and collect yourselves. We must think."

Pio Cavagna held up his hands like a referee. The children ran for chairs and pulled them up to the kitchen table.

"Think? Think of *what*? Pio, he's gone. He's been kidnapped! Someone discovered he was with us and they *stole* him!"

"We don't know that he's been stolen—kidnapped, Cecilia. All we know is that he isn't *here*."

She held a handkerchief to her mouth, as if to stifle a scream. In her other hand she clutched rosary beads. "Call the police!"

"No. Not yet."

"Then call those men, the ones who work for him, the priests . . . Ghezzi, Rocca," Cecilia pleaded.

"God forbid."

"Well, do something, Pio! My brother may be in mortal danger at this very minute, while you play at being a detective."

The younger children could hardly sit still. When they were satisfied that their father was not looking, they wriggled off their chairs, met in the middle of the kitchen, and pummeled one another in excitement. The disaster that had descended upon them sent the children into spasms of merriment. Their cheeks were flushed; their dark eyes glowed. What would happen? What would happen *next*? Where had Uncle Giuseppe gone? Who would find him? Would they bring him back? Maybe the *carabinieri*—in black overcoats, and peaked caps, wearing guns in leather pouches— would arrive at any minute in the drive outside with all their lights flashing . . .

Pio Cavagna glared at his wife. "If he is truly in mortal danger, then there is nothing anyone, short of the Lord Almighty, can do to help him. I am not *playing* at anything—and to insult me will hardly help us, Cecilia. Or your brother."

"So what do you want me to do?"

Pio did not reply at once. He put his hand to his cheek. A stubble had grown on his face. His eyes were bloodshot and weary. "As I say, I am thinking. Try to be calm."

"I am trying very hard, but let me put it to you this way: He is not only my brother, your brother-in-law, and the beloved uncle of our children. He is also Supreme Pontiff of the Universal Church, Successor to the Prince of Apostles, Primate of Italy . . ." Her voice broke. "And *we have been robbed of him*. How long do you think we can keep it a secret?"

"I haven't said we should keep it a secret. I haven't said anything. Only that I'm still thinking."

"Oh Pio!" Cecilia screeched, rising from her chair. "I cannot bear it another minute. What has become of Peppe? I am so frightened. . . ."

She began to move her lips swiftly in prayer. "Remember, O most loving Virgin Mary, that it is a thing unheard of, that anyone ever had recourse to your protection, implored your help, or sought your intercession, and was left forsaken. Filled therefore with confidence in your goodness I fly to you . . ."

"I believe I know what has happened here." Pio's tone was quietly, coldly rational. He sat down at the table, his long body folded into the chair, and brought a crushed cigarette from his pocket. Lighting it with a wooden matchstick that he struck on the heel of his shoe, he said, "Your brother has taken off of his own free will."

"Despise not my poor words, O Mother of the Word of God, but graciously hear—" Cecilia Cavagna stopped in the middle of her prayer. "That's crazy."

"I believe it is so."

All the children were silent now. The three youngest stood in a tight corner near the sink, their eyes grave, their mouths open, saliva glistening on their lips.

"*Il Papa* has run away from home?" their mother cried. "Is that what you mean to say?"

"Well, he has already run away from Rome. And examine the evidence. What have we? Your brother discarded his robes—folding them very neatly, I will add, on the bed. He took with him his breviary, his cross, and the ring. He borrowed my most comfortable boots. He made off with the truck ... Go outside and look at the ground again: There are skid marks everywhere. He also ruined the few blades of grass we have left. Who else would drive that way except a man who has not been behind the wheel in thirty years? Surely not a band of professional kidnappers. They would not have gone near that heap of tin in the first place. It hardly runs."

Cecilia looked at her husband incredulously. It was just like him to react in time of crisis with infuriating calm; to puff those wretched cigarettes and attempt to explain away an act of barbarism or madness. Pio's cool ignited her rage. She debated whether or not to pick up the sugar jar next to her hand and crown him with it. Her fingers fairly tingled. But no; it was too crude a gesture for the only sister of the Patriarch of the West; and besides, it would not knock any sense into her husband's hard head.

"There are no signs of a struggle that I can detect. Nothing has been disturbed," Pio went on in his laconic way. "We have received no threatening telephone calls, no demands for ransom. The only thing I don't quite understand is why he left no note, no letter of explanation. But then, why would he? Obviously, he does not want us to find him."

"Maybe he fell and broke his brains. Then he lost his memory, grabbed your pants by mistake, and drove off into the hills!" suggested one of the children.

"Be quiet!" Cecilia cried.

"It is possible, but unlikely," Pio replied, unwilling to reject, out of hand, his child's imaginings.

"No more unlikely than running away," his wife said. Her husband's slow, reassuring manner became progressively more vexing. "We know that your brother was seriously distressed. That is what brought him here."

"Who is not distressed? I wake up distressed, I go to bed at night even more distressed!"

"My understanding is that his problems were of a rather different sort than yours," Pio responded. "Nevertheless he has vanished. These are the facts. I do not claim to comprehend a profound crisis of faith. Mine is shaky at best. But I am not foolish, as you know: I look at the evidence and this is what I see. . . . There has been no foul play here, except perhaps the violence that your brother has done against himself."

Cecilia walked around the room in a circle, her eyes on the floor, touching those things that were most familiar to her—the faucet, the sugar jar, a can opener lying on the counter. The rosary dangled from her fingers. "Let us say that you are correct, Pio. Let us say that your theory has some merit—"

"I'm glad you've come around to my point of view . . ."

"I didn't say that. I said that I would suppose, for now, your theory has merit. . . . What can be wrong in telling the police?"

"As you yourself have pointed out, Giuseppe is no ordinary man." Pio developed a plausible scenario. "To tell the police is to tell the world. Soon all of Italy pours out in bands and caravans searching for him. The government offers big rewards for his capture . . . It quickly becomes dangerous—a hunt, a national game. They call in the Army! No, it has to be handled with much more tact—for your brother's sake, and for the sake of the country . . . and for God's sake," Pio added, grudgingly. "Just give me time to think some more."

The telephone rang. "Pio!" Cecilia exclaimed in a high, reedy voice, "while you are thinking and thinking, and getting nowhere with your thoughts, *they* are calling us! Perhaps to say his thumb will be in the morning mail!"

Once more, the sharp buzz cut through the humid air of the room like a laser. The thrumming instrument hung on the wall near the porch door. Husband and wife lunged for it together.

"Monsignor Ghezzi? Is that you, Padre?" Cecilia shrieked into the mouthpiece. Pio tried to wrest the receiver from her hand, but she held fast.

"Bite your tongue, control yourself! Say nothing!"

"Padre? It's my brother . . . *Il Papa, sì!* . . . He is *missing* . . . No, he has not gone for a walk! . . . No, there isn't a home for convalescents near here . . . What are you asking me? No, no hospital either . . . He is *missing*. Can you hear me?"

"*Stia calma!*" Pio hissed. "Cecilia!"

"That's right, *gone* . . . Yes, vanished into thin air!"

"Now you've fixed it," Cavagna whispered darkly. "Just remember, it was you who fixed it." He pulled another cigarette from his pocket.

．　．　．

Leo drove into the village of T———. It was situated high in the cleft of a mountain of volcanic rock. The trip had been tortuous and tiring, especially for one so inexperienced at the wheel. On his way up he had passed an abandoned mine, groves of sickly-looking olive trees, silhouetted against the night, the branches withered, the leaves sere, and, later, clumps of chestnut trees. The remains of several cars dotted the landscape like the bones of modern dinosaurs. It seemed like a lost country, severed from the world, and forgotten.

T———'s main street was flanked on either side by squat buildings and shacks. A few appeared to grow directly out of the rock. Paint peeled in long strips from some houses; from others, it was altogether worn clean. The walls of the stone buildings were cracked and coming loose. An aura of impermanence, at odds with the stone, hung over them, as if at any moment they might split in half, or crumble away. A number of dwellings had boards for front doors; rags covered the windows. The town seemed to have grown up haphazardly, constructed from whatever materials blew through the atmosphere.

The main street was unpaved and two parallel ruts were worn down its center, like train tracks. Angry black flies swarmed in the stagnant air. Even at night, when they were not visible, one could still hear them grumble. *Il Papa* drove very slowly, afraid of colliding with something, or someone, in the dark. A single street lamp, attached to the side of a building, illuminated a discarded refrigerator. Its door hung open and an orange cat nestled inside.

At the far end of the street an old café languished, four chairs and one table set in front. A fat man with a drooping tobacco-stained mustache and white hair reaching almost to his shoulders slouched in one of the chairs. He wore only an undershirt, and his black pants were held up by a pair of thin suspenders. Puffing a cigarette, he inhaled and exhaled without taking it from his lips, as if he had been smoking the same butt forever. He stared into space, his eyes fixed on some chimera in the distance—a man with too much time on his hands, all the time in the world, Leo thought. Tuesday and Saturday, Thursday and Sunday would be all the same to him.

Il Papa stopped his truck and stepped out. Pools of milky light spilled onto the street from inside the tavern. The fat man looked up at the stranger, his eyes squinting against the smoke from his cigarette.

"Lost?" the fat man grunted.

Leo's heart skipped. *"Mi scusi?"*

"You must be lost. It's the only reason anyone ever lands in this Godforsaken place." The man closed his eyes, the lids seeming to slip down slumberously.

There was a long silence. Leo hovered near the truck, pinned there in alarm.

"Where'd you come from?"

Il Papa mulled the question, turning it over, as though examining a foreign object. *"Roma."*

The fat man opened his eyes and sat up a little straighter. His gaze took in the clothes of the stranger, from the battered felt hat on his head to the slight bulge under his sweater, where the waistband was rolled, to his walking boots.

"The city, eh? You don't look like you come from the city. Well, I have been to Rome only once, and frankly I'm sorry I took the trip. . . . How long have you been driving?"

"Most of the day. Since morning." Leo ventured a few steps closer.

"How did you manage to get all the way out here? We're not on the road to anywhere." The fat man removed the cigarette from his mouth and tossed it on the ground. It continued to burn, sending a wavy gray tail into the dark.

"I am a salesman. I go everywhere." Leo marveled at the convenient way the words spilled from his throat.

"You won't sell anything here, my friend."

"I may surprise you. Sometimes I even surprise myself."

"They haven't any money to buy. If you'll take a half-dead pig or some olive oil in trade, maybe. What do you sell?"

Il Papa rubbed his forehead hard, as if the gesture might generate a convincing tale. "Religious articles: rosaries, Missals, crosses on chains for the ladies, keychains for the gentlemen, postcards of Vatican treasures, miniature portraits of the Blessed Virgin, guides to the Eternal City . . ." He tried to remember what goods were purveyed by the souvenir vendors of Rome. "I also carry a plastic replica of St. Peter's basilica . . . electric . . . it glows in the dark."

"Perhaps you'll let me have a look?" The fat man stroked his mustache with one hand and held out the other. "I myself have a few *lire*. I might buy . . . a cross . . . for the mother of my second wife."

"Mi dispiace. I cannot." Not ten hours out, and the rope of his own deceptions was already threatening to strangle him.

"Can't show your goods? *Cosa vuol dire?* Because you think I can't pay?"

"No, no, not at all ..." *What now?* "I was set upon—by ... by *bandits!*"

"Bandits? Where? When?" The man leaped from his chair with a grace and swiftness that belied his sleepy eyes and tremendous bulk. He trained those eyes, now alert, down the road in the direction from which the stranger had come.

"A little while ago. About a kilometer away. They took everything. Fleeced me. I haven't a postcard left."

The fat man looked a minute longer. All was blackness where the main street ended and the road wormed its way back into the heavily wooded hills.

"What kind of bandits were they?" he asked Leo.

Il Papa's mind raced. "A big one and a little one," he said at last, his heart racing faster than his mind.

"They got everything? Your whole sample case?"

"Both my sample cases," Leo heard himself reply. Then he remembered: "Except for the few *lire* that I keep here, in my shoe—in anticipation of just such eventualities," he added as an afterthought, pointing to his foot. The lace of his left boot had come undone and trailed in the dirt.

"They hurt you too?" The man nodded at Leo's leg.

"No. It's a bit lame from driving so long. They pushed me around a little, that's all."

The fat man began to cough convulsively until he was red in the face. Then he lifted his head, spitting a gummy piece of phlegm onto the ground. "How'd they stop your car?"

"Jumped in front of it from behind some trees, waving their arms," Leo answered.

"You said a big one and a little one?"

Il Papa's mouth was dry. He took a moment to review his story before replying. "Yes, big and little. Larger and smaller. Two different sizes, that's right."

"Two different sexes too?" The man's interest was further awakened.

"What?"

"Male and female?" He sat down again with the groan of a person grateful to be off his feet. He did not allow Leo time to respond. "I know who those two were: Caterina, the gypsy, and her lover, Carlo the Awful. They held you up."

Il Papa's brain bounded between excitement and astonishment. "Have I," he wondered, "as sometimes happens, lied my way into a truth?" Leo asked aloud: "Bandits of your acquaintance?"

"They live in a sort of cave built into the side of the hill at the edge of town. They scrounge for what they need, occasionally stealing from travelers in other towns. But they're really quite harmless. Did you get a look at their faces?"

"Their faces? No. The road was unlit and, uh, as it happened, they seemed to be . . . *wearing masks!*"

"Ah! Stockings. Ladies' stockings—stolen also, of course."

Leo felt on the brink of believing his own lie. "The male accomplice, what did you call him?"

"Carlo the Awful . . . He is very large and not good-looking. This, no doubt, accounts for his name." The fat man laughed uproariously, then stopped short. "A long time ago, it is said, he killed a woman. His wife, probably. No one knows. That was in another village, far from here, in the north. The story arrived before he did, on the tongue of a fortune teller. Caterina has him under a spell now. He does exactly what she likes and caters to her every desire." He winked at Leo.

Leo, trying to wink back, blinked both eyes by mistake.

"Every so often, those two come into the village. Mostly, they prowl through the streets, staring at us like animals. Sometimes they buy—a chicken, or some beans. From us villagers, they don't steal. We're staying here, we're not going anywhere and they don't want enemies. But many people are afraid. The children scream and run when they see them. Some women say that Caterina was born with three breasts. Others claim that she has two rows of teats on her chest like a cat."

The fat man's two chins jiggled when he moved his head. "If we had tourists, Carlo and Caterina would be our only attractions. I wouldn't mind them much if *he* were honest and *she* didn't cast spells. But then, what man is completely honest? And what woman wouldn't cast a spell on her lover, if she could? I myself have been the victim of several such attempts," he said proudly.

"It is a touching bond between them," *il Papa* murmured.

"You saw that, eh? Even in the dark, behind the masks."

Their conversation, especially his part in it, filled Leo with wonderment. This man not only believed him, but assisted him in his lie, and showed sympathy for his plight. They spoke as intimates, comrades, conspirators. Truths and untruths mingled recklessly, and no one was the worse for it. At least not yet.

Il Papa felt safe enough now to advance a few more feet until he was standing in the light that came from the café. Inside he saw more tables and chairs strewn on a dirt floor. There was an old fan on the ceiling that did not revolve, a small bar upon which sat bottles of wine and a steel espresso maker down whose sides ran fossilized rivulets of coffee.

The fat man let flies settle on his chest and shoulders. He thrust his hand into Leo's. "My name is Franco Pisticci. I run this place . . . but mostly I sit on my behind. At one time the government promised us heavy industry, a mine, machines for agriculture, a fancy hotel, and a steady stream of visitors. As you can see, the promises were not kept. And you, who are you?"

Panic percolated in Leo's breast. Pondering this question he looked down at the ground and, for a moment, did not even recognize his own feet in Pio's massive boots. "I'm Giuseppe . . . Ghezzi," he said.

Signor Pisticci cocked his head, as if pleased by the information. Then he ducked inside and returned quickly with a bottle, two glasses, and a corkscrew. It was obvious that he did not wish to lose the company of the stranger. "It's too warm to drink in there."

He motioned for *il Papa* to sit, placed the glasses on the table between them, opened the bottle, and poured carefully. *"Cin-cin!"*

"Cin-cin," Leo said, raising his full glass. He felt miraculously relieved of obligations, appointments, and tomorrow morning. What would come, would come.

—

Pisticci wiped his lips with his wrist. "So where will you spend the night, my friend?"

Finally, a question *il Papa* could not answer, even with a lie. He sighed. "You see, I lost my way. I was daydreaming and didn't watch the signs. . . . *Quanto lontano è il prossimo villagio?*"

"The next village?" Pisticci shook his head. "Too far to drive tonight. But don't worry." The café owner leaned forward and patted Leo's shoulder. "We're not entirely without resources for overnight guests. There's a woman, a kind of a widow, who lives at the far end of the street. She keeps a few rooms for guests, three or four beds, and serves breakfast too. Only the tax collector is staying there now. She'll have space. Donna Lucia's her name, Lucia Fedelio. When we finish the bottle, I'll take you there, if you like."

"Molte grazie," Leo said, feeling oddly protected and at home outside the walls.

As the two men finished the bottle, the tavern keeper told *il Papa* an intriguing story. "Donna Lucia's husband was a dreamer from the day she married him. He never earned so much as a *lira*. Other men, no matter how poor, they stick their hands in their pockets and you hear the jingle of a few coins. Alphonse Fedelio stuck his hands in his pockets and all you heard was the whistle of the wind. The few rooms Donna Lucia let were their only means of support. He was a man obsessed with flight; talked of little else," Pisticci recounted.

"The whole town knew that upstairs in the house, Alphonse was working on a pair of wings. Finally, one warm spring night, several of his cronies helped him—in great secrecy, of course—to carry them to the top of the mountain. These wings—each one of them—were nearly as big as you, my friend. And what an extraordinary, delicate craft! He had waxed the ribs of the wooden frame until they shone under the moon. The fabric of the wings was as thin as a summer dress; you could almost see through it. Steel wires, like a spider's web, ran this way and that. And to attach himself to his machine, he had fashioned broad leather straps with silver buckles. Nevertheless—triumph of craftsmanship though it was—we were all sure he would break his neck. But Alphonse took off . . . and he flew! He flew! All night long, he circled the village, cawing like a raven, waking people from their sleep. Dawn came up, and his cohorts watched as Alphonse Fedelio grew smaller in their vision, until he was only a dot on the horizon."

Pisticci paused, shrugged his shoulders, and drained the rest of the wine from his glass. "He wafted away . . . and never wafted back. Several years later, Lucia declared herself a widow—but only after she tried to have the marriage annulled. She traveled all the way to Rome and returned without the papers. The priests there refused to accept her story about a man who flew away. Life is amazing, don't you think?" Pisticci stood up and stretched his fat arms. "That they should have doubted such a woman? Come, let's go." The two men started to walk. "But please respect Donna Lucia's privacy. It pains her too much to talk about Alphonse. I just thought you should know."

The widow, Lucia Fedelio, was still young; he guessed no more than thirty or so, with olive skin and deep blue eyes. They browsed with surprising boldness over Leo's face and body, as Pisticci reeled off his name, occupation, and immediate predicament: "Signor Ghezzi . . . salesman of religious novelties . . . lost his way on the road." It was late. The woman wore a long white sleeping robe; her waist-length dark hair was loose, falling down her back.

"You will have to share a room with Galeazzi, if you want to stay," Donna Lucia said. "I haven't cleaned the others today."

"Tax collector, like I told you," Franco Pisticci whispered in *il Papa*'s ear.

Leo nodded, half-listening, conscious of the innkeeper's eyes upon him.

"All right then, follow me."

Her full hips swayed as she went before him up the stairs.

Emilio Galeazzi, a young man with wire glasses and a trace of whiskers above his upper lip, lay on the bed reading a book. He wore a white shirt, a skinny black necktie which was still knotted tightly at his throat, and wrinkled brown trousers. He looked as though he had come to do the accounts. When *il Papa* entered, Galeazzi politely closed his book.

"You have a guest tonight," Donna Lucia said. "To make up for the inconvenience, I'll take a thousand *lire* off your bill." She shut the door.

There was one window in the small room and, on either side of it, two iron bedsteads with thin mattresses and threadbare blankets. An old bureau stood against one wall, opposite a United States Army footlocker. Over each bed hung a wooden crucifix.

"Buona sera," the young man said.

The Pope extended his hand and for a moment was surprised when the man did not incline his head to kiss it.

"Good evening," he said, recovering himself.

"What is your business here?" Emilio Galeazzi grinned. "It's the first time I've ever had to share my room. Not many unforeseen guests . . ."

Leo told his story, this time with dispatch, as if he had been telling it for years.

"A fearsome tale," Galeazzi remarked.

"At least I escaped with my life." *Il Papa* sat down on the bed that would be his for the night. It was hard and narrow, he noted, not so different from the one he slept on in the Vatican. At the Cavagna farm his bed had been small too, but soft as a nest of down.

"You must be hungry after such a trip and all that aggravation." The tax collector went to the window and opened it to the night. Like a magician, he produced from the sill a large box of raisins, two fresh apples, a wedge of hard, crumbly cheese, and a bottle of mineral water.

Leo's stomach rumbled at the sight of it. He was ravenously hungry. Once more, as at the café, he gave himself over to the care of a stranger. "What a feast," he said with gratitude.

"In the places where I travel, one must always be prepared. Here, put that locker between the beds. It will make a table."

Papa Leo pushed the foot locker along the wooden floor. It was empty and rattled loudly. "How did such a box ever find its way up these hills?" he asked, sitting down again.

"How did *you* ever find your way up these hills? Strange things happen," Galeazzi said.

Leo stuck his hand into the box of raisins. They were plump, soft, and moist to the touch.

The tax collector considered the puzzle of the locker, removing the cap from the mineral water. "Listen, I once cracked open a chicken egg and a baby snake fell out. I nearly had *un attacco cardiaco*—and I was only eight years old. How did it get there? Who knows? One cannot always look for logical explanations."

"Almost never," Leo agreed in a comradely way, charmed by the irrelevance of Galeazzi's anecdotes. "A footlocker here, a snake in the wrong egg there. In a long lifetime, I have learned that one must come to expect the unexpected."

"Especially in these parts." Galeazzi lowered his voice to a whisper. "You haven't heard, I suppose, the story of Donna Lucia's flying husband?"

"Indeed I have."

Emilio Galeazzi nodded sadly. "Poor woman. Talk about the unexpected . . ."

Il Papa put a fistful of raisins into his mouth. They were succulent, exploding between his teeth and bringing tears to his eyes. "You have been in this village before, I take it." He sipped some water and picked up an apple. Emilio reclined on the bed.

"A few times. I'm a tax collector, but what can I collect? They send me to make seizures; when I arrive, there is nothing to seize. These people are very poor and don't see why they should pay— even if, indeed, they could. I try to be lenient . . . so I am always in hot water with my superiors."

Leo bit into the apple. He had never known such an appetite, and spoke with his mouth full. "Leniency. I approve of it. 'Render therefore unto Caesar the things which are Caesar's'—within reason."

"My superiors do not believe in this idea. I often return from these trips practically empty-handed. Once, in desperation, I almost accepted a wing from Alphonse Fedelio. But then I thought: 'What can I do with only one?'—and I gave it back. In the old days, from what I've been told, one might pick up a sack of flour, a pig or a duck. It was something. But today they won't accept that. I cannot go back to Rome now with a sow in the back seat and some bags of chestnuts in the trunk and say, 'Here are your taxes, gentlemen!' The computers would not know what to make of it."

"Frankly, I do not know what to make of the computers." Leo put down the apple and broke off a piece of cheese.

"Every year is a bad one for these people. There is no business here to speak of, no work. Their only industry is making macaroni, but no more than one ton a year reaches Naples. The lake down below has brought them nothing. It is only three feet deep. They use it to wash their clothes."

"Is there no farming?"

"Some own an acre or two, but the arable land is miles from here. The land closer to the village is worthless. Believe me, it's a miracle that these people survive at all."

"And you?"

Emilio sighed. "Me? My job is unrewarding, as I say. But I have a wife and three children to support, with another on the way. My father was a tax collector before me. . . ." He turned on his side. The springs beneath him squeaked. "Are you married?"

Leo shook his head.

"A free man, eh?"

"No, not free. Simply not married." *Il Papa* took another drink of water.

Later, the men rested in their beds. The window was open, but no wind blew.

Il Papa lay on his back, confronting the unknown into which he had willfully wandered. The girl on the altar appeared to him again, her contours blurred, her face out of focus. Then she slipped away like mercury.

Unbidden, a great sadness filled his heart. "Emilio? Is there a church in the village?" he whispered.

"Oh yes," the young man answered quickly. "There is a church, of sorts."

A church of sorts. A kind of a widow. What manner of town had he entered? "I must ask Donna Lucia the times of the Mass." Leo realized now, with sinking heart, that he could not celebrate Mass. Already, he was falling into ruination.

"I doubt there will be one. It is not the custom here."

"Not the custom? Such a thing is inconceivable . . ."

"Well, there it is. You had better talk to the priest, Aldo Guglielmo. He's rather unorthodox in his practices, or so I've heard." There was silence for a few moments. "Signor Ghezzi? Are you still awake?"

"Sì."

"Do you think it's possible we've met before? Did we share a compartment on the train between Milan and Venice?"

Leo grew cold in the warm room. He closed his eyes. "No. I have never been fortunate enough to take that train. We have never met. I am quite sure of it."

"Well then, it is a compliment to you. All this evening, I have felt that you were not unfamiliar to me. *Buona notte.*"

"*Buona notte,* Emilio."

VI

IT WAS WELL AFTER MIDNIGHT when a long black limousine roared into the Cavagnas' driveway, bucking a high wind. Even before it had come to a stop, the door on the passenger side flew open and Monsignor Ghezzi hurled himself from the car. His cassock, blowing wildly, exposed his thin, blue-white legs in black shoes and ankle socks. Monsignor Rocca stopped the automobile short and jumped out behind his colleague. Neither man said a word as they raced up the steps to the porch and into the kitchen. Pio and Cecilia, with their three oldest children, were seated at the table drinking coffee. They did not have time to open their mouths; Ghezzi spoke first.

"All right, tell me what has happened! Tell me everything you know!" His voice was hoarse and dry.

"Why don't you both sit down and have some coffee?" Pio suggested, rising from his chair.

"Coffee? Coffee?" Alfredo Rocca cried. His hair seemed to stand straight up on his scalp; his scar was black. "We don't want *refreshments*, Cavagna. This is not a social call. We want *answers!*"

"Naturally, you would like to find Giuseppe. But a little hot coffee will not impede your investigation," Pio said in measured tones.

"*Faccia presto!*" Ghezzi snarled. "Give me a complete report, every detail. Now."

Pio glowered at the two priests and walked to the other end of the room. "Start from the beginning, Cecilia. Then maybe they'll cool down."

Cecilia's eyes were puffy and red. She appeared to have shrunk a foot and aged ten years since *il Papa*'s disappearance. Rocca hardly recognized her. "There is not a great deal to tell. I arrived here at about four o'clock and found that my brother had . . . vanished. A few minutes later, my husband came home. We searched everywhere—the woods, the barn, the chicken coop—but without success. We did discover his robes and his slippers, and the *zucchetto*. Some of Pio's clothing was gone."

"Who is Pio?" Rocca interrupted.

Pio was smoking a cigarette and flicking ashes into the sink. He raised his hand.

"Go on, Signora. Please leave nothing out."

"As I said, some of my husband's clothes had disappeared—trousers, a sweater, a shirt, socks, boots, a hat—as well as *il Papa*'s breviary, his cross, the ring. Nothing else was disturbed." Cecilia paused, recalling the missing money. "That is all I know."

Ghezzi turned. "And you, Cavagna? What do you know?"

"No more than my wife. I can add only that I believe my brother-in-law took the truck."

"*Only* that he took the truck?" Ghezzi's voice quivered with sarcasm. "What truck?"

"The one I use on the weekends . . . to haul manure," Pio responded drily.

Francesco Ghezzi reflected on that for a moment and brought his handkerchief from his sleeve. Rocca stood stiffly at attention, a leather portfolio clasped under his arm. "Wait a minute." Ghezzi turned to his partner. "Alfredo, I think you had better get all this testimony on paper. Sit down and make notes."

Monsignor Rocca took the place that Pio had abandoned at the table. He opened the portfolio, removed two sheets of unlined paper, and unsheathed a fountain pen. "I'm ready."

"Have you followed the facts so far?"

"Sì . . . Signora Cavagna comes home, finds Holy Father missing. Husband arrives moments later. Search ensues." Rocca narrated as he wrote. The kitchen was silent except for the droning of his voice and the scratching of the pen. "Finds items of clothing gone. Finds truck gone."

"This 'truck,' Signor Cavagna, is it just a truck like any other truck?" Ghezzi asked, gently probing the inside of his nose with the handkerchief. When he was upset, the warts became more bothersome.

"It's a small truck with a bed . . ."

"A *bed*?" The priest grew pale at the information. "Tucked into a vehicle? What is this? I'm sorry, you must understand, I am not acquainted with farm machinery."

Pio spoke with his eyes on the floor. "My truck has an open area in back, that's all."

"I see. I thought—well . . . You know your own business, of course."

Rocca vigorously crossed out some words he had just written, squirting a small constellation of ink blots on his paper.

"What makes you think that the Holy Father borrowed your truck himself and that he was not, let us say . . . taken away in it?"

Pio ran the butt of his cigarette under cold water from the sink. "I made a careful examination of the drive out front; there are skid marks everywhere on the ground—evidence that the truck was started and stopped abruptly many times. Only one person, besides a child or a drunk, would drive that way. We have received no calls. Don't you suppose that his captors would have made themselves known by now? They would have sent one of his ears, his cross, a note of extortion to you . . . the Vatican, the government. No, this is not the work of professionals. I have a strong hunch, so to speak, based on the facts."

Monsignor Ghezzi strode up to Pio and addressed his chin. "Hunches, so to speak, will get us nowhere, Cavagna. And your other 'facts' are—please forgive me—flimsy!"

Pio returned the priest's hard gaze, as if to say, *But they are the only evidence we have.*

Francesco Ghezzi and Alfredo Rocca spent what was left of the night on the Cavagna farm. They shared the room that His Holiness had occupied just the night before. There was one small bed.

The men lay on their backs, side by side, rigid as two trees. The mattress was so soft that they slipped into the center of it. Ghezzi stared straight ahead, his mind working ceaselessly. Although he was loath to admit it, Cavagna was probably correct. In Ghezzi's opinion *il Papa* was capable of almost anything. He had run off before, as if practicing his moves; why, then, was it so far-fetched to conceive of him fleeing again? This time, permanently—swallowed up in the maelstrom wearing a farmer's hat and muddy boots.

Ghezzi's agitation grew. Does flight constitute abdication? What are the rules that govern Papal defections? Which part of canon law covers such gross outrages? Although tormented, Ghezzi almost had to laugh: In their intricacies, the questions were practically Talmudic in nature; and probably only *il Papa* himself would know the answers.

In their cramped bed, Rocca could not keep his eyes open. He was aware that his companion was still wide awake, yet his jaw fell slack and his head inclined to one side. Rocca's chin rested lightly on the other priest's shoulder. A faint whistle escaped from between his lips. He moved his leg and one toe prodded Ghezzi's ankle. Ghezzi started, then withdrew his foot. He felt Rocca's warm breath on his neck.

Dawn came. The room filled with a greyish light. A bird began to sing. A cock crowed. Through the open window a gentle wind riffled the white curtains. The house was quiet, still drowned in the last minutes of a troubled sleep.

Rocca stirred, then dozed again.

"Alfredo? Are you there?" Ghezzi inquired. Monsignor Rocca smacked his lips a few times in response. "It's getting light."

Rocca opened one eye. *"Sì."* He rubbed the one that was still closed. "I think we ought to have left last night." Then he sat up halfway, assaulted by consciousness. "We've let the Holy Father get too far ahead of us."

"How far could he have gone?" Ghezzi asked. His voice was uncustomarily drowsy. He sounded as though he were speaking from the bottom of a deep well, or from underneath the sheets. Rocca, both eyes open now, looked at his bed partner.

Monsignor Ghezzi curled one arm behind his head. His gray hair was tousled; a lock fell rakishly on his forehead. Rocca had never seen him without his glasses, without his priestly garb: How vulnerable, naked, frail, and peculiar he looked! His throat and arms were as pale and hairless as a small boy's. He wore a thin white undershirt.

"I suppose you're right ... how far could he have gotten?" Rocca repeated. "But you are certain it is essential—that is to say, appropriate—to inform no one?"

They spoke in the husky, intimate tones of two who have been kept awake all night long by a common purpose, and who have, side by side, watched the sun rise. They shared the most sensitive of professional secrets now, tugging at the tension like two ends of a short string.

"Who could we inform? The secular authorities?" Ghezzi pointed his toes, stretching. *"I poliziotti? I carabinieri?* No, I've turned it inside out a thousand times: It would be a disastrous mistake. On that point, I agree with Pio Cavagna, probably for the first and last time: We must handle this business ourselves. If the world were ever to discover that the Holy Father has ..." he lowered his voice, "broken out ..."

Rocca's next thought brought him fully awake. "I do not dare imagine what would happen! Our posi—the position of the Church—is unsteady at best. Even the devout have begun to leave in large numbers. If we were to let on now that *il Papa* has left too ... My God, we'd be finished!"

"*Sì*. But I do not have to—I do not want to—dwell on your unseemly constructions, while the very future of the faith may be at stake." Monsignor Ghezzi sat up in bed, as if struck from behind. "Not to mention our own lives! Everything I have worked so hard all these years to build!" His voice shook. "A place for myself, the respect of society. I will not have *him* tear it down!—" He paused in mid-sentence. "If it were only Leo himself, if he were the only one involved, I'd almost consider forgetting—"

"Forgetting? ... What?"

"Never mind. The rest of the world is involved, so I am going to get up and get washed and get out of here." Ghezzi swung his legs over the side of the bed. Monsignor Rocca kept his head turned until Ghezzi had put on his soutane and closed all thirty-three buttons.

. . .

Leo awoke just as the sky was growing light. On the bed next to his, Emilio Galeazzi slept heavily, his breathing deep and noisy. The footlocker still occupied the floor between them. The water bottle was empty. The white meat of a half-eaten apple had turned brown, and the sweet fragrance of the fruit reminded Leo of his youth. He felt refreshed and rested. Once he had fallen off, stretched out on his side, his sleep had been blissfully sound, and he woke up in the same position.

Examining the walls around him, Leo mused on his situation. There were some large gashes in the plaster as if it had been pulled apart by giant hands or ruined in a war long over. He felt caught between two waking dreams: the one he was living and the one he had just left behind. His arm had fallen asleep beneath him. He cupped and uncupped his hand, feeling as though he held a ball of pins. This was the only physical reality. The rest of him was numb. Then he saw Alfredo Rocca in his mind's eye, accompanied inevitably by Francesco Ghezzi. It had not occurred to *il Papa* until this moment that, of course, they would try to come after him. Yet, if he were to remain in this remote and ravaged village, what then? And if he were to move on, how long before the masquerade would collapse?

.   .   .

"Let's get going right now!" Monsignor Rocca suggested, quite heartily. His taste for the hunt, it seemed to the others, had already gotten the better of him.

"Not so fast," Ghezzi replied, ominous. "First we will return to the Vatican. A necessary side trip, I'm afraid."

Pio ground out his cigarette in an ashtray made of brown clay and blew out a last lungful of smoke.

"Aren't you wasting precious time, Padre?" he asked. The three men sat at the Cavagnas' kitchen table, drinking espresso out of small white cups.

"No, Signor Cavagna. I simply refuse to race off *half-cocked*," Ghezzi said, indulging a penchant for the American idiom, "on what could well turn out to be a fool's errand. As it happens, there is an . . . important informant in Rome whom I must see. He may hold the key. Besides, it's only two hours' drive. We can be there and back before sunset."

Pio regarded the aging priest with reluctant admiration. The man knew his own mind; perhaps he knew even more than that.

.   .   .

For breakfast, the innkeeper served the salesman, Giuseppe Ghezzi, and the tax collector, Emilio Galeazzi, *caffelatte,* bread and butter, hard cheese, and one boiled egg apiece.

Lucia Fedelio had given birth to three children in her young life, but only one had lived past infancy. Isabella, stone deaf, moved about the room heavily. When she placed the bread before *il Papa,* her developing bosom brushed his cheek. Isabella's skin was bumpy, her teeth protruded over her bottom lip, her thick, coarse hair hung in two stubby braids; she had the ungainly look of sudden adolescence.

To make her burden worse, the girl had lost her father early—whether to a pair of wings or simple wanderlust hardly mattered. Leo wondered at the paradoxes of life: that a man presumably lighter than air could have left behind this poor child with no more buoyancy than a block of cement. Yet, at the same time, she seemed fragile, somehow ephemeral, as if she might evaporate without warning. A strong force could move across the earth a bit too angrily and wipe out Isabella and all those like her.

Meanwhile, she went about, modest, unperturbed, and imperiled, "a pale shadow," Leo thought, "trapped in flesh she has not made her own." The girl appeared to him to belong to some ancient race, bound together not by blood but by a sort of luminous suffering. Theirs was a passion hidden even from themselves and, perhaps because of that, they endured.

"Has she always been this way?" Leo whispered when the girl turned her back, realizing, as he said it, that she could not hear him.

Lucia Fedelio hovered near the breakfast table, watching Emilio as he ate absorbedly, chasing a lump of cheese around and around on his plate. Her silken hair hung in a long unplaited tail down her back and her eyes were bright as she enjoyed the male company. This lovely woman's gentle mouth and round, healthy cheeks seemed to have so little to do with the poor mute to whom she had given life! *Il Papa* strained to see God's hand at work—aware that children like Isabella were, to some, a sign that He did not exist at all. Leo recalled that, as a young priest engaged in pastoral work, he had always been hard put to comfort the parents of a sickly or deformed infant, uncertain how to assure them, in their anguish, that they had not been overlooked.

"She's been deaf and dumb since birth," Donna Lucia replied, matter-of-factly. "Her two brothers were perfect, jewels of children, but they were taken from me three winters ago. First one and then the other in the flu epidemic. There is no real doctor here and no hospital or clinic nearby. Mario in December, and Rinaldo in January. Only Isabella is left, and all that I have in the world." Donna Lucia hesitated, not sure that either man appreciated hearing her sad tale.

But Giuseppe Ghezzi, the good-looking older one, wanted to hear more. Evidently hungry for conversation and curious about her circumstances, he invited her to sit with them at the table. She observed him from under her eyelashes, intent and curious too, although not quite looking at him in a direct way. He was different from ordinary men—polite to a fault, somewhat withdrawn and given to reflection. As he ate, he would suddenly stop, as if captured by some deep thought, then return after a while to the plate in front of him. Who was he? Donna Lucia wondered. She was not sure even that he was a true native of Italy. As he spoke, she listened carefully for the accents of another language, but to no avail. His Italian was without flaw, sometimes even lapsing into Neapolitan dialect. Donna Lucia, encouraged by his interest and clear concern, revealed more of her life and her daughter's than she had ever revealed before to anyone.

"Isabella is usually a good girl, but sometimes she goes wild . . . weeping, howling, beating her head on the floor as if driven crazy by her own silence. I am the only one who can return her to herself, and even for me it takes a long time—hours, sometimes a whole day." The mother spoke with her eyes on the table.

Embarrassed by the intimacy of her revelations, Emilio changed the subject. "Donna Lucia," he said, wiping his lips, "Giuseppe would like to attend Mass. I told him he would have to ask Aldo Guglielmo."

"It won't do any good. I would ask him myself, but he frightens me," she said.

Il Papa stiffened. Since his ordination, he had never gone a single day without celebrating Mass. Now there was not even a Mass to attend. "Why does Guglielmo frighten you?" He leaned away from the table, having eaten too much, and too quickly.

Donna Lucia seemed relieved to turn from the trials of her daughter. "He came here many years ago, exiled."

"Exiled? For what reason?"

"This man was nothing but questions, as if he had just been born into the world," the woman thought. She lowered her voice. "Nothing remarkable. He had a love affair with a girl and a child was born."

Leo put his elbows on the table and cupped his chin in his hands. For the first time, his eyes met Lucia Fedelio's.

"Priests in the countryside occasionally father bastards, you know; here it is less of a dishonor. But he was from the city; from Milan, I think, maybe Turin. There it is scandalous, to say the least. They sent him away, with the girl and the child.

"Don Aldo lived here with her. A year or so after they came, she left him with the little boy. He began to drink. Then his son died." Donna Lucia looked at Emilio, unsettled by Leo's gaze. "He was a beautiful child, as sweet as any angel. Perhaps because his father was a priest, do you suppose?"

Leo shook his head. "Priests are not so different from other men, I should think. They do not father angels, of that I am certain."

"Well, even now it breaks my heart to think of it. . . . Since then, Don Aldo refuses to perform his priestly duties. He wants to be paid for everything. So?" She held out her eloquent hands. "Is he right? Is he wrong? A priest too must live. He cannot eat the Blessed Sacrament, God preserve us. But no one has any money for him. We can't afford to support a doctor, much less a priest. And if you ask him even the tiniest favor, he barks like a dog and sends you away. Mostly he stays up on the mountain near our sorry church. He rarely comes into the village. . . ." She let out her breath as if to encompass the whole world's troubles. "He is the way that he is."

After breakfast, Donna Lucia walked with him to the door. *"Arrivederci,"* she said, in a throaty voice.

Leo rolled restlessly on the balls of his feet, his heart drumming.

Franco Pisticci was sunning himself in front of his tavern when *il Papa* came down the street. He had tipped his chair against the wall and his feet rose off the ground. Another clumsily hand-rolled cigarette dangled from his lips. A family who lived in a house across the street from the café was just then carrying a square table and some chairs into the road. Leo watched as the grandmother, her face as grey as an old pot, tossed a tasseled blue cloth over the table. The grandfather emerged with a dish of olive oil and a piece of crusty bread and took up a position in one of the chairs, aimlessly scanning the horizon. Nearby, a donkey decked out in brass bells strolled, unattended, urinating in a loud yellow stream.

Leo's truck stood just where he had left it, in front of the café. On the hood, a scrawny, underfed rooster paraded shakily back and forth, as if showing off its last vestiges of virility before surrendering to the next life. Its crown was not bright red but an anemic shade of pink. The day was clear and brilliant; however, a chill had set in and a sharp tang cut the air, as if the sea were not far off.

Leo shivered and drew his brother-in-law's sweater closer. Pisticci's only concession to the drop in temperature had been to pull on a short-sleeved cotton shirt over his undershirt. When he saw Leo approaching he smiled.

"Winter is coming now for sure," he said affably. Pisticci glanced at his belly and caressed it like an old friend. "Lots of flesh keeps out the drafts. I'm one of the lucky ones. Every year there are great losses." He blew a thick stream of smoke out through his nostrils and, without prompting, went on. "An old man goes out to tend his miserable acre; if he does not return by nightfall, we know that someone will bring home his body in the morning. Children freeze to death in their beds." He spoke with solemn resignation, almost casually.

Il Papa had read such stories in the newspapers, enclosed in boxes like obituary notices. These tragedies had pricked him for a moment in the region of the heart—sharp needles, quickly retracted. But this morning the pain was knifelike and did not dissolve.

"And you, Signor Pisticci? Have you a wife, children?"

"Six of them. With two wives. Two of my children are dead . . . so are my wives. The other four children, all boys, got out of here as soon as they could." He recited his story—once again, of deaths in life—without emotion or irony, as if it were no more than simple arithmetic: add, subtract, divide. "I rarely hear from any of them. If this means good news or bad, I have no idea." Pisticci dismissed the issue, almost lightly. "In our lives, good news, bad news . . . there is not much difference. The good is never so good and the bad comes so often . . . one grows accustomed." Tossing his head back, he closed his eyes and raised his face to the sky, as if sunbathing—or counting more wasted lives.

"Your café, does it sustain you?" Leo asked.

"Well enough," Pisticci replied. "Nothing else I tried was better." He launched into a litany of occupations, dredging his memory slowly, the way a steamshovel turns the earth. "Snail-catcher . . . welder . . . used-parts dealer . . . grave digger . . . grape-sorter . . . cigarette-smuggler . . . boot-polisher . . . tree-chopper . . . spaghetti-maker . . . lavatory attendant . . . pimp . . ." He scratched his head and looked at Leo. "But I never amounted to anything. All of these pursuits required energy—which with me was always in short supply. Now, with the café, although I don't make any money, at least I can sit still." Like Donna Lucia, Franco Pisticci accommodated his burdens artlessly, even with a certain grace.

"How did Aldo Guglielmo lose his son?" Leo asked the café owner.

Franco Pisticci sat up. His feet and the legs of the chair hit the ground with a thud. "Where did you hear about that?"

"From Lucia Fedelio. I said to her that I needed to go to Mass, and she told me about your priest."

"He's no priest of mine."

"Donna Lucia implied he was . . . something of . . . a drinker."

"He's a charlatan, that's what he is, taking up valuable space on earth. . . ."

"Defrocked maybe, but probably no charlatan," *il Papa* murmured. An expert in linguistics, he knew the etymology of that word: from the Latin, *cerretamus*—a seller of papal indulgences to sinners slated for punishment.

"Would you like to know the story of how Guglielmo's boy died?"

This little town, too small to appear on most maps, teemed with stories, Leo thought, and men and women whose only relief was to tell them.

"Guglielmo's girl walked out on him. One day soon after, he was smoking, drinking, feeling sorry for himself, and fell asleep on the ground outside his house. The cigarette in his hand set fire to some dry grass, which, in turn, set the house on fire. That bastard woke in time to save himself, but not his son, his little Vittorio. Flames were visible for miles. The whole town came running. We did what we could. It was not enough. Guglielmo screamed . . . for days, I think. 'Cries of grief' describes nothing. He seemed to be looking into . . ."

". . . into the pit of hell," Leo finished, without realizing he had spoken.

Both men were silent.

"Nevertheless, for all his agony, which seemed real enough, I despise the man," Pisticci said finally. He threw the butt of his cigarette over his shoulder. "So, do you still wish to see him?"

Leo nodded.

"Why, for God's sake? To pray? To receive the Sacrament? Do you really believe in these superstitious rites, that they will get you anywhere in this world? Do you really think He takes our burdens on His own shoulders?" Pisticci snorted. "Well, my shoulders don't feel any less weighed down!"

Il Papa frowned. He was drawn to the man who had glimpsed the inferno, and wanted to hear his story from his own lips. "If Don Aldo were actually the reprobate that the townspeople believed," Leo thought, "he would no longer possess the right to perform priestly functions." "Will you tell me where to find Father Guglielmo?" he asked.

Pisticci set his mouth in a hard line. "I've grown to rather like you in this short time. You're a good and simple man. I can tell that you care for people, even for strangers. So here is some friendly advice: Leave Don Guglielmo alone. You will only regret it if you so much as go near that son of a bitch."

Leo thought for a moment. "Please tell me the way," he said finally.

The fat man stood up. He pivoted *il Papa* around by his shoulders. "It is at your own risk. Follow this road. At the end of it, take the left fork, the one that leads to the hills, not the one that goes into the valley. Farther on, you will see my house: It is the only one around that is not made of stone. Pass it by. Do not stop; there is nothing much to see. Keep walking. Soon enough, you'll come to Guglielmo's shack. The church is in a grove of trees behind it. *Buona fortuna.*" Slamming the door behind him, he was swallowed into the darkness of his café.

VII

"YOU!" FRANCESCO GHEZZI SCREAMED, pointing a well-manicured finger. "You were the last man to be alone with him! What did he say?"

Though fearful, the bishop refused to reply. He was seated in a low chair that might have been built for a child. His knees were drawn up to his chest. Biondi's bloated ankles hung over the tops of his black shoes. The stiff collar above his purple soutane cut sharply into his jowls.

They were huddled in a room at the very apex of the Apostolic Palace—a neglected place, almost never used. The only furniture in it had the look of having been recently pulled out of storage: two low chairs, a red velvet stool with one leg missing, a wooden desk. The walls were dark green, bare of pictures or decorations. In one corner a stack of old issues of *L'Osservatore Romano* moldered, bound with cord. On the desk, old jelly glasses, grime-misted and filled with dust, were arranged in a circle, as if awaiting a celebration of ghosts. A green shade was drawn over the single barred window. The only light in the room emanated from a globe balanced in the slender arms of a naked brass nymph. When Ghezzi entered, he had twisted her to face the wall so that now the three priests beheld her chaste back and cushiony buttocks. It was a gloomy setting, but one came here for privacy. Only two or three members of the pontifical family knew of its existence.

"You understand I can say nothing," Biondi whispered.

"I don't understand that at all! Now I will implore you one more time to tell me everything the Holy Father said when you last saw him."

Again the bishop would not respond.

Ghezzi put a hand on his hip, assuming a studiously informal pose. "Tell me, for instance: Did he make his confession?" The monsignor's tone had changed without warning. He took a more disarming tack.

"I came to *hear* his confession . . ." The bishop held his big hands in his lap and kept his eyes upon them.

Monsignor Ghezzi grew harsh again. "Is it impossible for you to give me a direct answer? I asked a direct question: *Did he make his confession?*"

Biondi hesitated. It was not easy to keep up with his questioner's chameleon-like swings of mood. "No! He did not make his confession. Nevertheless, what happened between us must be held in confidence. . . ."

Approaching his victim, Ghezzi bent down. The bishop felt the priest's gaze peel him raw. "I'll have you thrown in jail, Biondi. I'll have you locked away for the rest of your life, if you don't tell me what the Holy Father said to you. The fate of us all may rest on it."

A dreadful silence descended upon the room. Beset by anxiety, Monsignor Rocca turned a button on his gown so roughly that it came off in his hand. He lowered his head, impotent and unhappy.

Biondi addressed Ghezzi with dignity, pasting together the shattered pieces of his sanity like a collage. "This isn't the Middle Ages, you know, when bishops were carted away like so much trash, Francesco. You do not frighten me."

"What must be done will be done." Ghezzi's tone was menacing and clipped. "I have many friends."

Rocca raised his eyes from the hole torn in his cassock. He wondered: Did his colleague actually possess such power? As closely and as long as they had worked together, some things about Monsignor Ghezzi remained mysterious. Rocca had never seen the inside of the priest's apartments; he had never heard him speak of his family, although he knew that his father was still alive, and that he had many brothers and sisters in Genoa. But Ghezzi concerned himself only with those matters that concerned the Vatican.

"If a man has to be locked up before he comes to his senses, then he will be locked up," the monsignor continued in a dark but level tone. "If he needs to be punished, then he will be punished. Do not misjudge me. I mean what I say. Our very lives are threatened, as I may have pointed out before, no less than the life of our Church!"

Biondi longed for a cigarette for the first time in twenty years. "You are trying to force me to violate my own ethics," he said. "Whatever passed between us passed between *us*. Whether His Holiness confessed or not, I hold to the same principles: Worthy or sacrilegious, our encounter must remain private. I can make no exception—not to save your life or mine—or even for the common welfare. Pope or no Pope, *I will not do it!*"

Having said that much, Biondi seemed to regain his composure. He looked up at Ghezzi. "As a bishop, I have certain privileges of . . . seniority. And you? A mere monsignor. What is that? Nothing. *Nothing.* A purely honorary title, a member of the papal household. You have no office, no jurisdiction—and no power, except the power that you have usurped!"

Rocca winced, and the scar on his face tightened into a neat crease.

When Ghezzi spoke again, his lips barely moved. His eyes glowed with murky, passionate fire. Somewhere deep in his heart he seemed to nurture a perverse appetite for the very confrontation that was now provoking his fury. "We will see about my jurisdiction, as you call it. We'll just see how far it extends."

The bishop saw that Ghezzi's fingernails had turned almost blue.

"I am not through yet, Biondi. You know of the dog thrown into the ring who fights to the death for what he believes? I am like him."

"That dog does not have beliefs, Francesco. He fights because he is trained to kill," Biondi replied.

"But he fights, Pietro. The thing is, he fights." Ghezzi moved to the door. "Let's go, Alfredo."

The two men left the room, Rocca's head bowed in shame for his companion. Biondi heard a key turn in the lock.

An hour later, the key turned again. Monsignor Rocca came in carrying an oval silver tray covered with a white napkin. The bishop stood by the window. The shade was still drawn. Rocca set the tray on the desk and removed the cloth. There was a mug of steaming tea, a bowl of greenish soup with threads of vegetables and stringy meat floating in it, and four golden cookies on a flowered plate.

"I've brought you something to eat," Rocca said. "I'm sorry it's not more."

Biondi glumly stared at the food. "I don't want any of that. Take it away." Monsignor Rocca picked up the soup bowl and took a step forward. Biondi held out his hand to halt Rocca's advance. "Does *he* know you're here? That little rat? Did he authorize this visit?"

Rocca shook his head. "No. He's busy elsewhere."

"Arranging with his 'friends' for my punishment . . ."

Rocca shook his head again.

Biondi's voice grew confidential. "You must tell me, Alfredo, what in God's name has happened to *il Papa?*"

"*Il Papa* is quite, uh, quite as usual. Don't fret."

"Look, I am not a child or an idiot. Your partner has taken me hostage for good reason. *What has happened to the Holy Father?*"

Rocca's eyes met Biondi's. "I am not at liberty to speak. I am under strict orders." Ill at ease, he traced Leo's baptismal name with his finger in the dust on top of the old wooden desk. He knew full well that, sooner or later, they would have to deal honestly with the bishop.

"Whose orders?"

"Monsignor Ghezzi's. Whose do you think?"

"Is the Holy Father ill?"

"No."

"Then what has he done now? Where is he?"

"How should I know?" Rocca eyed Biondi cautiously, unsure of his opponent but convinced that, at least for the present, he could emerge the victor in this contest.

"Has he tried to take his life, Heaven help us?"

"God forbid!"

"Has he abdicated?"

"No . . . not really." Rocca instantly realized his indiscretion. His face turned the color of tallow.

Biondi, pensive, rubbed at his cheek. He seemed in no great hurry, suddenly, to continue the interrogation.

Monsignor Rocca set down the bowl of soup that had grown cold in his hand. "No, *no!* You're barking up the wrong tree. Abdication . . . is . . . a formal procedure." He waved his arms stiffly in the unmoving air, as if to erase from the bishop's mind whatever dangerous thoughts his slip of the tongue had planted there.

Biondi stared at the panicky man. "Calm down, Alfredo. You've revealed nothing."

Rocca backed away, toward the door. "*Sì, sì.* There is nothing at all to reveal," he said, his eyes on the doorknob. "Why don't you lift the shade, Excellency? You have a good view of all Rome from up here."

"I know already what is out there," the bishop mumbled.

. . .

The path on which Leo walked was as narrow and cramped as an alley, lined with little houses in worse repair, if anything, than those near Pisticci's café. They were stooped with the years, their once hard angles blurred by time and the elements. Some were split down the middle like pits of rotten fruit.

As *il Papa* went, the passage widened and he came upon two larger dwellings—veritable castles in comparison to the rest—with columns in front and turrets, like watchtowers, on top. These must have been constructed long ago by wealthy landowners, Leo surmised. But they had since fallen into dereliction, too, and were now occupied by squatters. A girl with ulcers on her legs sat on the stoop cleaning her feet with a rag. An older woman emerged from the courtyard within and called to her children, who were nowhere in sight. Her voice was weary, indifferent.

"Vergilio! Renato! I'll throw your food to the cats if you don't come home for supper. . . ." Two urchins, crouched in the shade of one of the ruined castles, were playing a game with tin cans. They ignored the threats. Farther on, an old woman with a kerchief over her head sat on a low stool in front of her house peeling onions and slicing them into a wooden bowl. As tears rolled down her cheeks, she brushed them away with the back of her wrist and kept working.

Other women walked on the road. Some, with tired faces and dull expressions, went about their errands silently. Others, whose eyes were still bright and figures still trim, promenaded in clusters, gossiping, giggling, spinning tales. ". . . and so he swore that the next time he would cut off both her ears with a meat cleaver!" Leo heard one of them say, and laugh. He walked quickly—uneasy, yet enchanted by this street of women. He tried not to notice that they watched him shyly, questioningly, as he passed.

The road turned and gave on a piazza. Paved with broad flagstones, it was bounded by low walls and buildings and, on one side, by a sheer drop into the valley below. Here, near one wall, the men congregated. Some of the older ones played cards, speaking not a word. Others chatted, their tones thick, like honey poured from a jar. The younger men laughed roughly, sharing bottles of red wine, which they passed from hand to hand. Between swigs, they pushed one another around with the careless violence of those who have not enough to occupy their days. They bet earnestly on local events: When would Benedetto have another one of his raucous sneezing fits? Was tonight the night that Cristina and Lorenzo would go to bed? What were the odds that old Alphonse Fedelio would ever waft back again? What time would the sun set? How many stars might appear in the sky?

A middle-aged man in a dark shirt and a knit cap stood at the wall, somber and immobile. He stared into the valley, seeming like all of them to wait without hope for something to happen. Watching him, Leo remembered his uncle, a shopkeeper in Massa Marittima, always anticipating customers who never came. Not rich enough to close his shop, but not rich enough to keep it open either, he simply waited, speechless, vacant, unexpectant.

There was a fountain in the middle of the square in which the possibly religious statue of a female reposed, but *il Papa* could not fix her identity. Her nose was badly chipped, her cheeks were pitted, and her chin had been worn away by water that dribbled for centuries from her parted lips. A little girl, with legs so thin that the flesh seemed soldered to the bone, skipped around the statue in the shallow pond. She held her cotton skirt in her hands. A young boy bathed his face in the water.

Leo wandered toward the wall where there were fewer people. He did not wish to talk to anyone. He had engaged in too many conversations; the salesman's charade had begun to drain his energy. For the first time, surrounded by the men of the town, his isolation lay like a stone on his back.

Leo looked over the wall. A ravine yawned below. It was wide at the place nearest him and choked off by rocky brown cliffs farther away. He saw now that, like the village itself, the piazza had been built into the side of the mountain. Everything here appeared to exist at the edge, teetering on the brink of extinction. In the ravine were some of the "miserable acres" that Pisticci had mentioned. But, looking down on them, Leo was certain that the café owner had exaggerated their size. These patches of soil could not be calculated in acres but, at best, in feet. They were situated among boulders, low scrub, and dried streambeds. Another mountain loomed beyond the cliffs; small settlements dotted the face of it like smudges. The Supreme Pontiff stood for a long time studying the view and listening to the voices of the men, who—unlike the women—seemed intent on disregarding the presence of a stranger.

He turned around. In the fountain, the girl continued to play. The boy had finished washing and was wiping his face on his sleeve. "C'mon Pasqualina," he called, holding out his hand, "it's time to go." She ignored him. "Come *on,* Pasqualina. *Andiamo!*" She shook her head. "You want me to climb up there and pull you down? *Pasqualina?*"

Leo watched the children a moment longer, admiring the young man's tenacity, his strength of will. The scene in the waters of the fountain seemed to *il Papa* staged for his benefit alone. Nobody else on the piazza was aware of Pasqualina and her solicitous young companion.

Leo jammed his hands in his pockets and walked on. The thin, translucent walls of his mind, which once had admitted only the palest colors and the muffled noises of the vivid world outside, seemed ready to burst.

· · ·

Cecilia Cavagna lay prostrate on her bed, a damp cloth over her forehead. She moaned softly.

Pio turned from the closet. "You know, your brother helped himself not only to my favorite boots but to my favorite sweater as well—the one without buttons." His tone was that of a husband trying to maintain his equilibrium and sense of humor against impossible odds.

"It was a rag," she murmured. "Where are those maniacs? What's taking them so long?"

"It's early yet." Pio folded a pair of pants into an old suitcase. "Ghezzi assured me they would be back before suppertime and I believe him. We will find Giuseppe. Soon. I promise." His words hung in the air like smoke after a fire.

· · ·

Monsignor Ghezzi strode into the room, shutting the door behind him. "Wake up! Get up!"

Biondi was snoring in the little chair, his chin resting on his chest, his long arms limp at his sides.

"Snap out of it, Pietro. We're going."

The bishop did not respond swiftly. His brain oozed with fatigue and confusion, as pus from an infected wound. Monsignor Ghezzi, at the window, jerked at the shade, and released it with an ear-splitting crack.

"Uhhh!" The bishop protested.

Ghezzi inspected the tray. "You didn't eat. You will destroy your health." He lifted a cookie from the plate and thrust it at his prisoner. "Here, have a bite."

"You have a bite," Biondi said foggily.

"It's good. It's just a nice, fresh little butter cookie. Sister Angelica outdid herself this morning," Monsignor Ghezzi said. "I had one not ten minutes ago." He popped a whole one into his mouth, seeming a different man altogether than the villain who had visited Biondi only a little while earlier.

The bishop rubbed his eyes as he attempted to put his mind in order. Was *il Papa's cameriere segreto* a madman? His latest change of mood, this abrupt solicitousness, caught Biondi off guard. Had *he* done something to the Holy Father? When Ghezzi commanded, "We're going!" what did he mean? Go where? What was next on this incomprehensible agenda?

Biondi struggled to his feet. His legs had knotted; pains shot through his groin.

"My first—my *only* responsibility—is to *il Papa*. He is my single care and my trust. I will not move an inch until I know where I am bound and why."

"You will accompany Monsignor Rocca and myself. We are . . . leaving here."

"Leaving Rome? Where the devil are you—are *we*—going?"

Biondi's simple question seemed to transform Ghezzi into a very old man. For a moment, he appeared to totter. His cool eyes lost their keenness and turned in on themselves, as if attending a secret vision. "Even I do not know where we are going, precisely," he admitted. "By now, I suppose you must have guessed: The Holy Father is missing."

"But the other times . . ."

"This is not like the other times. This time is different. He has totally evaporated, like water in a dish."

"I see," Biondi said in a whisper, his body growing cold. If what Ghezzi told him was the truth, then he had no reason now to continue to resist. It was better that he should be with them. He—who was *il Papa's* confessor, and far closer to him than either of these men—must not be left behind. He could not leave the Holy Father to Ghezzi's less than tender mercies.

"Come, Pietro, collect yourself." Ghezzi sighed so deeply that he drew up a cough. "You may wait in my office until we depart."

The monsignor went to the door and opened it. The bishop did not move.

"Pietro! Are you crippled?"

"I only want to understand. What plan have you in mind?"

Ghezzi did not turn around. "We're going after him. Unfortunately, there is no alternative."

Biondi nodded wordlessly and followed Ghezzi from the room.

. . .

Il Papa sat down on the ground in front of Franco Pisticci's house. More a hovel than a human habitation, it seemed to be made of metal—tin perhaps—salvaged from the hulks of automobiles. A chimney, actually a broken, blackened tail pipe, emerged through a hole cut into the flat roof.

Despite the café proprietor's admonition, Leo could not help resting here for a minute. He leaned back against the trunk of a tree, contemplating Pisticci's dwelling. The foliage caused the sunlight to fall in a dappled pattern on the rusty earth. A squirrel ran near his hand, eyeing *il Papa* in a friendly, exploratory way. Its coat was brown and lustrous, its ears like tiny petals, its pink mouth guarded by rows of sharp, perfectly white teeth. The squirrel reared on its hindquarters displaying a rounded belly. Even in this emaciated environment, the little creature glowed with health, a living testament to the power of survival. Animals! To Leo, they seemed reverse mirrors of men, relieved of the humiliations, complications, fears, greed, and all the thwarted passions that ruined human lives. He listened for a while to the songs of earthly things; then, turning, looked out over the wide sweep of the valley where an autumn wind bent the grasses.

At last he stood up, brushed the dirt from his trousers, and moved on up the road, toward his meeting with the mysterious priest, Guglielmo.

· · ·

Monsignor Rocca took the wheel.

Francesco Ghezzi sat beside him, Rocca's leather portfolio on his lap, bulging now with dozens of annotated scraps of paper, a fistful of road maps, and two skinny tourist guides to the towns of Southern Italy. The bishop sat in the back of the boxy, green Fiat, an overnight case at his feet. He had rolled up the window on his side of the car. Outside, the city sights and sounds were unfamiliar, jarring. On a normal day, at this hour, he enjoyed retiring to his apartment for a pre-prandial nap.

The men rode silently, each one alone with his thoughts. The fiery rays of an evening sun blinded Rocca, who lowered the visor. The streets through which they drove teemed with Vatican personnel, all bound for home. Monsignor Ghezzi offered a whispered prayer, as they drew close to the Arch of Bells, that the Swiss Guards stationed there would not recognize the passengers in this particular sedan. Their faces, after all, were well-known to many of the workers and inhabitants of the city. There was no special danger from the Guard, but Ghezzi was unprepared to make small talk or to offer an explanation for their sudden departure.

His prayer was answered. There was a good deal of bustle at the gate; amid the comings and goings, they passed without inquiry or inspection.

Once safely away, Ghezzi breathed an audible sigh of relief that gave the others permission to speak.

"Slipped one over on them, eh?" the bishop said, in a tone as ingratiating as he could muster. He had swiftly decided that the most pragmatic course was to make peace with the two priests. He would demonstrate his involvement in their plans, in whatever lay ahead. He would not remain the odd man out, divorced from his companions, dragged along as an unwilling victim. No, he would cooperate. In that way, he could be of more use to *il Papa*.

Monsignor Ghezzi swiveled in his seat. "First, we will stop at his sister's house," he said, outlining the first step of the mission, "to pick up her husband."

"Why?" Biondi asked.

"As you know, when he . . . faded out, the Holy Father was spending a few days with his sister, Cecilia Cavagna. Signora Cavagna's husband, Pio, is somewhat more familiar than we are with southern geography. Besides, if we did not allow him to come, *she* would insist on joining us, and that would be . . . grisly."

Biondi cleared his throat. "I, for one, will welcome an experienced navigator. But why the South? Why not the coast? Why not the North? The Lake District . . . he is partial to water. As a boy, he sailed . . ." Despair settled like sediment in the bishop's chest at every thought of Leo, now just a grain of sand among millions, billions.

"We have to begin somewhere, sir," Ghezzi responded. "Are you proposing that he left us merely to resume a youthful pasttime? The Cavagnas themselves are to the south. *Il Papa*—if he wished to escape, if that was truly his wish—would doubtless not head back, toward Rome, but would flee farther from Rome. Doesn't that make sense?" Ghezzi turned in his seat again and faced the rear. "Or do you honestly believe he went away in order to indulge a passion for *water travel*? Maybe we should go to Venice? Perhaps he's disguised himself as a *gondoliere*."

The bishop grew angry, then shriveled. Actually, nothing made sense. Or, rather, one possibility made as much sense—or nonsense—as another. *Il Papa*'s disappearance, his desertion, was still raw and undigested.

"A puff of white smoke announced his election," Biondi said

aloud, wistful, "and he has remained as elusive as that ever since. I have been his confessor all this time and am better acquainted with him than most, yet he has always slipped away, even from me, like a handful of smoke." He stopped then, realizing that he acknowledged feelings that were more wisely kept to himself. "I . . . I apologize, Francesco, for going on. It is all so new to me. You and Alfredo have by now accommodated some of the trauma. I'm sorry; your plan seems excellent."

Rocca nodded with vigor. He had to make himself heard, he knew—issue some sort of opening shot—or be relegated for the duration to the permanent status of chauffeur. Even here, in this closed space and under these crisis circumstances, one still had to maneuver for position. "*Sì, sì,* we have confronted the calamity with, if I may say, aplomb! As *il Papa* himself once said to me, about facing the worst: 'If the floor caves in beneath you, you do not sit in the hole, laughing, and say, "The floor did not cave in, what's for supper?" ' " Nobody laughed.

"He *said* that?" Ghezzi asked in a tone of disgust.

"*Sì!*" Rocca continued, prattling on for Biondi's benefit with unself-conscious enthusiasm. "Of course, we examined numerous courses of action before settling on this one. The influenza story we gave to the press, and even the story we told within the Palace, were worked out well beforehand."

Rocca hit a bump and the clerics, as one man, shot up toward the ceiling of the automobile.

"Just what tale have you given to the Palace?" Biondi inquired.

"*Il Papa* has chosen to go into seclusion at an undisclosed location in the North," Ghezzi said, casting an evil eye at Rocca. "He has moved from the Vatican because, while convalescing from his illness, he must have complete and undisturbed peace and privacy."

"And why—if you will forgive me for playing the devil's advocate—has he not gone to Castel Gandolfo," Biondi asked, "as is his custom?"

"Tourists. Too many of them. 'As is his custom,' " Ghezzi mimicked the bishop, "he would be passing out blessings like candies, shaking hands, and kissing all the little babies. The press, and everyone else, would become suspicious, if they did not see him in the streets. Listen, don't worry, they believe what I say implicitly . . . that we are on our way to His Holiness."

The bishop sucked his teeth, making inadvertent sounds of skepticism.

VIII

ALDO GUGLIELMO SAID NOTHING AT FIRST, as he dabbed with a
cloth at a little pink hole on his jaw. Leo and he stared into each
other's eyes through a crack in the door.

"Cut myself," the priest explained finally, his expression morbid.

"*Che?*" Leo blurted out, as if awakened from a trance. He had expected another sort of man, ruder-looking, older.

"Nicked myself . . . shaving." He opened the door wider.

Father Guglielmo had an exquisite, fine-featured, almost feline
face. Perhaps that was why, Leo concluded, he seemed excessively
concerned by the notch he had just put into it. His flawless porce-
lain complexion appeared all the more so framed in the dark rectan-
gle of the doorway. His cheekbones were set very high; the light
blue eyes, vaguely slanted, were fringed by long, heavy lashes. He

had thin, sensitive lips and fair brown hair that grew halfway over
his ears. But his earlobes were purple, full, and angry, as if engorged
with blood.

"You have found the rectory. Want to come in, or do you prefer
to stand there, gaping?" Guglielmo asked, seeming half-amused.
He spoke as though to someone he had been expecting, someone
he knew.

Il Papa was taken aback. Guglielmo did not snap, bark, or close
the door in his face. He stepped aside to admit him into his home.
He appeared to be sober. The rough and casual welcome from this
rather elegant man startled Leo. The priest was neither friendly
nor unfriendly. He had the manner of a man who allows the undertaker into his home: without welcoming the presence, he accepts its
necessity, and so treats the visitor civilly but with a certain re-
serve.

Entering, Leo cleared his throat nervously and, unthinking,
passed a hand over his face as if to draw a mask. "Thank you for
receiving me without warning," he said.

Father Guglielmo led Leo into the space behind him, extending
his arm with a lumpy gallantry. "Unexpected visitors . . . Well, I've
got nothing left to lose, so why not?"

There was only a single room. Franco Pisticci had not misrepre-
sented the priest's living quarters any more than his own. Both
were just shacks—four thin walls gracelessly erected against the
rain, wind, heat, and cold. For a few moments, Leo was blinded by
the dark that surrounded him. Presently, he discerned a cot in one
corner of Guglielmo's room, then a rocking chair, a square table,
and a straight wooden chair. On the far wall, over one window,
hung a small crucifix. Two fat candles burned on a battered bureau.
A kerosene lamp sat on the table; its flame sputtered, starved
for fuel. The eaves of the roof extended so low over the three
small windows that Leo could not imagine sun ever penetrating
the gloom. The place reminded him of the catacombs: dank,
humid, abysmally dark—a region where light would never come, a
region for the dead.

Guglielmo left his guest where he was and disappeared into the deepest part of the house. Leo heard shuffling and scraping; a drawer or a cupboard opened and closed. When the priest reappeared before him, he held two mugs and a pitcher.

"Whiskey?"

Leo grinned lopsidedly, "You decant it yourself?"

Pisticci. Guglielmo. They might not have much else, but there were always a few drops at the bottom of a bottle to keep a man warm.

. . .

"From now on, we will use aliases exclusively when addressing one another. No more 'Father this' and 'Father that.' It's too dangerous, and besides, we will have neither the time nor the energy for formalities," Ghezzi said. He, Rocca, and Biondi, were seated on the frayed couch in the living room of the farmhouse. Cecilia Cavagna stood behind the armchair in which Pio sat, gnawing on the edge of her handkerchief. "For this purpose," he opened Alfredo Rocca's portfolio and removed a slip of blue paper, "I have taken the liberty of determining these names for each of us. You, Pietro," he said, turning to the bishop, "your name is LoBianco. Pio, henceforth you'll be known as Mingione. Alfredo, you are Capovilla. And I am—" he blushed, "Della Chiesa. Not extremely imaginative, I know, but serviceable—and accurate." He crumpled the paper in one hand and stood up. "I want to do away with this now."

Without being asked, Pio reached into his pants pocket and withdrew a long match with a bright blue head. Ghezzi took it from him and struck it expertly on his thumbnail. The others looked on, incredulous: Where had the priest learned such a worldly trick? Rocca nodded to himself. It was yet another riddle. Who could be certain how the older priest spent the hours when he was out of Rocca's sight? Ghezzi touched the flame to the balled-up paper. It ignited, and he dropped it into the middle of an ashtray. "We must destroy every shred of evidence," he said.

All was silence as the paper burned. Taking a moment to watch

the little conflagration, Ghezzi seemed engrossed in a private reverie. He turned to the other men. "I suggest that you repeat these
names to yourselves over and over again. Become as well acquainted with them as you are with your own. We can make no
mistakes. . . . Now, Signor Cavagna, uh, Mingione—where are the
clothes?"

"I have laid them out upstairs," Cecilia said, gesturing over her
head with her damp handkerchief. "For you, Excellency," she said
to the bishop, "I have made some . . . modest adjustments . . . in
the trousers. They will not be handsome with the seams let out, but
I hope they fit."

"Come, gentlemen," Monsignor Ghezzi ordered the other
priests. "We must change." Rocca and Biondi rose like two con-
demned men. "As soon as we have gone, Signora, burn our cassocks. Burn them well and bury the ashes."

. . .

"Whiskey?" Aldo Guglielmo asked again, jiggling the pitcher before *il Papa*. Although weary from his long trek up the mountain,
Leo declined.

Guglielmo set the mugs and the spirits on the table. "You don't
mind if I have a little?" He did not wait for a reply, but poured
himself half a cup. "Sit here," he said to Leo, motioning toward the
rocking chair. "Tell me, *che cosa desidera?*"

Leo sat. The chair, on loose joints, rotated beneath him, like
something alive. "What should I want? I have simply lost my
way."

"Perhaps. But it's not easy to get lost around here. Only one
footpath leads up and down the mountain. There is another,
mostly for donkey carts, but it's hidden and rarely used. Both end
here, at my house, and the church."

The priest took a long swallow. "No one comes up anymore—
not that many ever did—unless he wants something. They used to
come looking for God, but when they did not find Him—only me,
His unfortunate representative—they stopped coming altogether."

The priest polished off his whiskey like someone who drank for a living. "So you see, I cannot remember the last time that anyone paid me—how shall I say it?—an innocent social call."

Irritation mixed with pity simmered in Leo's heart. "Nevertheless, may we consider this a social visit?"

"It would be a lie," Guglielmo said sharply, pouring the last of the spirits into his mug.

He grew more maudlin as he drank. "I mean, they still come around sometimes, in extreme circumstances, of course—when a relative is ill, or a parent dies. But even then, quite often they do without me. And when a child is born, if it should die without being baptized, they would rather consign it to limbo, it seems, than give it into these unsteady hands."

"Your hands may be unsteady," Leo observed truthfully, "but you have the demeanor of a man one can trust," he lied.

"In any case, I am not esteemed. You must have gathered that by now. In the town, they consider me the bearer of misfortune—and they have too much of that."

Guglielmo's eyes dropped and moved over the floor as if looking for something he had lost. "So enough," he said, without glancing up. "Why have you come here?"

Leo hesitated. "To see for myself," he replied.

"To *see*? To see what? The town pariah? I am no object of curiosity."

"No, that is not why.... Calm yourself," Leo pleaded, now unsure—if, indeed, he had ever been sure—why he had taken the arduous trip up the mountain to find this acerbic, excitable fellow. What *was* he seeking?

"Let's stop the fencing, Signore. I have no time."

"I am Giuseppe Ghezzi. I sell Missals and other ... other religious articles."

Guglielmo's tone quickened. "Souvenirs? Little models of the *Pietà* ... ?"

"And rosary beads, prayer cards ... I am also an acquaintance of Donna Lucia Fedelio's and of Franco Pisticci's," *il Papa* said.

"I don't care who you know. If you've come to sell, the answer is no thanks, I don't want any."

"I have not come to sell," Leo's voice shook. Now he wanted nothing more than to retrace his steps down the mountain and away from Don Guglielmo.

The other man looked up from his perusal of the floor. "Listen, I ask very little . . . only to be left alone, in peace." His tone had grown steely. "Soon it will be evening and the trip back to the village is treacherous. There is nothing to light your way. Leave here now, while you can. As you see, I am not equipped for overnight guests."

Il Papa walked as fast as he could down the steep path. He did not know whether he was running from his frustration, from Aldo Guglielmo, or racing against the night. Several times he lost his footing and slipped. Once he stopped to regain his bearings and, in the gathering dusk, through a break in the trees, saw the brown valley spread out before him. In the distance, an old woman was leading a mule with water barrels strapped to its back. Another woman was also still at work: She raised a mattock over her head, then, hunching forward, brought it crashing with all her might into the earth.

Leo was saddened and outraged by the sight of them trying, even at this hour, to eke a living out of land that so cruelly resisted their shovels, their hoes, and the water they collected with such care to moisten its crusty surface.

What would these people make of the Church if they really knew it—with its seductions of power and prestige, its displays of wealth and triumphalism, its many-layered bureaucracy? How would they understand it as a church of the poor, who would inherit the earth . . . that earth from which they hardly took enough to survive? He thought of the Vatican and felt disgraced.

Was there a way to wipe out centuries of worldliness? Leo wondered. There had to be—for the true Gospel began somewhere beyond all the majesty, the pomp, the lush rituals, the drama and ceremony. Passing Pisticci's house, absorbed in his own thoughts, *il Papa* stumbled on the exposed root of a tree, cutting the palm of his hand against some sharp rocks on the ground. He bound a handkerchief around the wound and went on. As he walked across the piazza once again, Leo noticed two lovers seated at the edge of the fountain, holding hands and talking quietly. It was as if the little Pasqualina had grown up and come out of the water to be with her suitor under the moon.

When Donna Lucia saw Leo's bandaged hand, she gasped. Blood had dried on his handkerchief. She removed it, bathed the cuts in soapy water and covered them with clean strips of cloth. Isabella sat by his feet, watching.

As Donna Lucia ministered to Leo's injury, he tried to describe his conversation with the priest. But he could not. His throat constricted at her touch. His nostrils filled with the scent of her freshly washed hair. Even his vision seemed to cloud, yet at the same time grew sharper. He observed that the ends of Lucia Fedelio's hair were still wet. They stuck together in thick, luxuriant points, as if dipped in wine.

· · ·

Monsignor Rocca explored the length of the dashboard with his fingers, searching for a switch that would turn on the headlights. By accident, he tripped a lever with his thumb; the empty road was illuminated. They were driving on a ridge. On their right, high in the sky, was a sliver of crescent moon, a wink in the heavens.

The four men crouched, imprisoned, in the tiny Fiat. The bishop and Pio sat in the back, shoulder-to-shoulder, their knees wedged tightly against the front seat. Monsignor Ghezzi occupied the place next to Rocca, a great map, veined in reds and blues, spread over his lap like a quilt. In the well at his feet lay the two tourist guidebooks, open on their faces, their spines broken.

"After a few miles, we will arrive at a three-way intersection. I believe this is where you should bear to the left, Capovilla," Ghezzi said, pointing to a green dot on the map. "The books report that five kilometers farther on there is a *pensione* . . . It gets low marks on all counts, particularly the cuisine; but then we are not traveling as kings."

The quiet of the crowded automobile was broken only by the high, metallic straining of the engine that by now (they had driven all day and gone without dinner) had become a part of the silence.

"The innkeepers may be asleep at this hour," Alfredo Rocca suggested, lulled by the driving into a semi-stupor.

"Then we shall wake them," Ghezzi replied. "How does one fold these ridiculous things?" he asked nobody in particular as he fumbled with the enormous map. "Crease here, crease there . . . this way? . . . that way? If one could only remember how one began. . . ."

"Here, let me," Pio said, impatient, unable to resist interfering with Ghezzi's amateurish efforts. He reached over the seat and wrested the map from the priest. In three deft moves, he had formed a neat rectangular package, which he returned to the front seat.

"Ah, Mingione, you are most dexterous," Ghezzi murmured sardonically, as he turned the map over in his fingers, examining the other's handiwork.

"No, not particularly. It's the workingman's life, Padre."

"Della Chiesa," Ghezzi reminded him.

"You have never had occasion to fold one, Della Chiesa, so there is no reason that you should know how. By necessity, one becomes proficient at those tasks one does often. I would fumble if I were suddenly to have to consecrate the Host."

"Heaven help us," Ghezzi said, appalled.

"I'm sorry. *Sono stanco.* . . . There is room for both, your life and my life."

"You are tired, Mingione," Ghezzi interrupted, "so your tongue flops around in your mouth like a dying fish."

For a while no one spoke. Then the *pensione* was upon them. Its windows were unlit.

"Are you, forgive me, a Communist?" Ghezzi asked Pio in an intimate tone, as the men stepped from the car, stretching and groaning under their breaths after their long incarceration. "A Marxist? An anarchist? Go on, you shouldn't feel mortified to tell me."

"Well, I do not shoot at bureaucrats, if that's what you mean."

Rocca and Biondi began to pound vigorously on the front door, and to call out to the upstairs windows.

"But your sympathies . . . ?"

"Let's not debate our ideological differences on empty stomachs," Pio suggested.

A somnambulant man with a bare, sunken chest and an unshaven face answered the door.

"It'll be double the price, for waking me up," he said, as he led the party of four up a narrow flight of stairs. "It's unholy, that's what it is, unholy. Decent people are in bed in the middle of the night, not gallivanting around like wild dogs."

A day and a half passed. The weather grew colder. Brown leaves carpeted the ground. The sun had lost its summertime strength, its rays lengthening early in the days. The air became crisp and thin, shocking to the lungs.

Francesco Ghezzi borrowed a telephone in the back room of an *osteria* where they were eating lunch. He closed the door behind him and placed a call to Rome. The connection was not achieved easily. He had to hang up and wait five minutes. When the phone buzzed and Ghezzi was invited back on the line, discharges of static and high-pitched, distant voices assaulted his ear, sounds of fishwives haggling over the price of olive oil or peppers.

He stood at the window, the weighty, old-fashioned receiver cradled in the crook of his neck. Outside, an American in light blue trousers and white shoes quarreled with his wife, a thin woman whose many gold chains hung like a coat of armor over her narrow bosom. She held a long cigarette between her lips; her nails were painted brown. Their argument had started in the familiar whispers of tourists who do not want to humiliate themselves in a foreign country. Now it had escalated to roaring dismay. The couple had evidently come many miles in the hope of repairing what they now saw was beyond repair. Ghezzi could not make out all that they said, although he was fairly fluent in English. He watched the American heave several suitcases, all in matching patterns, into the trunk of his car. Each time he tried to slam it shut, the lid popped back in his face. The more furiously he pushed, the more it fought him. When, finally, it closed, the man discovered he had locked his keys inside. For the first time, the woman laughed. Ghezzi marveled that some people wore their stupidity like a badge of honor, as if they belonged to a private club.

"Tuttobene here!" A voice crackled over the line. At first the monsignor, absorbed in the domestic drama outside, did not realize that at last his call had been completed. He blinked and returned his attention to the noises in his ear.

"Tuttobene? Tuttobene? Is that you?"

"Ugo Tuttobene, *sì*. Who is this? Speak up."

"Ugo! It's Francesco. Francesco *Ghezzi*." He raised his voice. "Can you hear me now?"

"Francesco! I can hear. Where are you? I was getting worried."

"Are you alone? Can we talk freely?"

"*Sì*. Do you have news for me?"

"No news." Ghezzi conceded, trembling. The strain of the last days was more than he cared to admit, even to himself. "We go about the countryside, we ask questions, we offer a description of . . . the missing person, including even the limp. But there is not a sign of him, no one yet who comes close. It seems he does not stop to eat, or sleep, or go to the bathroom. . . ." Ghezzi's voice broke. "Have *you* anything to report?"

"Nothing. No ransom demands, no phone calls, threats, or letters. I am convinced that he was not abducted. . . . Listen, has it occurred to you gentlemen," Tuttobene asked with a professional flourish, "that the party in question may have already altered his appearance?"

"Oh no. He isn't wily that way, not a criminal type, you know. His mind doesn't work in those directions." The priest sniffed. A puzzled look crossed his face. "Well, what would he do anyway? Grow a beard? It's forbidden. A mustache? Purchase a false nose?" He shook his head. "No, I don't think it's conceivable . . . and what about the truck?—although in these parts it would not stand out much. Every day such wrecks go by. Still, no one seems to have seen it."

"He may have sold that vehicle and bought another."

"Who would buy it? No, that would be the last thing on his mind . . . commerce, trading. It is not in his character." There was a brief silence. The telephone line hissed, echoed, and snapped.

"Francesco? Would you like me to step in now?"

"Maybe."

"I am trained in this kind of business. It would be a discreet operation, as I promised before you left Rome. I will bring in just five or ten of our best men. They are totally reliable. When their lips are sealed not even the hand of God Himself—you'll pardon me—could pry them open."

"Perhaps . . ." Ghezzi wrinkled his brow in indecision.

"We have up-to-date methods . . . entirely modern, I assure you. Scientific. Bloodhounds too, and helicopters if necessary, to comb the mountains and villages. It may be he is in hiding some place where you cannot see him from the ground."

"Helicopters! Ugo, unless he is running through a meadow, in his robes, I do not understand how you can hope to spot one tiny, nondescript man from the air."

Tuttobene did not respond immediately. "Your point is well taken, Francesco," he conceded at last. "However, we are able to cover great distances with helicopters in an extremely short time."

"No, absolutely not."

Tuttobene was pathetically eager for the assignment.

"I assure you of the most *complete* discretion."

Ghezzi took a deep breath. "No helicopters, thank you. Now tell me, Ugo, what's happening at the Palace?"

"I was over to your office this morning. Everything seemed as usual—as far as I could tell, without arousing suspicion."

"I called yesterday."

"So they said."

"I could have only a brief conversation, but I think I set their minds at rest. They believe we're all safely with *il* . . . with the party in question. I dictated a new statement and ordered it released this afternoon. It will appear in tomorrow's newspapers: He is resting well and working hard. The fever has entirely subsided. He has taken a stroll, and spoken with his sister by telephone. When I left Rome I also left behind several recent photos of . . . you-know-who—walking with me and other members of the staff. One cannot tell from these pictures whether he is in the Vatican gardens or in the streets of Milan. They will be doled out, one by one, to the press."

The American and his wife got into their car, wrenching the doors closed behind them. "Where could they go," Ghezzi wondered absently, "without the keys?"

"How clever!" Tuttobene was impressed by the monsignor's strategy. "You have the brain of a master tactician. . . . So, Francesco, what is it you would like *me* to do?"

Ghezzi turned from the window and transferred the receiver to his other ear. He spoke very softly. "It would take how many men, did you tell me? Five, or ten at most?"

"At most."

"But what would you say? I do not want them to know the truth. Pour it into their ears, it will come spilling out of their mouths. Besides, they'd never believe it. On what pretext can you lure ten officers away from Rome long enough to mount such a campaign? It seems impossible to me, without involving the entire department."

"This is my profession—doing the impossible. Francesco, my dear friend, how much longer can we delay? At this rate—I mean to say—what will you do if you find him?"

"In truth, I don't know."

"And if you don't find him, what then?"

"Either way, Ugo, we are up the Tiber without an oar," Ghezzi whispered.

"And your companions? Are they of any help?"

"My *companions!*—that is a charitable description of the vile bunch I am forced to tolerate. . . . This Cavagna, I am certain, is on the side of the devil. He will not confirm it, but I don't doubt that he keeps anarchists, or worse, in his cow barn. I would not even be surprised, between you and me, if he encouraged his illustrious relative in this escapade! . . . As for Alfredo, he drives with the skill of a monkey. The coordination of the pedals eludes him totally, and we are all in a chronic state of nausea. Except Alfredo, of course, who adamantly refuses to relinquish the wheel, and who seems to be enjoying himself more than he has since we've met. Biondi's legs—not to mention his mind—are giving way. So every day that passes renders him of less and less use to us. He seems to think that his squeals of pain are as pleasing as *bel canto!* . . ." He paused to catch his breath and, in that moment, reconsidered. "Well, Ugo, perhaps now *is* the time for you to step in."

"Thank heavens!" Tuttobene's tone was suddenly carefree, boyish, as if he would burst into laughter.

"But Ugo! Ugo! It is imperative to exercise the utmost caution." Ghezzi's tone grew black. "If anything goes wrong, if you slip up in any way, I will never forgive you."

"Naturally. When is the last time you forgave anyone?" He did not wait for a reply. "Cavagna? Does he know about me?"

"No, he doesn't know your name or even of your existence. It's crucial that he doesn't find out. The man is a bloodthirsty nihilist and I suspect that, for philosophic reasons, he would just as soon his brother-in-law remain a fugitive—"

The doorknob turned slowly. Ghezzi jumped at the sound. A shrill gurgle of surprise escaped his lips.

"What's wrong?" Tuttobene asked.

"I must go now. *Addio.*" He replaced the receiver with a clatter as Pio entered the room.

"Who the hell were you talking to?" Pio demanded. His voice vibrated with anger. "I thought we agreed that no one is to know."

Ghezzi swallowed hard and began to sweat profusely. His heavy glasses skidded to the tip of his nose. He drew himself up and faced his accuser squarely.

"Have you any coins in your pocket, Signor Mingione? We must leave these people something . . . for the telephone."

. . .

Ugo Tuttobene, a deputy commissioner in the *carabinieri,* let himself sink deeply into his leather chair. It was lunchtime. Headquarters was quiet, nearly deserted.

Tuttobene was a short, dark man with a luxurious mustache that stood out from his cheeks. His hair was thick and black, styled in meticulous waves and curlicues. He wore a trim black uniform with gold buttons; three medals of various sizes and configurations were pinned to his left breast. Each one contained a story, which he was pleased to tell, whether asked to or not. A black peaked cap, adorned with a golden bird just above the visor, lay on the desk before him. The office was large, but without much furniture. A wrinkled flag of Italy hung behind the desk, and in one corner a fan, mounted on a metal pole, gave off a deep-throated rumbling.

Tuttobene swiveled lazily in the big chair, closed his eyes, and brought the fingers of both hands to his lips in a pyramid. It was in this position that he closed his eyes and plotted how—now that he had seized the gauntlet—he would conduct the most momentous manhunt of modern times.

. . .

Il Papa sat at Donna Lucia's kitchen table shelling peas. He split the pods down the middle, at the seam, and pushed the hard green pellets into a ceramic bowl. He liked the feel of them as they broke from their moorings and fell away under the gentle prodding of his thumbs. "How long can I stay here? . . . Almost two days have passed, and I am no more prepared to return to Cecilia's," he mused, as he worked, "or to Rome, than I am to leave this house and continue my journey." Nevertheless, visions of the place that he had left nagged Leo constantly: the Grotto of Lourdes, where he often went to pray, his bedroom, the basilica, Monsignors Ghezzi and Rocca, the nuns who so tenderly cared for him. Still, none of that inspired in his heart a desire to return to that time when his life was immaculate and orderly but not his own and the hours went by in lockstep, rigidly divided into blocks of waking, sleeping, working, eating.

Here, the days were long and free; time was like a cradle in which one gently rocked. And although, in Rome, he had begun to fear that he might be getting sick or going mad, in Donna Lucia's humble house he felt clear-minded and remarkably well. The hours dissolved one into the next, like honey on the tongue.

Lucia Fedelio stood at the threshold behind him, so quietly that he was unaware of her presence. She rejoiced that her visitor showed no signs of going away, for she was not eager to have him gone. Nevertheless, he had confessed that his funds were low and, for this third night's lodging, had given her no money at all. In a short time, his manner had relaxed perceptibly; he had settled in, as if belonging, soon offering to perform household chores in exchange for room and meals. It had been years since so attractive a man had lived in her house, and one of such obvious intelligence and grave charm. Donna Lucia was prepared to keep her guest for as long as he would stay.

She watched him accomplish each task slowly, but well, as if unused to, yet charmed by, working with his body and hands. He appeared to take sober pleasure in mending a piece of broken pottery, sweeping a floor, chopping wood, fixing vegetables to cook. Often in the past days, Donna Lucia overheard him talking to himself in a low, intense voice, as if involved in inward arguments or lost in his own world. Yet this man was not indifferent to the life around him. He wanted to know about her neighbors in the town and listened carefully to all she told him, storing the information in some private file for future reference. Every hour they found it easier to talk. A friend had traveled to Naples and returned with cans of paint. Tomorrow, Giuseppe Ghezzi had promised to paint Lucia Fedelio's bedroom walls.

Who was this salesman of religious merchandise? she asked herself. Where did he come from? She had never seen his wares, nor did he speak of his past or his future. When he was robbed, why had he not returned to his home office to report the theft and replace the stolen rosaries and Missals and keychains? It was his livelihood, after all, or so he claimed. Was he hiding here? Had the assault upon him ever really taken place? Why was he so content to remain in their poor village? What did it offer him?

Donna Lucia knew that he had withheld some part of his chronicle. But that knowledge did not make her uncomfortable. If the tale he told was incomplete, he himself was not. "Here is an excellent man," Donna Lucia said silently. "Who he may be is his own secret, but he must have good reason to keep it so."

Suddenly Leo sensed her standing there. He was not sure if she had shifted her weight, or shuffled her feet, or coughed. But a shiver of recognition crept up the back of his neck as her gaze rested on him. He smiled. "Don't hide, Lucia Fedelio. Come out of the shadows and talk to me."

For the first time, they were alone together. Having collected all the taxes he could, Emilio Galeazzi had left early that morning, before sunrise. Until now, Galeazzi had shared meals with Donna Lucia, Leo, and Isabella. The night before, sitting together in the parlor after dinner, the two men had talked about national politics, local government.

"A black market exists in everything, from milk to coffins," Galeazzi had informed Leo. "In these mountain villages, there is practically no commodity that is not scarce, therefore precious. Even the mayor sells leather shoes that he brings from Naples and Rome. But he charges almost as much as the finest shoestore on the Via Veneto."

Donna Lucia sewed—poorly, lunging at buttons and the holes in socks as if they were opponents. Isabella played with a family of headless dolls that she herself had decapitated. Was it an unconscious response, Leo wondered, to her own state of silence?

Now, he turned in his chair to look at the innkeeper, who still hung back at the threshold of her kitchen. *Il Papa* extended the bowl of freshly shelled peas, like an offering. "I think I have done ..." he began, but his sentence remained unfinished. The screams of children came through the open window.

"Donna Lucia!" Their voices were high and panicky. *"Lucia Fedelio!"*

Goose pimples sprouted at the small of Leo's back. His limbs were icy with foreboding.

A boy of about eight, followed by a small gang of other children, appeared at the door. They were breathless and frightened.

"What is it?" Leo asked, leaping to his feet.

"Isabella! She fell down!"

"Where has she fallen? Where?" Donna Lucia shook the boy by the shoulders.

"Over . . ." Sobs and hiccups wracked his body. "She's over . . . there . . ." He pointed out the door.

"Over *where?* What is it, Ettore?" Donna Lucia shook him again, harder. His head wobbled on his neck; rivers of tears streaked his dirty face.

Another child, a girl, spoke up: "She fell down the cliff behind Pisticci's café! We were playing, just playing. No one meant to hurt her! It wasn't our fault. All of us were running . . . then she tripped in the wet dirt and lost her balance. She's there . . . at the bottom . . . and she won't move or answer us!"

Leo, Donna Lucia, and the children raced down the street. In spite of his weak leg, Leo ran hard and fast, forging ahead of the rest. But soon, under the weight of apprehension, he began to slow his pace, as though the worst had been already confirmed.

Pisticci saw them as they rounded the side of the café. The fat man waved his arms and bellowed, "Here! Down here! Hurry!"

Leo drew alongside the café's proprietor. A moment later, Donna Lucia came up next to them. "Please . . . help her!"

It was his passionate wish to help the girl. But alone? He searched the crowd for another likely man; only Pisticci, who hovered on the fringe, looked less than ninety years old. Leo peered into the ravine. Isabella lay there, one arm curled under her body, her legs akimbo, her head crooked to the side at an unnatural angle. Her eyes were closed.

"Come on, Franco! We must bring her up." Without considering how he would proceed, Leo began the descent. The incline was steep, the earth dry and strewn with many jagged rocks. At his first steps, the ground tore away beneath his feet. He stopped and looked back. Pisticci stood at the top of the hill, unmoving. "Come!" Leo yelled. *"Venga qui!"*

The fat man's face was white. His voice slipped into a high register. "I have a weak heart . . . and a weak stomach."

Il Papa was riveted now on a single concern—to rescue the child from the pit. He started down alone. Only later did he wonder at himself, at the way he sprang to life and took command of the perilous situation.

Pisticci edged toward the precipice, his head hanging low, like a dog's. He followed Leo, almost involuntarily. Tumbling over one another, sliding and falling in the dirt, at last they reached Isabella.

Leo was out of breath, panting. "See if she's . . ." The rest of the thought jammed before it reached his lips.

"See if she's what? *What?*" Pisticci stared at Leo.

"Listen to her heartbeat." He could not bear the weight of the discovery.

Pisticci shook his head. "If I bend over, I'll faint and then you'll have both of us out cold in this ditch."

Leo dropped to his knees, half in exhaustion, and placed his ear on Isabella's chest. As he sought desperately for the sign of life, he tried to block out all other sounds—the women's wailing, the birdsong, the rustle of the afternoon breeze in the treetops. He heard nothing; he could not discern a heartbeat. "Dear God, do not take this child from us," he prayed silently. "It is too soon for her. Her mother has lost two already. . . ." Then he heard it—only a flutter, the beating of butterfly wings: muted, shallow, thready. He listened for a moment longer to make certain that he was not deceived. Below his cheek he felt the slight rise and fall of Isabella's chest as she took air into her lungs. A broad smile parted his lips. *"Miracolo!"* he exclaimed to himself. Leo lifted his head. "She's alive!" he called. "Alive! Alive!"

As if from one body, a cheer burst from the crowd.

Leo ordered Pisticci to take the girl's legs and he grasped her under the arms. They inched their way up the slope, pausing twice

to gather strength and then, like underwater divers hauling treasure, continued their slow, treacherous ascent. As they neared the
rise, two younger men came running and catapulted themselves
over the precipice. They swooped down, kicking up clods of earth,
and reached Leo and Pisticci quickly. Carried by the four men, Isabella was soon lying safely on the ground at her mother's feet.

Someone brought an old blanket. The girl was placed on top of
it and the young men formed a makeshift stretcher by gathering
the ends on their shoulders.

Her hair was matted with blood.

Word was transmitted from the bedroom: Isabella had sustained
a deep gash on the back of the skull. Many women had come to the
inn to wait. Shapeless and silent in their tents of dresses, they did
what they could for the child and the mother, moving about the
house, like shadows, efficient and serene. With their help, Donna
Lucia had put her daughter to bed. Wielding a long, squeaky pair
of scissors, they cut away the hair around the wound and cleansed it
with warm water. Franco Pisticci brought a bottle of cheap brandy
from his tavern. "It is the only one I have right now," he said, giving it to Donna Lucia. "Wet her lips . . . it might bring her around
. . . anyway, it can't hurt." The mother nodded her thanks—since
the accident, she was almost as speechless as Isabella—and disappeared into the sickroom.

As the sun set, the women of the village brought their few men,
crowding the little parlor and kitchen. They ate Donna Lucia's
food and drank her wine and chatted noisily, as if at a party. There
was not much talk of the accident. Leo sat in a chair in the corner,
again a stranger among them. Silently, he offered a prayer for the
injured girl, feeling his petition as poignantly as when he prayed for
the whole world, in Rome. As it grew late, the guests drifted out of
the house, leaving behind dirty mugs, empty wine glasses, the skins
of oily sausage, olive pits, rinds of salty *pecorino* cheese, and bread-
crumbs everywhere.

When all was quiet, unable to consider sleep and seeking a small chore, Leo got up and began to collect the glasses. Although dulled and tired by the day's events, he worked out a simple housekeeping plan. First, he would polish the glasses with cinders, as he had seen Donna Lucia do. There would be almost no running water at this time of night. Then he would wash the tabletops, with what little water trickled from the tap, disposing of sausage skins, pits, cheese. Finally, he would sweep all the floors and set the furniture to rights. The visitors had left the place in disarray. This work would not relieve the suffering of the child and the woman in the bedroom just above his head, but it would make him feel less futile.

At midnight Lucia Fedelio came downstairs, accompanied by two older women dressed in the customary black from their head scarves to the hems of their long skirts. In the kitchen they discovered Leo at the sink.

"She is unconscious," Donna Lucia said in a monotone. "I talk to her but she does not hear me. Her eyes do not move. I prick her with a pin; she feels nothing."

Leo gave the mother a glass of red wine and some bread with a little cheese on a chipped plate. The women made her sit. One of them touched *il Papa*'s elbow and promised him that they would return early the next day.

He saw that the skin of Donna Lucia's face was stretched taut as a painter's canvas, eliminating even the natural wrinkles in her lips. Anguish heightened her beauty: Her hair was blacker, her eyes were wider and darker, her cheekbones sharper.

"Isabella will awaken presently," Leo said, although he did not feel sure of it.

"You risked your life for my poor *bambina,* who neither hears nor speaks," Donna Lucia murmured. "And only God Himself could have done more!"

Leo was moved. "All your neighbors have gone home. It was like a celebration. I thought it strange. They were eating and drinking and talking. . . ."

Donna Lucia bit into the bread and sipped the wine. "Don't

think badly of them." Her voice was deep, her accents guttural. "They have seen it all too many times. Each time one grows a little more resigned." She looked up at him. "Where you come from, Signor Ghezzi, life must be kinder."

The innkeeper rose, snapping the circuit between them. "I must go back to my daughter. In the morning, if she is no better, you will go to the priest? Please beg him to come."

IX

UGO TUTTOBENE WAS SNATCHED from his reverie by his aide, Federico Ottaviani, who set up a clatter serving the deputy commissioner's afternoon coffee.

Ottaviani, a young man of twenty-five, had puffy eyes, wet red lips, and a broad, pasty, off-center nose that seemed to have been slapped onto his face by a cartoonist.

The coffee service—Tuttobene's private property—was suited to a prince's court more than to a police station. A silver pot with a long graceful spout occupied the middle of a silver tray. It was flanked on both sides by china cups, handpainted with rosebuds. There were linen napkins in a flowery shade of pink, sweet biscuits in a basket from which fragrant steam curled up, heavy cream, butter, and four flavors of preserves—strawberry, raspberry, wild blueberry, and apricot.

The tray slipped from Ottaviani's hands and landed on the deputy commissioner's desk with a crash. Tuttobene opened one eye.

"Buon giorno," the commisioner said, with the air of a man who has made a career of cultivating impassivity in the face of bullets, bombs, and other sudden tumult.

"I beg your pardon, sir! My clumsiness . . ."

"It's all right, Federico. I'm accustomed to it," Tuttobene said cheerfully. The young man wore a uniform similar to his commander's, but without the medals. He mixed the commissioner's coffee with a little hot milk and placed the cup in front of him.

"Sit down, join me." His superior motioned to a chair next to the desk. "You're too thin. Doesn't your mama feed you?"

Ottaviani thanked him, sat down, and helped himself to the largest, brownest roll in the basket. He painstakingly bathed one side of it in wild blueberry preserves and took a big bite. The fruity purple syrup forced its way between his lips. He chewed with enthusiasm, smiling all the while and nodding at his superior as if to encourage him to continue speaking.

"Your mouth is full, Federico, but your ears are open, I hope, and prepared to hear some news?" Federico waved his head up and down in long expressive strokes. Tuttobene took a deep breath. "Then listen carefully: I have come into possession of information that—should it fall into the wrong hands—could prove deadly to all involved." Ugo Tuttobene reached into the top drawer of his desk and removed a thick black cigar, which he began to suck, twirling it in extravagant circles between his lips. "I would very much like to confide in you, Federico, but before I do so I must feel confident that I can count on your silence."

"Yes sir, of course, sir." The young man spoke wholeheartedly, as though leaping fences.

"And whatever I may ask you to do, you will carry out my orders without a word?"

"You won't hear a word from me. I'll lay down my life."

Tuttobene extracted a red enamel lighter from his pants pocket and lit the cigar. He took three long puffs, held the smoke in his cheeks, and finally exhaled, examining Ottaviani's face through narrowed eyes, as the fumes dissipated. Once he had made his assistant his confidant, there was no turning back:

"The Pope has been abducted, Federico."

Federico dropped the biscuit in his hand on the carpet. Under the best of circumstances, he had a poor record for holding onto things. "The Holy *Father?*"

"Himself." He tapped a perfectly cylindrical grey ash into the saucer of his coffee cup.

"Oh God, my dear God, this cannot be true!"

Yet easier to believe than the truth that *was* true, Tuttobene thought cagily. A kidnapping, yes. Perhaps. Within the realm of possibility. A plot against the Pope was not so far-fetched. But how could Federico, with his limited imagination, be expected to accept that *il Papa* had, plainly and simply, picked up his skirts and taken off?

"Do you remember, not too many days ago, it was reported that His Holiness, recovering from influenza, would travel to an undisclosed location?" the deputy commissioner continued calmly.

"I read it in the newspaper."

Tuttobene pondered a moment, organizing the details of the narrative that was still taking shape in his mind. "Well, he never arrived at that undisclosed location, wherever it may have been. His automobile was ambushed by a band of thugs. Everyone else in the party was killed—bodyguard, a bishop . . ." He hesitated, then plunged recklessly onward. ". . . a cardinal! The Holy Father was taken captive."

Unconsciously, the young man leaned over, swiped the biscuit off the floor, and stuffed it all into his mouth, never for an instant taking his bulging eyes off Tuttobene. "Who else knows of this abomination?" he asked, spitting crumbs.

Tuttobene shook his head gravely. "Almost no one—for the most obvious reasons. And it has to remain so. *Il Papa's* captors are already making wild, obscene demands. . . ." Tuttobene had by this time grown quite enamored of his yarn. He played with it, as if twisting a lock of hair around his finger. "All the jails must be emptied, they say. Murderers, thieves, rapists, enemies of the state—everyone's to be set free. The Apostolic Palace itself must be, in their language, 'liberated.' They also demand the use of an airplane, an official craft.... As you can see, it could turn into a national disaster, a political as well as a religious calamity."

Ottaviani swallowed the biscuit, but still he could hardly speak. "Where is His Holiness—imprisoned?"

Tuttobene filled his mouth with smoke and blew one ring, then another. "We believe he is somewhere in the South. It may not surprise you that I have been entrusted with the mission of leading a small, highly trained and trustworthy force of men to scour the countryside and bring *il Papa* back—alive—to the Eternal City."

"It does not surprise me," said the young man. He crossed himself three times. "May God help you."

Tuttobene lowered his voice. "But since there is no time to lose, I have discarded the idea of assembling a force. Some others in this department might receive the news of the abduction, how shall I say, *badly*. Fall to pieces, you know. So I have selected you. I depend on your stability, Federico. You and I will go out on our own."

"I am honored, sir! But ... just the two of us?"

The deputy commander rocked back in his chair and held the cigar at arm's length, gazing at it intently, as if he could read a message in its glowing tip. *"Sì.* Otherwise one day soon, the fisherman's ring will turn up in the Vatican post office, its seal removed." He closed his eyes ceremoniously. "And then we will know that we have lost him forever, by failing to act in time."

The young officer sprang to his feet. *"Guerra!* It's a holy war! A crusade has been thrust upon us! We will smash the bastards and return Leo to his throne!" His feet began to move in a nervous little gavotte. "Give me my charge. I am at your command."

Tuttobene opened his eyes and stared at Ottaviani: The man's face was puce, and he was breathing hard, as though sexually excited. Federico had believed every word; he had gobbled the tale greedily, the way he had eaten the roll, the way a dog takes its dinner.

Ugo Tuttobene thought quickly. "Tell me, when is the last time you flew a helicopter?"

Don Aldo, slumping in a chair in front of his house, clasped his hands behind his neck. "Yes," he said wearily, "the girl lived with me. She was not my wife, though, or even my woman. Valentina was little Vittorio's sister. Or so they both agreed when I found them—wandering alone—on my way here, all those years ago. But we three arrived together, so nothing could convince my friends down there in the town of the truth."

"People believe what they see," Leo concurred, not quite certain himself where the truth really lay.

"So you have before you an exotic version of the traditional *confinato*," Guglielmo went on wryly. "And since you've come back so soon, let me set you straight on another point: I was never exiled. I was sent here from Rome. But these people were so stunned by the sight of me with the girl and the boy in tow that they would consent only to *their* version of the thing—that the church had disowned me. Valentina finally left, that much is true. The boy . . . Vittorio . . . died." Leo saw Guglielmo's eyes mist. "Then it was over for me. I gave up trying to convince them I was not the man they imagined. What did it matter anymore? Well, I am no good now even to myself. . . ."

He paused, lost in thought. "Why should I go down to their village? Except to sell some eggs." He poked an elbow in the direction of a few chickens that were foraging on the hard, dry earth. "And to do a little business among Signor Pisticci's bottles. He maligns me night and day, yet for a few *lire* he gives me what I want." There was an empty glass on the ground beside Guglielmo's chair.

Leo pondered for a full minute before speaking. "I accept your story, Padre," he said at last. "But you should go 'down there,' as you say, because a child is very ill. She and her mother need you." He sensed the impending failure of his mission as soon as the words left his lips. "Your past may be unfortunate, even tragic, but you are still a priest and these people are your flock."

"*They* are my only flock," Guglielmo replied, indicating the chickens. "Did you haul yourself all the way up here again to try to help me redeem my vocation? Is that it? Worry about saving your own life, not mine! The mother wants my *services,* Signor Ghezzi, as if I were a plumber or a butcher or a mechanic . . . or a witch. She hopes that I can perform a miracle." A smile twisted his lips. "That is what she's looking for, you know. A little mumbo-jumbo. *Magico.* That's what people believe in—amulets, charms, incantations."

Guglielmo sat up straight in his chair. "I say *no.* I refuse, as I told you once already, to have anything more to do with it—any of it— ever again!" He struggled to his feet. His legs slid this way and that as he walked toward the door of his shack. "Please, leave me alone." He wheeled around. "Why should I? Why *should* I? Go have a glimpse at their church. They do not even care enough to keep it up. It's no better than this 'rectory.' Take a look. Go around to the back," the drunken priest babbled, waving his arm. "Go see what has become of it!" He closed the door.

The church—hidden in a grove of tall trees—was a small stone building, two stories high, with a few broken windows and an aspect of utter neglect. It had escaped Leo's notice on his first visit, so absorbed had he been with Guglielmo. Now he saw an edifice sagging under a roof that had partially collapsed. Leo walked slowly around to the front. Roaring lions had been carved in bas-relief on the heavy wooden doors . A live lizard sat motionless on the threshold, soaking up the last rays of afternoon sun. Its flat, unblinking eyes held *il Papa's.*

.   .   .

Alfredo Rocca peeled an orange and began to recount some extraordinary tales of Papal history. He had become the group's unofficial bard, reciting such stories again and again in the belief that somehow they held a measure of comfort, or at least diversion, for his colleagues.

St. Gregory the Great had fled Rome in a wicker basket . . . Stephan VII ordered the corpse of his predecessor, Formosus, exhumed from the grave, attired in papal robes, and brought to trial. Formosus was found guilty; one finger from his right hand was sliced away, and his body was thrown into the Tiber. . . . The Pierleoni, a family of Jews, installed three Popes on the throne: Anaclet II, Gregory VI, and Gregory VII. . . . Sergius III, while *he* was Pope, lived with his mistress. . . . "Alexander VI was not famed for his chastity either," Rocca went on. "Happiest in the company of other men's wives, he fathered at least four children. . . . And Julius II beat Michelangelo with a stick when he felt that his work on the Sistine Chapel progressed too slowly. . . ."

"So?" Monsignor Ghezzi asked, looking up with disapproval. "Sometimes, Capovilla, with your revolting stories—all of which I have heard before—you make me feel like beating *you* with a stick."

Rocca removed the last bit of rind from his orange and bit into a section of the fruit. Juice dribbled down his fingers. "I only mean to make a point: by comparison," he lowered his voice now, "our leader, Leo XIV, is a normal, sane, and conservative man . . . on a sort of extended holiday. That is all I mean."

They were in a café near Posillipo. Ghezzi and Rocca, alone, were eating oranges, grapes and slices of pineapple at a table set for four with tall glasses and paper napkins. Pio Cavagna and the bishop had gone to bed. Outside, the first certain signs of winter, freezing rain and blasting winds, had chased everyone off the streets. The other men in the café were huddled around a tall hearth, talking, throwing dice, sipping *grappa,* the fiery peasant brandy. Near the door sat the town lunatic—the male widow. He was clothed in black, in women's attire, a kerchief tied over his closely shaven head. In mourning for seven years for his wife, who was a man, he was uncertain where he belonged, whether in male or female society. The male widow came to the café every evening, the priests learned. Although he did not drink or engage in conversation with the other men, he liked to remain in their company. When the café closed, unwilling to walk in the haunted streets by himself—afraid that the ghost of his dead lover would swoop down and, with fingers like talons, carry him off by the throat—he would follow the men home. He walked a few steps behind them like a woman, until he reached his own door.

Monsignor Ghezzi frowned, washing down a piece of pineapple

with some wine. "Yes . . . In history, there is always someone who has got there first. Whatever one does, however bizarre, however outlandish, cruel, or evil, it is never quite original. And seldom the worst act of its kind. So?"

"So perhaps he will simply come back, as Gregory did."

Ghezzi appeared impatient, irritable. He spoke rapidly, crossing and uncrossing his legs. "Here is where you alter history to suit yourself. Only after he'd been apprehended by a search party such as ours did Gregory agree to return. And even if we were to find the Holy Father, I would be most surprised if he were to reverse himself—like that, you know." He snapped his fingers under Rocca's chin.

Ghezzi's eyes took on a baleful aspect, as though receding back into his skull. "To what end? I do not believe, Capovilla, that his fever has yet run its course. He is in the grip, I think, of something quite alarmingly new. The missing party was never an adventurous man—that is to say, his deeds have never been especially, outstandingly, bold. The baptismal certificates, perhaps . . ." Ghezzi pulled on his earlobe, thinking. "And while in Rome, what has he done? Broken a few rules of minor consequence, yes, but beyond that . . . ?"

The priest paused long enough to order another pineapple for himself and Rocca. "So where is the precedent for his present behavior? There is none—only in your history books. For *il Papa,* it is a terrifying break with the past. Therefore, I do not foresee that he will present himself at St. Anne's Gate, saying with a pretty smile, 'Here I am.' " Ghezzi sipped his wine. "However, I do find myself wondering every so often, quite against my will—for I recognize the danger in idle speculation, a danger to which even he fell prey—*what in the world must he be up to now?*"

The room was hot and the pineapple cool. Perspiration stained the armpits of Ghezzi's shirt. He was almost certain that he saw the male widow wave at him from across the room. He looked away, embarrassed. "I try to imagine—I try *not* to imagine, rather—the sort of . . . situations he has met, how they may have altered his mind, his personality."

Rocca was beginning to feel the spirits. "God knows!" he said. "If we ever see him again, we will be obliged to live with any alterations we may find. Even in the old days you couldn't count on *il Papa* to be the same man from one day to the next—"

Ghezzi could not make up his mind: Was the male widow simply playing with his shawl, mopping his own sweaty forehead, or beckoning to him with the end of it? "How can we conjecture—we who have spent our lives in devoted service, we who have so little experience of the world—what our old friend may have taken it in his head to do, once outside? What are his fears? His temptations? Whom has he met . . . ?" He did not finish his sentence. The male widow had got up from his table and seemed on his way across the room. Ghezzi glanced hurriedly at his watch. "We have to make an early start in the morning. Let's go, Capovilla. You have eaten enough fruit to flush out the bowels of an army. It would make another man ill." He nudged Rocca out of his chair. "Tomorrow we will adjust our course and head higher into the mountains."

. . .

A light rain was falling when Leo came down from Aldo Guglielmo's church into the village. The drops felt bulbous and insistent, as they pelted his shoulders and head. Two dogs barked in the night; a horse whinnied, answering. What disturbed them so? Leo asked himself. All of nature seemed distraught.

He walked slowly, not eager to return to the inn, resisting each step because of what he might discover when he arrived. The dampness had caused his hip to ache. As he went, dragging his right leg a little behind him, he peered into the houses that lined the cobblestone street. Whole families crouched around small charcoal fires, crowded together against the rain and cold. As Donna Lucia had explained, winter here, greeted with fear and superstition, had all the makings of an annual tragedy. After centuries, these people were still unprepared and unequipped for anything more menacing than the Italian sun and warmth. Their villages had been left behind in another age, abandoned by a modern society with neither time nor money to reclaim these ancient pockets of poverty. Even Lucia Fedelio's house, which Leo now approached, was rude and unheated. It smelled salty, moldy, a trace fetid, as the sea smells in foul weather.

The innkeeper met him at the door. Her hair was disheveled; dark circles ringed her eyes like ripples in a pond. She spoke in a whisper.

"She is worse, Signor Ghezzi. Where is Don Aldo?"

Leo stared at her helplessly. His voice was thick with feeling and defeat. "You do not see him here with me. That is his answer."

Donna Lucia closed her eyes. When she opened them, tears spilled down her cheeks. She went back to the kitchen and leaned against the stove. "What now?" She turned to Leo. "The wound has begun to fester, I think. Isabella hardly breathes. The women—the older ones who know more than I—tell me to prepare myself . . ." Her voice trailed off. "Twice today, they thought her heart had stopped. They hit her on the face, on the soles of her feet. She breathed again, thank God! But if the time comes when they will pound and pound and . . . We must have a priest. There is only Guglielmo. Don't you understand?"

"I understand," Leo said, tormented. "But there is another kind of help. Why have you not sent for a doctor?"

She had only contempt for his ignorance. "There is one doctor here. He is old, and performs one sort of surgery. For a very large fee he will replace the virginity of an unmarried girl with the hide of a goat. In the cities are the real doctors, those with medicines for all disorders. Here, we have no choice but to help ourselves." She turned to peer into a pot of water boiling on the stove. "So if she is not to live, I want her at least to have what anyone else—"

"Listen to me, Donna Lucia," Leo said.

She spun around, her face wet and glistening. "I have listened and listened, and I have trusted you, but what has it availed me?"

"I am not the man I said I was." He sat down at the table.

Unexpectedly, the innkeeper almost smiled. "I did not think that you sold picture postcards, Signor Ghezzi." Then she did smile, but it was grim. "Oil paintings, maybe . . . Well, I have neither the time nor the patience to hear your confession tonight." With a towel in each hand, Donna Lucia lifted the big pot from the flame. "The women need some water upstairs."

Leo saw now that his vocation had pursued him; he was its captive. That must be the meaning, he decided, of Guglielmo's refusal to perform the sacrament. "I am a priest, Donna Lucia," *il Papa* said.

She put down the pot and faced her boarder. A cloud passed behind her eyes.

"What sort of priest?"

"A priest of the Church."

"Do not say so only to comfort me," she warned him. "If this is another lie, it is an unforgivable one." Although her tone was severe, her expression was rapt. "You'll fry in hell if what you say is not the truth."

"I swear to you before Almighty God." He sank into the nearest chair, resting his elbows on the table. "I am . . . finally . . . telling the truth." Leo rubbed his eyes hard. Colored lights burst in his brain like fireworks. "It was my intention . . . I would have much preferred . . . to keep my identity to myself. But now this is no longer possible."

Lucia Fedelio sat beside him. A strand of her hair, wet with tears, brushed his arm. Her voice was low. "I did not think you were . . . such a man. I thought quite the opposite. I thought you had run away from your wife."

It took him a moment to reply. When he removed his hands from his eyes, her face was a blur before him.

"I am who I say I am. .If you choose not to believe me, I shall understand."

"What one believes, just as who one loves—the choice is not always free." She shook her head, looking away from him. "Where is your church? Have you a church?"

"Yes, indeed, I have a church," he said. "But why I have left it and why I am here . . ." He shook his head silently. "I beg you to trust me. There is good cause."

Donna Lucia wiped her hands on her apron and pushed back her hair. For a moment there was silence. A fly buzzed overhead. It hit the ceiling, making a noise disproportionate to its size.

"What will you do for my child?" she asked.

"I will pray for her," Leo said. "I will pray for her to recover." He pushed his chair back and stood up. "Go upstairs, attend to Isabella."

"No! Please come with me right now."

Leo took the woman's hand. "First there are practical ways to help Him do His work. God will not appear with a washcloth to clean her bruises. Take care of your daughter, then send the others away." He gripped Donna Lucia's other arm. "I will see her, but only if you *promise* me that you will not give up hope. Isabella is alive. When she fell, the blow shocked her, but I do not believe she will die. She will live."

"I promise," Donna Lucia said. High color washed her cheeks and the tips of her ears. She returned *il Papa's* gaze. "*Sì*. I promise."

They went together into Isabella's room. Bedsheets had been draped over the windows to dull the light. A smell of sickness hung in the air, acrid and stinging yet sweet. The nightstand was laden with an assortment of comforts: a bowl of soapy water, a damp cloth, a string of rosary beads, a charm that Leo took to be the hoof of a small animal, a crucifix, a small, garish portrait of the Blessed Virgin, and Franco Pisticci's bottle of brandy, by now half empty. He wondered for a split second who could have been drinking it, and decided that Isabella's nurses must have found it restorative.

Once inside the sickroom, Donna Lucia shrank into a corner and lowered her head in prayer. Leo went directly to the girl's bed, his back to the mother.

The change he saw in Isabella since the day before disquieted him. Her hands were clenched in tight fists; she had rolled to one side and her knees were drawn halfway up to her chest; the hair on her head, where it had not been cut away, was dirty and matted. His gaze traveled the length of her body until he noticed a bright red smear on the back of her white nightdress. Without thinking, he averted his eyes, uncertain and embarrassed. Then, steeling himself, he examined the menstrual stain again—it was quite fresh. Clearly, her body had not ceased to function. He was overwhelmed by the feeling that, at the sight of the blood, an even greater intimacy with the child, and with her mother, had been visited upon him. He pulled a chair to the side of the bed and sat down. His fingers were shaking.

Donna Lucia saw that the priest took both of her daughter's hands in both of his, and that he talked quietly to her, as though she could hear. But he spoke in such whispers that she could not tell what prayers he offered. She watched him bend forward, touch the bandaged area tenderly, and kiss Isabella's forehead.

In a little while, Leo got to his feet and turned to leave the room. Donna Lucia's heart beat wildly, and the conviction seized her that she had witnessed a mysterious and sacred rite.

Far into the night, they sat drinking what was left of Pisticci's brandy.

"Now that you have seen my daughter, do you think she will live?" the mother whispered.

"There is a God Who hears our prayers, and Who sees into our hearts, and Who takes pity on us in our need. He will help Isabella," *il Papa* said.

Donna Lucia's eyes shone with gratitude, and something more than that. "Should I call you 'Father' now?" she asked.

"No. Everything must continue as before," Leo replied, knowing as he said it that what was between them had already been transformed.

X

THE BISHOP AWOKE. A double layer of curtains were drawn over the windows of the room he shared with Pio at the *pensione* in which they had spent the night. His limbs had swelled dangerously during sleep. Biondi groaned and eased himself onto his back. Since they had left the Vatican, the bishop had not rested more than two or three consecutive hours. He longed for his own bed in his own small apartment on the Via Rusticucci where, day or night, he could hear the soothing, familiar rush of Roman traffic. He wished to return to the time before *all this,* when he knew when to wake up and when to sleep, when to eat, and when to pray. His longing for the ordinariness and routine of everyday life bordered on lust. Confusion, fatigue, and sadness fought for space in his tormented mind. A great, muscular force pulled on him—on the very tissue of his heart, Biondi felt—until he was certain it would cease to beat.

At night, he drifted off, listening to voices that argued with one another about topics that he could not sort out, in a language that was foreign to him. Yet all the time, he recognized that it was his own voice he heard in many guises; and even as he slept, the sensation of being incomprehensible to himself cloaked Biondi in frustration, sometimes in rage. And so he woke at regular intervals throughout the night, gasping as if he had been running.

Now the bishop sat up in bed, rearranging the pillows behind him into a bolster. In the next bed, Pio Cavagna stirred and opened his eyes.

"Che ore sono?"

"Almost five o'clock." Biondi's flesh puffed up like the edges of an egg soufflé around the face of his watch.

Pio's eyelids drooped. "Go back to sleep. We have another hour at least."

"No. You sleep. I cannot."

Pio raised his head from the pillow.

"Insomnia?" he asked compassionately.

The bishop nodded. "But never before in my life. Until now. I worry for him constantly." His voice cracked.

Pio nodded in agreement and rose in bed. His mouth tasted sour and felt gummy.

"Please!" Biondi exclaimed, as his companion prepared to get up. "Do not ruin your rest on my account. My anxiety will keep me company." He gave forth a little laugh. "My anxieties are so many, they can keep each other company!"

Pio ruffled his hair and cleared his throat. He fumbled along the bedside table for a package of cigarettes he had left there. "It isn't on your account," he replied. "I was about to get up." Pio inserted a cigarette between his lips and lit it. He turned on a lamp on the table, and exhaled a long, perfect stream of blue smoke.

"Smoking? So early? I was a smoker myself twenty years ago, but at least I used to wait until after breakfast."

Pio shrugged. He was wary of these priests with their excessive, sometimes lugubrious concern for others. With the cigarette suspended precariously in his lips, he slid off the bed and stood up. He wore a pair of trousers and a sleeveless undershirt. "Without a cigarette I couldn't make it as far as the breakfast table."

Biondi spoke again, assuming a tone of tact. "Monsignor Ghezzi—Francesco—he seems irritable with you," he began.

Pio was pacing the room in slow, loping steps. He stopped short. "Oh? What did he say?" he asked.

"He implied that, ah, you and he had had an argument." Biondi paused, as if in private debate. "Yesterday, when you were changing the tire . . . he drew me aside. . . . He led me to believe that you may be—were—are—"

"An anarchist?"

Biondi flushed. "I did not say that, sir."

The Pope's brother-in-law drew on his cigarette several times before responding. He held the butt between his index finger and thumb, his face pink. "Ghezzi sees trouble lying in wait for him even on the steps of the Scala Regia. But you can forget about it. I do not shoot guns. It is all inside of me."

"Francesco said only that you were—that you were not—*with* us, one hundred percent."

Pio hesitated before he replied. "I want to find Giuseppe as much as anyone. I would like him to return to Rome, for I doubt whether Cecilia will survive it, if he does not. However—if you will allow me to be honest—I do have some doubts about whether that is where he belongs." Living at such close quarters had given the men a certain fraternity. "I think that perhaps my brother-in-law may be on a pilgrimage into the heart of passion. In my opinion, he does not know himself. He has spent his life in dedication to others, but Giuseppe Bellini he sees through the wrong end of a telescope." Pio drew deeply on the cigarette. "I do not presume certainty; however, I believe it may be such considerations that have led him on his quest. And I believe he may return the better for it . . . for having left us. Although this is not the popular view."

The bishop looked wretched. "Yes, I too found the Holy Father, how shall I say, perplexed, at our last meeting," he admitted, settling on this most discreet statement of the truth. Then his candor got the best of him. "But looking backward—in hindsight, you know—that was hardly a surprise. The . . . changes, the . . . cataclysm, if you will, had been coming on for quite a while. I realize only now that I learned to value—yes, to love—his struggle. Although I did not help him understand it, it brought me closer to him, you see."

Pio stubbed out his cigarette in a dish. "Well, don't blame yourself," he said with a gruff kindness.

"How can I not?" Biondi asked. "I failed the one who matters most to me in the world! Truly, it is my tragedy as much as his."

"So far, it is only a crisis, not a tragedy." Leo's brother-in-law sought a less taxing subject. "You do not look well this morning. How are your legs bearing up?"

"If it were just the legs, I would say, 'Cut them off, the stupid things!' Quite frankly, my legs are the least of it." His voice dropped. "You know, I fear terribly for him every moment that he is away," he said, unable to let the topic rest. "Of course, the Church has withstood many crises and survived," he remarked more hopefully. "Mad Popes, evil Popes, Popes who hid women in their chiffoniers, Popes who died under inexplicable circumstances after barely taking office. Celestine V actually abdicated." Biondi drew in his breath. "But never, *never,* a Pope who . . . simply . . . blew away, like a bit of dust in the wind. . . ."

The bishop, tempted, picked Pio's package of cigarettes off the table, nervously crinkling the cellophane. "I am not like Ghezzi, or even you, both so tough-minded. And I was surely unprepared to join a search party for His Holiness so late in life. My legs are killing me!" he blurted out. "But I will go on forever, until we find him. If all of you go back to Rome, defeated, I will not give up! I will go on alone, if need be."

Pio removed the package of cigarettes from the bishop's lap and lit another one, dropping the wooden match into a dish. The room was so still that a sound could be heard as the stick fell. "Perhaps everything is fated, as you suggest," he said.

Biondi nodded. "If a man is destined to drown," he declared, picking up from where Pio left off, "he will not die of pneumonia. We are left to wonder at the inscrutable designs of the Lord."

Pio shrugged and rubbed out his half-smoked cigarette. "Be that as it may," he said, "I'll go downstairs and see if I can find us both some coffee. At least that's an easier matter to investigate."

·   ·   ·

A day and a night passed. On the morning of the second day Isabella opened her eyes and mewed like a kitten. The old women screamed in disbelief; they had consigned her to eternity. Donna Lucia and *il Papa* came running. Everyone stood around the bed, watching anxiously. Isabella blinked and flexed her arms. Her legs stirred beneath the blankets. She grunted and tried to raise herself. The women said they had never seen anything like it. "Truly, she has come back from the dead," one of them exclaimed. Donna Lucia wept and laughed and cradled her daughter's head in her arms. By late afternoon Isabella was sitting up in bed sipping soup.

Donna Lucia found Leo in the parlor, praying. He looked up and met her eyes.

"You have given us a miracle," she said in an undertone.

"It may well be a miracle, but if it is, it has nothing to do with me."

"This I do not believe," Donna Lucia announced.

A silence opened, into which they both poured unspoken words. Regret wrung the woman's heart. She knew more surely all the time, that the priest could not travel the distance that separated them. But later, when she was alone, after Leo had gone to bed, she asked a favor.

"Holy Mother, please do not allow this man to leave us. Keep him here in my house. Do this for me, Blessed Mother, and I will light a candle to you every day of every year! I ask it not only for myself," she went on, after seeming to come to the end of her entreaty, "but for all my neighbors as well."

·   ·   ·

Up, up, up they went. They were airborne! The rooftops of Rome receded beneath them. The blades of the helicopter emitted a deafening noise, a tremendous churning and tumultuous roar that made conversation all but impossible.

"Are you sure you know what you're doing in this damned crate?" Ugo Tuttobene bellowed. "Why the hell didn't you tell me you were a beginner?"

Federico Ottaviani did not look up. His young face was a study in terror: his brow was knitted, his lower lip trembled, his face was claylike as a dead man's. In one hand he held the stick; his feet played on the pedals. Suddenly the ship pitched forward.

"I know! I know! I am *not* a beginner! I'm an intermediate! I trained for fifteen hours in one almost like this!" Ottaviani yelled, as Tuttobene grabbed his thigh.

"*Almost* like—?"

"Relax! Hold tight! Keep your arms and feet inside! And take your hand off my leg!"

The ship reversed itself at the final moment and climbed still higher. Over his left shoulder, Tuttobene could see the Propaganda Fide College on Janiculum Hill. It shone white and imposing against the sky. To his right he observed the great dome of St. Peter's, veiled in a light fog, yet seeming to gleam in the afternoon sun. The city grew smaller and smaller under them.

"Head south," Tuttobene cried. "South! . . . Can you hear me?"

"*What?*" Ottaviani was riveted on the stick, the pedals, and on the field of little dials and meters with their accusatory stark white numbers and insanely fluctuating needles. It was not a simple matter to gain his attention.

The altimeter showed them flying very high, then sinking like a stone again. The compass swung first northeast, then east, then hurled itself, like an hysterical person, to the south. The airspeed indicator reported that they were racing through the skies faster and faster, then slowing suddenly to a snail's pace. When Ottaviani composed himself enough to coordinate all the functions properly, they moved up and forward. When he became confused and frightened, the aircraft began to drop like a large, somber insect in a death-spin.

Ugo Tuttobene squeezed his eyes closed. His stomach heaved in nausea and panic. He silently mouthed a prayer. "Dear Father in heaven," he began, "we are on a mission in Your name, in the name of Your universal Church, and in the name of the Servant of the Servants of God, *il Papa*. . . . Forgive me for the false tale I told Federico! Forgive me for disobeying Francesco Ghezzi's instructions. It was not evil that overcame me, but the need for a willing ally and swift transportation. It was all in a holy cause that I chose to embroider the truth and commandeer this machine. I beseech You, O Lord, that if we should die in Your service, make it swift and painless! And welcome us into Your loving arms!"

As he finished, Tuttobene had a vision of himself and his companion immolated in a mangled, blazing wreck in the middle of St. Peter's Square as tourists, nuns, and priests looked on in speechless horror. He felt certain that they would perish ignominiously, heralded in the headlines of the world press only as two deranged thieves of government property, gone up in flames, their true purposes forever obscured.

"We are going to die!" Tuttobene bellowed, before he could stop himself.

"So be it!" the pilot called back over the shriek of the propellers. "Our deaths will be noble ones." The ship swayed slightly to the right and shuddered. "As my dear mama says, 'Funerals await even the best of us . . . and all our lofty ambitions as well!' "

There were no doors on the helicopter, but only small apertures through which the passengers and pilot could enter and exit. Just then a great gust of wind blew into the cockpit. Ugo Tuttobene's black peaked cap, decorated with the golden bird, had been resting on his lap. In a flash it was carried away, out of the opening at Tuttobene's side, and into the atmosphere. It dipped and swirled, waltzed and skated; the bird caught the reddish rays of the sun and glinted, as if mocking him. Finally, like a shred of tissue, it commenced a casual drift to earth. The deputy commissioner watched with pain and longing as his officer's hat, the symbol of his rank, grew tinier in his sight and finally disappeared altogether, some-where in the gathering darkness and the twinkling lights over the city of Rome.

. . .

It was the sort of day to which Leo would never have succumbed while at the Vatican: grey and cold, but windless, still. In his room at the inn, he gave himself to a quiet melancholy. Sleep beckoned him with warm fingers. He felt exhausted, wearied by anticlimax, after the emotions spent in Isabella's rescue. Although he had prayed for it, he was no less amazed than anyone by her precipitant recovery.

Il Papa yawned again and again trying, out of the habit of disci-pline, to stay awake. A faraway ringing in his ears reminiscent of a muffled alarm clock, and a pushing—or was it a pulling?—sensa-tion in his gut, drew him closer to an unavoidable appointment. His limbs felt like glass and his flesh raw, susceptible, as if nerves were exposed. His heart ticked rapidly, high in his chest, near his larynx. He shivered, aware of experiencing pains in the back of his neck, behind the ears. He guessed that he was running a fever.

Leo struggled up, and glanced out the window. Most of the trees had shed their foliage as winter bore down upon the earth; they stood like skeletons against the slate sky. In the distance, over the ridge of mountains, a single cloud—long and thin as if stretched by superhuman hands—lay suspended, unmoving.

Il Papa's attention was deflected by the cries of children running down the street. They chased a dog. One of the girls was dressed in a nun's habit and wimple; a small boy wore a monk's robe and cowl. Some parents in the southern villages outfitted their offspring in religious garb, in fulfillment of an ancient vow. But even Leo could not recall the exact nature of the pledge. The boy in the monk's robe had no shoes and lagged behind the others. The cowl slipped from his head and flapped loosely on his back. From Leo's second-story window, his costume appeared to have been stitched together from old sacks, or dishcloths, or perhaps canvas. The chil-dren carried pebbles in their hands and tossed them at the dog to make him run faster. When a pellet reached its target, the animal yelped in pain. Soon the children turned into an alley; their shouts grew faint.

The trees moved arthritically in a mild breeze that had blown up. The air, which had been autumnal in the morning, now had a moist and frosty sting that promised more bitter weather to come.

A draft stole through the floorboards. Leo returned to the bed and rested his swollen head upon the pillow.

He awoke several minutes later to a gentle rapping on the door. For a moment, he thought he was back in his bedroom in the Apostolic Palace.

"Grazie, grazie," Leo murmured, his eyes still shut, feeling no urgency to rise and confront a visitor. Then, lifting his eyelids a crack, he saw where he was. "Ah . . . who is there, please?"

"It is me, Lucia. May I come in?"

Leo roused himself, sat up in bed, and asked her to enter.

The woman's fine face was full of expectation, but he recognized apprehension in it, too.

"Forgive me for disturbing you, Padre."

"I am your guest; and you are never a disturbance. But please, it is better not to address me as 'Padre.' "

Donna Lucia let herself into the room and closed the door.

"There is someone here who must see you."

Through his fever, Leo felt the chill of fear. "Who is this?"

"Anna."

A throbbing began in his temples. He rose from the bed. "Who is Anna?"

Donna Lucia extended her arms in helpless entreaty. "She is very young and in a few months will give birth. She has no husband—"

His suspicion mounted. "Why, exactly, is this my concern?"

"Last night she dreamed that the child would be born with no arms. And deaf, like Isabella."

Leo's voice was shallow and uninflected. "Listen to me: I can play no part—"

"No one else but you can save the baby."

"Donna Lucia, a pregnant girl's nightmare does not predict the future," Leo said sternly. "All pregnant girls have nightmares, I am told."

It was as if she had not heard him or refused to hear. "You saved Isabella," she said, with the complacency borne of perfect logic.

Il Papa took the woman by her shoulders. "You told her so, this Anna?"

The innkeeper did not answer. With her lower lip between her teeth, she kept her eyes on her shoes. Her body stiffened under Leo's touch.

"Speak to me. You told her so?—that I *saved* Isabella?"

Donna Lucia nodded, silent.

"And did you tell her also that I am a priest? Did you?"

Lucia Fedelio began to cry. "Please don't be angry with me. How could I help it?"

"You promised you would keep my secret," he said, dismayed.

"I had no *choice*! She came to me early this morning in a desperate condition. She threatened to kill herself and the child. These may seem like empty words to you, but girls like Anna are impulsive; they do what they say they will." She raised her head and looked at Leo. "To do away with oneself and one's baby? Is this not a sin? A crime against life itself?"

There was silence. He turned his head from her.

"I do not know what kind of a priest you are! So tight-lipped, so reluctant, and with so many secrets."

Leo loosened his grip on Donna Lucia. "You should not have told this woman that I saved your daughter. In the first place it isn't true." It seemed to him that nothing could be less desirable just now than to be declared a healer, a holy man with extraordinary powers. He had no such divine gifts; even his temporal ones were in doubt.

Donna Lucia clenched her fists and closed her eyes. "I am not so convinced of the supernatural, but neither do I resist it when I see it at work. *I saw what I saw!* You touched Isabella, you prayed over her, and before we knew it, she woke up and made sounds. What appeared hopeless, you reversed overnight. I witnessed it! Now let go of me."

He set her free.

"Donna Lucia, I did not save her. I did not snatch your daughter from the jaws of death. She was simply not as badly hurt as we first thought. Do you understand me? No doubt she had what is called in medicine a concussion. Have you never heard the term?"

"No."

"It's a hard bump on the head, not very serious. People recover naturally from such accidents. Sometimes, as with Isabella, it takes days. I cannot *save* anyone. I have no such, uh, aptitude. And you must not go about telling ... innocent ... gullible people that a priest who lives in your home performs—"

"Miracles! Yes, miracles!" Lucia Fedelio stepped back and faced him, undaunted. "You cannot disclaim what you have done, no matter how ignorant ... innocent you believe we are."

Leo thought quickly. How could he cause her at least to lower her voice?

"If you stubbornly refuse to listen to reason, I shall have to leave here," he said.

She gasped, stricken.

"Yes, I shall. Don't you realize the danger of raising hopes in people's hearts that cannot be fulfilled? It only leaves them more unhappy than—"

The bedroom door flew open and a hugely pregnant girl, her face streaming, burst upon the scene. She hurled her small, misshapen frame at Leo's feet.

"Padre! Padre! I could wait no longer!" She looked to be no more than fifteen years old. "Last night I saw my baby born without arms. He could not hear!"

"My dear, my dear. Dreams are no more than—dreams. We all have them." Leo wondered if he truly believed what he said to the girl. But whether he believed it or not, his words only made Anna's cries louder. Her weeping filled the room. A thick, lemony waterfall poured from her nose, cascading over her upper lip.

"My child must not come into the world without his arms! Al-

ready, before he is born, he is missing his father! What *more*? Why should other children be whole and able to hear their mothers' voices, but not my son? I don't want him to be like Isabella!"

The girl looked up at Leo pleadingly. "You can prevent it," she whispered. Her round, olive face resembled a chimpanzee's. How could she know the sex of the child, he asked himself. Has this, too, been revealed to her?

Donna Lucia joined Leo in trying to calm Anna, but it was no use. At last, together, they managed to encourage her to sit down on the bed. *Il Papa* gave her a handkerchief from his pocket. He glanced at it briefly, for it had a familiar feel: the fine handiwork of the papal tailors. He laid it in Anna's open palm. Somehow this modest act, the proffering of a bit of white linen cloth to the young woman, made them both feel better. She mopped her face.

"I saw it as I slept," she repeated in a choked voice. "He came out from between my legs ... all covered in blood ... and he was—*not normal!* That is the way he will be born, I know it, unless you help me!"

"Let me tell you something, both of you," Leo said as gently as he could. "There are a hundred possible natural reasons for Isabella regaining her health. This was no miracle. Christ crossing the waters ... the multiplication of the loaves and fishes ... the raising of Lazarus from the dead—these were miracles! Sometimes we can clearly see the hand of God moving in the affairs of men." He waited for a sign of understanding or recognition on the part of the women—a nod or even a flicker of an eyelash—but none was forthcoming. They only stared at him. Perhaps if he took a harsher tack? "There is a phenomenon known as 'hysterical cures.' Have you heard of it?" He knew the futility of asking them. How could they have heard of such a thing? They had barely heard of the invention of the telephone.

"*Hysterical* cures?" Lucia Fedelio replied angrily. "Isabella could not have been hysterical, Padre! She was fast asleep, halfway to heaven. *I* am the only one who was hysterical!"

The benighted Anna bobbed her head in agreement. Leo considered: If he recited some prayers, if he performed a rite of exorcism or healing over Anna and her unborn baby, by the next day Donna Lucia's parlor would overflow with supplicants begging for his aid. He would be unable to refuse anyone. He would not wish to refuse anyone. On the other hand, what could he offer them?—magic tricks? Like a fire in a pile of dry twigs word would spread, down the mountain, out from the village to neighboring villages. It would become a festival, a carnival of frustrated hope.

They would not expect him merely to resume his old pastoral duties. That, he admitted with a sudden lifting of his heart, did not seem unattractive. They would expect marvels: "You saved Isabella; you made Anna's child whole. Now you must help us as well!" One 'miracle' would beget the next, confirming the primitive beliefs of these simple people, their increasing reliance on occult rituals, until he himself—God forbid—might come to honor powers that he did not possess.

It would be untenable fraud, even heresy. Beyond that, how long could he hope to avoid attracting the attention of the ecclesiastical authorities? It would not please them to find a living, breathing miracle worker residing no more than a day's trip from Rome! For a while they might ignore the whole affair—and rightly so. These alleged wonders always seemed to happen in the countryside, among people with little education and less worldliness. It was true, Leo said to himself, that intellectuals and those who fancied themselves sophisticates were nearly always immune to the remarkable. Too many complex ideas and preconceptions mediated between their hearts and their experience of the world. They could not make the leap of faith that encompassed miracles, or even God. The Blessed Mother had appeared at Lourdes, not on the Via Condotti, and there was good reason for this, both in heaven and on earth.

Leo called Donna Lucia to the window, where he was immersed in these reflections, out of the earshot of the mother-to-be. "There is nothing I can do," he said with finality. "You brought this young woman to me, now you must take her away. I cannot deliver her from her nightmares, and I cannot vouch for the health of her child. I am a priest, Lucia, not a wizard." He had called her by her name without realizing it.

She glowered at him now, while Anna—sensing his rejection—prepared to escalate her campaign.

Although enervated, Leo stood as erect as he could, making a conscious effort to appear commanding. It had been easier to exercise control within the Vatican than here over these recalcitrant, impassioned women.

Anna had begun to rant and babble incoherently. "I do not ask for money or power, or even for *love*! But if my child is born maimed, all the other children will beat him and steal from him! He won't be able to hear the birds singing . . . or to throw a ball! They will taunt him—children are so wicked! He will starve when I am gone. I have no luck, I will die young! O Mary! O merciful Mother of God! They will take from his pockets, cheat him!" Anna's eyes seared Leo. "The world overflows with strong men like you who trample on the weak!"

The girl flung herself to the floor again and tore her hair. She began to rap her head on the floorboards until Leo and Donna Lucia feared that she would injure herself. With much straining, they drew her to her feet. She wobbled heavily in their arms like a sack of wet meal.

"Ai! . . . Ai! Always misfortune! It follows me like an assassin, ready to take me from behind and stab me in the belly. My poor *bambino*," she spoke to her unborn child. "Why do they punish you for *my* sins? Why? You are innocent. They call me 'Whore. Daughter of whores, *mother* of whores!' but it is false." She mooed like a cow.

Leo turned to the innkeeper, sensing himself carried by events over which he had lost authority, toward acts he was loath to commit. "My heart breaks for this girl, but I cannot attend to her—"

"Have you too been banished, is that it? Like Guglielmo?" Donna Lucia cried, furious. "Has the Holy Father excommunicated you? Are you a priest or are you not?"

"*Il Papa* has nothing to do with it," he said, feeling crazily, dizzyingly split. "It has nothing to do with . . . try to understand . . . I . . . I cannot indulge in rituals which . . ."

Donna Lucia ignored his protests.

"Can you *hear* Anna?" She beseeched him. "Your heart breaks? I have seen boulders break more easily. It does not even thump, if you ask me. It lies there, a dead thing in your chest."

The ominous sound of breaking glass caused them both to turn from the window.

Anna had shattered a water pitcher that she took from the night-stand next to the bed. Now she was holding a shard of glass, as long as a kitchen knife, to her throat. She talked calmly to Leo, as if measuring her words in teaspoons.

"You do not wish to help me. So I have only one course left: I will kill myself. I will kill myself *and* my baby. Because what can I expect of life? *Nothing.*"

The girl began to press the jagged glass into the flesh of her neck. Leo's head pounded. Either his temperature was very high or it had suddenly plummeted; he was covered from head to ankles in a cold sweat. He knew very little, he acknowledged, about the psychology of distracted women, but he knew that he could not allow Anna to risk real injury.

Before he could reach her, she forced the glass harder into her flesh. Droplets of blood formed on her skin and began to course down her neck in thin streams.

"*Alt! Si ferma! Non si muova!* I will do whatever you ask!" *Il Papa* cried.

He wrested the glass from Anna's hand. The cut was not serious. She wiped the blood with his handkerchief that she still held clutched in her fist.

"Please," he said, "sit down, sit down. I will do what you wish."

She walked slowly, with an air of quiet triumph, to the bed. Half-reclining on the edge, lifting up her blouse, she presented her large naked stomach to the Servant of the Servants of God.

Donna Lucia stood behind him, peering over his shoulder, satisfied that she was about to witness her second miracle.

Leo said nothing. He stared at the round white mountain of Anna's abdomen, its navel distended like an accusing eye. Then, turning away, he examined the bloody piece of glass he held in one hand and the bloodied handkerchief in the other, which Anna had returned to him as politely as a schoolgirl. Leo marveled at the richness of the blood on the glass, now turning brown. How quickly, how neatly, it bonded and coagulated on the smooth surface, so unlike its natural home in the veins! He put forward his hand and with the cloth dabbed at the new blood that had sprung out on her throat.

But still he said nothing. The church did not encourage exorcism. As he leaned over the girl, Leo could not summon up a single prayer. What was he to do? How was he to deal with this ... flagrant *absurdity*? He tasted the word, testing its heft, and as he did so, saw that it was not for him to determine the reason or unreason of all the things of life.

Anna gave him his direction.

"The arms are, I think, here," she said, taking his hand that held the handkerchief and touching it to two places on her stomach. "And the head is here, I'm sure of it."

Leo took a deep breath. He moved his lips, reciting the only prayer that came to mind. He spoke in Latin, hoping that this would lend an air of gravity to his ministrations. *"Sancta Maria et omnes ... et omnes sancti intercedant ... intercedant pro nobis ... ad Dominum. Amen."*

He made the sign of the cross with his thumb over the places to which she had guided his hand.

Anna stood up, smoothing her skirt.

"Now my son will be well," she remarked, smiling at the priest, abruptly coquettish. "Thank you very much, Padre."

"Prego," Leo replied.

Anna left the room, flouncing, slightly dazed but proud.

Donna Lucia touched his arm. "You are a fine man. You have done a holy act."

Leo's eyes filled, perhaps triggered by the fever. He said nothing, overcome with emotion.

"Lie down now," Lucia Fedelio ordered like a mother. "You look very tired."

"I don't feel at all ... myself," he admitted, as she closed the door quietly behind her.

Il Papa stretched out on the bed. Or was he feeling more and more himself? He shivered, as if having just shed someone else's overcoat—too close around the shoulders, too short at the knees. It seemed a prodigious effort to stay awake. Then the fever overtook him.

Less than an hour later, the door crashed open and Anna came to stand over his bed.

"Back again?" he mumbled at the girl. "Who is it this time with bad dreams? Your sister?" He had been sleeping; his temperature had not abated, and in the darkening room he saw imperfectly. Lucia Fedelio hovered near the door, wringing her hands, crooning apologies.

A dead, plucked chicken dangled from Anna's hand. "It's for you. He's the best I could find so late in the day."

Leo put his face into the pillow. "*Tante grazie.* I appreciate the thought, but I cannot accept your gift."

Anna screwed up her face ready to cry.

"Then the grace is no good! The grace will do no good, if you refuse to take it. My baby will be born without limbs and deaf!" She began to keen again, as if the rites had never taken place.

A triphammer banged in Leo's head. "Grace costs nothing," he explained from deep within the pillow. "Grace comes free, you see?" His words were muffled. "That's the point of it: freely given and freely received. If it's grace you want, then you should understand that it does not demand the payment that you offer."

"It's not payment, it's a chicken," Anna said indignantly.

"Then it does not demand the chicken," Leo groaned.

"No! Nothing in the world is free—everybody knows that—including grace! You must take what I have brought."

With that, she tossed the dead bird on the blanket under Leo's nose and trotted smartly from the room, as if her act resolved their theological dispute in her favor.

Il Papa opened his eyes and with morbid curiosity examined the poultry the girl had deposited on his chest. Its waxy skin was pocked with goose bumps; perhaps at the moment of death it had experienced a mortal chill.

"Did you die for me, little bird?" he muttered to himself. For a moment, he saw Edoardo again, strutting about near his coffee cup during breakfast at the Apostolic Palace. "To pay for . . . *what?*" Donna Lucia silently removed the chicken. "To pay for grace with death?" His eyelids drooped. "Still, through me, it may be that help has come from Him."

He experienced a lightness in his breast that did not come merely because the weight of the bird had been lifted.

For more than three days *il Papa* lay in the small boat of his bed, cut loose by fever from the moorings of consciousness. Yet he guided his vessel with care, over stormy midnight seas, and from the crow's nest of his illness surveyed his life. Past and present mingled in fantasy and hallucination.

Much transpired during these hours, both inside and outside the sickroom. For Leo, time became a shadow play that bore only a distorted resemblance to what, up to then, had been his existence. He traveled back through the years—but the progress was halting and erratic. A series of dislocated images rose up to ravage him: Men and women he knew well—Cecilia, Ghezzi, his parents—appeared more and less than human, like characters in a poorly drawn cartoon. Their features were overblown, their voices shrill and quick.

Leo followed his own evolution as he would have watched a film: One scene showed him as an adolescent; the next as a toddler of two; then he was sitting on the stoop of his childhood home as a young man of seventeen. Several times he spoke his family name aloud, "Bellini, Bellini," sharpening the machinery of memory.

He slipped in and out of delirium. During the hours of light, he was occasionally aware of daytime bustle: voices, footsteps in the hall outside his door, the aromas of food, the barking of dogs, a subdued rustling around his bed. These sounds and sensations, dimly perceived, buoyed Leo close to the surface of consciousness and then ... night and darkness came, and with it a restless, edgy peace. He felt heat and cold; someone ran a warm, rough washcloth over his chest, his face, across his lips, and wiped his fingers gently. He attempted to imitate the normal responses of health, to form a logical sentence, but it was useless. He could not. He rode, sometimes heavily, sometimes lightly, on the waves of sickness, wrapped in the soft heat of the fever like a baby in bunting.

Six years old. In one year, his mother would be dead. His devout grandmother presents him with a child-size altar, linens, candles, prayer cards, and a Missal so that he can play at being a priest. The game is an old family custom that his *nonna* perpetuates. This night, the small Giuseppe stands before his parents and his sister saying Mass at his altar. His father, taciturn, a non-communicant, sits in a chair at the far end of the room, reading the newspaper. His mother watches him, transfixed. His sister smirks and sticks out her tongue. He takes the game one step further than most children, by preaching. Although the sense is not clear, he is impressed by his own seriousness, his flair for the pulpit ...

Eleven. Tall for his age. His father, not recovered from the loss of his wife, sits before the green glowing dial of a radio that plays softly. The older man speaks not about the love of God, but the love of moderation. He is oddly remote now, wary of expressing strong emotions. He never raises his voice anymore, either in joy or anger. His father seems to Giuseppe to dwell in a place where pain and suffering can no longer intrude—a shadowy glade, he gives his son to understand, of safety, if not delight. Observing and listening, Giuseppe learns that it is sometimes warm there, but never hot. The father tutors his son on the static geography of the place and describes the roads that lead to it ...

Thirteen years old. Giuseppe sits in a classroom. He is not proficient in this subject, mathematics. He tries to make himself small and unremarkable behind his desk. He studies his book intently, pretending absorption, but actually the figures swim before his eyes and make no sense. Although he has been in school every day, he believes he has missed something crucial to his understanding. He sighs. This is not unusual: In life, often, he feels he has missed something crucial to his understanding. Psychically, as if practicing hypnosis, he attempts to deflect the attention of his teacher from him.

Sixteen. On a day in July, he sits in a park on the grass next to Carla Galvani. She wears the thinnest of summer dresses and one of the cap sleeves rides high, exposing a slim, rounded, nut-brown shoulder. Placing his hand on its slope, he shudders exquisitely, and feels that here, perhaps, he has discovered something crucial to his understanding ... But she turns from him and runs away. He feels his life dribble into the ground through the soles of his feet—to be washed away later, he imagines, mixed with the earth, by men with hoses ...

Eighteen. Giuseppe enters the seminary. His father, ill now, has drifted into torpor and a state of depletion. Cecilia weeps, pleading with her brother: "There is only you and me. First I have no mother, now my father is wasting away before my eyes. I need you. Another year, what difference will a year make? Nothing prevents you from devoting some of your day here to prayer, if that's what you want. A religious vocation doesn't mean you have to lock yourself up in a cell!"

Giuseppe bows his head. Yes, it is all true. But he continues to stuff his few belongings into a case.

"The Church has no wish to annihilate families," she cries, angry. "A boy belongs first to his home and then to the Church."

He agrees with his sister about the wishes of the Church, yet he refuses to alter his plans. In her eyes, he knows, he must appear cold, driven, perhaps even fanatic. But he cannot find words to describe to Cecilia—his flesh and blood—the truth of his situation: that the inner flame on which he burns has grown lower and lower in the years since his mother's death, providing hardly enough heat to keep a man alive. Has she, his own sister, not noticed the symptoms: the numbness that flows from a clammy chill around the heart, the tentative, groping emergence from the tight circumference of his life, always followed by the swift retreat? He slides away from her, slips away, all the while nodding agreeably, agreeing ...

In carrozza! In carrozza! Last call!

The wheels of the train are rhythmic beneath him. Giuseppe stares, unblinking, from the window. The sound grows louder, arching over him, as if he has merged with the wheels . . . and from somewhere else, above his head, a high-pitched whining comes, like an immense chain saw. Modern engineering! It is an ache now, a disruption, settling into his bones. He must complain to the conductor. Where is the conductor? *Where is the conductor on this train?*

XI

THE LITTLE HELICOPTER swooped over the village of T—— causing a terrific din, skimming the treetops, and veering dangerously close to the low buildings. The blades sliced the air at a tremendous speed, churned up clouds of dust and tore stones from the ground, hurling them like bullets across the roads.

People came out of their houses to point at the sky in fear and wonder. A cluster of children gathered in the middle of the main street. They screamed with laughter, as if at an aerial show staged for their entertainment. The craft, bucking, its engine sputtering, gained altitude. Victory dissolved into defeat as suddenly it tipped, nose down, scattering the crowd.

In the sickroom below, Donna Lucia dropped a washrag on Leo's forehead. Running to the window, she stuck her head out. As the ship seemed to pass within yards of her face, nearly grazing the house, she drew back, glanced at her patient, and emitted a low moan.

The helicopter struggled up again and the children reassembled, clapping their encouragement. The steel-frame-and-glass bubble of the cockpit glinted brilliantly in the dying light. For a moment the craft hovered in space, bobbing, as though held fast at the end of a string.

The roar ripped into his brain, waking *il Papa*.

"Il treno?" he croaked, confused. "What is happening out there?"

"Nothing. Nothing that concerns you," Donna Lucia answered in a broken whisper. "Some madmen, some crazy acrobats performing in the sky." She closed the window and drew the curtain, after taking one more incredulous look at the wobbling aircraft.

Leo tried to raise his head. *"Che cosa ha detto?"*

"Stay where you are," she cautioned, picking the cloth from his brow. "Go back to sleep." The metallic whining grew fainter. "Sleep now, Padre, there's nothing to worry about."

Assured, Leo drifted back.

Men in brown hoods, like monk's habits, pursue him through the streets of a deserted city. The wet pavement reflects streetlamps and a full moon. The hooded men brandish spears on which gleam tiny crosses sharpened at the tips into points. *Il Papa* carries a jug of wine and a cake under his robes. He does not understand why these monks chase him, but fears that if he stops running they will steal his cake and wine and impale him with their weapons. Someone calls to him, it may be his grandmother, it sounds like her voice: "Think of this: To begin to offer the sacrifice of the Mass is to begin to suffer, Giuseppe!"

. . .

Federico Ottaviani succeeded momentarily in stabilizing the helicopter. But even as they soared higher, he warned: "I think we're going down!"

"What?" A by now familiar panic seized Ugo Tuttobene in the gut. "What do you mean 'We're going down?' We seem to be going *up!*" But his voice held a question: Tuttobene recognized that the data of the senses did not play a part in Ottaviani's calculations.

" 'Up' is a temporary condition, sir! Sooner or later, all 'ups' become 'downs.' It's a law of nature. And I don't believe I can keep her airborne much longer. We're out of fuel!"

"How do you know?"

"The gauge, sir, the gauge."

"Do you know how to read your damn gauges? . . . Everything I have seen so far suggests that you do *not!*" Tuttobene leaned back in his seat with a certain warped pleasure, mystically convinced that, by pointing out Ottaviani's incompetence to him, he, Tuttobene, had improved their chances for survival.

"This particular meter I *can* read, sir! Look, see, a tiny red needle, here, tells me." He took one hand off the controls to point to it.

"Get your hands back on the wheel!"

"The winds are bad as well."

"Winds? Where are the winds? I see nothing. I hear nothing. No blowing of the winds."

Federico Ottaviani removed his eyes from the dials to gaze with bovine regret upon the ghost-white countenance of his commander. "*Sì*, there are strong currents out there. You cannot see them because they are invisible; you cannot hear them because the blades make too much commotion. But you can *feel* them—the way they blow into the cabin, the way they push us about. And the gasoline tank is quite empty!" Ottaviani was wheezing like a man with lung disease. "There's nothing more to do . . . I am unspeakably sorry, truly I am."

"Do not apologize—just fly! You had better not kill us both, you imbecile—and stop *staring* at me!"

The young man returned his attention to the controls.

"Tell me something." Tuttobene took a deep breath. "Are we going to crash?"

"Crash?" Ottaviani said the word as if he had never heard it before. "*Crash?* I don't believe so, sir. I will do my best to bring us in lightly. But this ship is not a feather, you know, and the ground is not made of cotton wool!"

The pilot gazed down and was stunned by what he saw. Directly below them, a narrow road was bounded on one side by a steep embankment and on the other by a sheer wall of cliff.

"And this does not look like an ideal . . . place to set down." He paused. "If I could have chosen . . . I would not have chosen terrain so . . . rugged." He hesitated. "Of course, in these circumstances, one cannot choose . . . I mean to say—" He chewed his lips. "A field would have been better. Flat. No bumps. Some margin for error. *This is one hell of a rotten place to land!*"

"Well, that's just grand," Tuttobene said, "seeing as how error is your strong suit." His voice was filled with the vibrato that precedes a scream.

Ottaviani began his attempt to ease the craft to earth. It tilted to the right and then to the left. "I will do what I can!" he shrieked, "but I am afraid it will not be possible to put down without some damage—"

"Damage! To what—to *whom*—do you mean to cause damage?"

Federico's eyes popped. He considered briefly the wisdom of praying for death; it would be preferable perhaps than to suffer the consequences in this life of the long misadventure with Tuttobene. At least he would answer to a greater, more forgiving master.

"We shall not perish!" Ottaviani screamed instead, as if trying to inveigle His favorable attention. "But I think . . . the helicopter may sustain . . . that is, we must be prepared to explain to . . . to the authorities . . ."

The dark earth loomed before them. The pilot felt hemmed in on all sides, as if entering a tunnel. He could almost count the bits of mica embedded in the wall of granite.

All was still.

After a thunderous explosion, a searing of the atmosphere, the magnificent gnashing of steel against rock, a shattering, deadly quiet descended. The cosmos seemed to pause to take account of its bruises. All natural activity slid to a halt. Birds did not sing. Snakes did not slither. Ants in their hills, putting down their staggering loads, looked up, shaken.

The tail of the ship, its small, vertically mounted blade crumpled but intact, pointed straight up at the sky, like a warning finger. A fine white dust fell, a snowfall of debris.

One of the large blades lay, bent in two, a few feet down the road. Another blade nested in the branches of a nearby tree. A cloud of brown smoke issued from the wreckage. Broken glass was everywhere, some pieces big enough to form a seat for a child, others torn into shards, or smashed to pellets the size of hail.

Ugo Tuttobene and Federico Ottaviani sat, strapped in their seats, alive but in shock. Tuttobene had received a long cut in his eyebrow and a purple welt on his cheek. Ottaviani had sustained a gash in the palm of his hand and blood leaked from another cut on his scalp. He clung with his good hand to the control stick, which was now attached to nothing; bright red, blue, green, and purple wires hung from it.

Tuttobene spoke first, hoarsely and slowly, sounding in considerable pain, each word formed with great effort. "For this . . . I will have your commission. I will have your career. I will have . . . everything . . . in your life that is dear to you. If you own . . . a dog . . . I will blow his head off. I will have your precious . . . mama washing the floors . . . of the bathrooms . . . at Aeroporto Fiumicino for the rest of her life!" He seemed about to expire, but added one final thought. "I will have your *testicoli* . . . I will have them stuffed and . . . *mounted,* do you hear? Hanging over my *desk!*"

The younger man clenched his teeth in agony. A driving pain shot through his left leg. His left arm hurt too. *"La gamba mi fa male,"* he whimpered. "Also my arm. I think my entire body is broken." His brain was foggy, taking stock of the damages.

"I myself am bleeding everywhere. Only my heart does not bleed—for you." Tuttobene breathed in experimentally. An excruciating stab, like an electric prod, accompanied his inhaling. "My ribs . . . Oh God, my ribs. My ribs are inside my *lungs!*"

They sat there for several minutes, the silence punctuated occasionally by Ottaviani's groaning.

"What will we do, sir? Forgive me, but night is not far off. We cannot stay here. There may be wild animals in the mountains. They'll smell our blood and eat us alive!" Ottaviani slipped his hand into the holster at his hip. It was empty. The gun had fallen out during the crash. He scanned the ground around them but the weapon was nowhere in sight. Growing cold he hoped he might pass out. That way, tigers could chew off his fingers and toes and he'd never know it.

"Animals are smarter than that: They would not want you for supper." Tuttobene lifted his head and looked down the road. "But never mind. I think I hear them coming."

Ottaviani twisted his neck around, not easily. "Who is coming?"

"How do I know *who*? It must be some villagers from the settlement we flew over a few moments ago." Tuttobene rested his head on the seat back, relieved.

"Did you see them? Did you see them?"

"No, but I can hear the sound of their feet, running, and their voices. Now listen carefully," he continued, "not a word about our mission. You keep your mouth closed and I will do the talking."

"What will you say?"

"I don't know."

"May I suggest?—"

"No. *No.* One more suggestion from you ...! Just be quiet, that's all. Pretend you're dead or something." Tuttobene closed his eyes and awaited rescue. "I'll take care of them."

Tuttobene reached down to his hip. His holster was still in place about his waist. His fingers traced the handle of the pistol. It felt solid, comfortable, as though created to be held in his hand. Ah yes: *Guns belong in the hands of those who will use them.* The sound of voices came closer.

He saw a small horde bearing down on the decimated helicopter.

"There it is!"

"There they are!"

"*Ch'è successo?*"

"C'è stato un incidente!"

"Hurry! Hurry up! *Faccia presto!* "

. . .

The tramping of feet.

Il Papa awoke again, but remained drowsy.

What ruckus was this in the hall outside his door? The heavy footsteps, and the voices?

"Watch it!"

"Cauto!" Ottaviani swooned.

"Alt! His leg!"

"Hold on there! You're going to drop me!" Tuttobene wrung his hands. One man supported him under the arms, another had him under the buttocks.

"Attenzione!"

Tramping ... tramping. The wall that faced the corridor reverberated as someone or something fell mightily against it. But Leo sank back on his pillows. He could not summon strength enough to investigate.

"The man with the worse injuries, he's wearing a gun!" Franco Pisticci said.

Donna Lucia ran her hands through her hair. It had come undone from the knot she sometimes made, and hung down her back in thick waves. "Holy Mary, I cannot stand another one! Already I have two patients." She indicated, with a flip of her hand, the bedrooms upstairs. "The priest is still delirious, and Isabella can hardly walk. I am running a hospital here."

"Did you hear what I said? One of them has a *gun*."

Donna Lucia gave Pisticci a bowl of *risotto* with peas.

"What makes you think so?" She had grown accustomed to the tall tales, the lurid fantasies of men.

"When I helped bring them up the stairs with the others, I accidentally touched the thing. In all the uproar, you know. Then, later, as we were putting them to bed, I saw it." Pisticci shoveled a forkful of rice into his mouth. "He insisted on removing the holster by himself. Wouldn't let anyone lay a hand on him until he had it off."

Lucia Fedelio covered her face with both hands. "I do not want guns in my house. There is enough trouble here. I am going up there right now and tell him to get rid of it—or get out."

"No, I wouldn't do that quite yet."

"Why not? This is my home."

"In the first place, they have fallen out of the sky only half an hour ago. Such an experience does not put a man in a generous mood, or instill in him the warm spirit of cooperation. In the second place, neither one can move. They were carried here, as you know. In the third place, the one with the weapon seems, as it were, attached to it." Franco Pisticci took another mouthful of supper and asked the innkeeper if she might spare a little wine. She placed a glass and a bottle before him. "Besides, I don't really think he will aim at anyone tonight. His shooting days are finished, for the present."

Donna Lucia sighed. "Did you inquire if these thugs have friends? Family? Maybe they would like to send a message or two? Perhaps someone will come and take them away? I have my hands full, as it is."

"They mentioned no friends. Of course, they were too weak and dazed for polite conversation. Actually, they did not even ask for a telephone. Or a doctor."

"Well, that was good of them." Her voice dropped, irritable. "Although they may die without one. And if they die, who are they? At least did they give their names and addresses?"

"No," said Pisticci, not overly concerned. He shoveled up more rice, pushing the stray grains through his mustache with his finger.

"More secrets." Donna Lucia smiled grimly. "Everyone who passes through my house lately seems to have a mystery in his back pocket."

"Perhaps it is wiser always to let the truth emerge of its own accord, naturally and gradually." Pisticci paused, reflecting. "It usually does. It's practically a rule of life. A man falls in love with a woman and although his wife may be the last to know, sooner or later the truth emerges—naturally, and gradually." He laughed softly.

"But this town, from all we have seen in the past few days, has declared itself exempt from the rules of life."

The café owner offered a few more scraps of information. "The older one said that they were on a training flight." He snorted and tossed his head. "But as we just saw: Practice does not make perfect. . . . The younger one says virtually nothing. Just *'sì, no, grazie.'*"

"He talks to himself? Another one who talks to himself?"

Franco Pisticci shook his head. "He doesn't talk. He only answers: 'Does it hurt here?' *'Sì.'* 'And what about here?' *'No.'* 'Do you want a little whiskey?' *'Grazie, grazie, molte grazie!'* He took the whole bottle to bed with him. He lets the older one do the actual talking."

"I tell you, it is too much for me," Donna Lucia replied and sat down across from her visitor. "I no longer feel in control of what happens even in my own home."

Pisticci scraped the bottom of the bowl and poured himself another glass of wine. He patted her hand. "When they come to their senses a bit, then we will find out more. It's best to wait a few days. We should not force anything. They have been through quite an ordeal."

"And so have I," the innkeeper muttered. "I only wish they had taken their mess elsewhere, far away from this town and from me."

"God gives His crosses to those who are able to carry them," Pisticci replied gently.

"One cross at a time, please," Donna Lucia said weakly. "Ah, Franco. Do you think I am crazy that sometimes I see God's face before me, grinning, as if He were playing a practical joke?" She got up, found a glass, brought it back to the table and poured herself some wine. "If those two new ones stay for a month, will I see a single *lira* from them?"

"No," responded Pisticci, as if it were not a rhetorical question. "But at least they are harmless right now. The young one probably has a broken arm. The older one thinks he may have fractured some ribs. . . ."

"And it does not surprise you that they have not begged for someone to set the bones?"

Pisticci blew out his cheeks and rolled his eyes, assenting. "In any case, they will be on their backs for a while. But if you are frightened or would like help, I will gladly spend the night here."

"You are a good friend. However, the Lord has helped me so far. He will help me now." She put down her wine. "Nevertheless, I have wondered lately, why is He testing me, always testing me, testing my limits? Sometimes I feel as though my strength must come to an end."

A crowd had gathered in front of Pisticci's café. A festive mood prevailed. Some of the townspeople had fashioned makeshift torches out of pitchforks and spades, swathing the metal prongs and scoops in oily rags and setting them aflame. Several men stood about in their shirtsleeves, though the night air was wet and cold. There were women celebrants, too, drawing their shawls close to keep warm. Children scampered under the legs of adults. On the edge of the crowd even Caterina, the gypsy bandit, and her lover, Carlo the Awful, prowled, eavesdropping on the conversations of others. Caterina wore a cape of rags, her face blackened with soot. On the end of a bit of rope, she dragged a mangy, hobbling, three-legged mutt. Carlo the Awful, an imposing wall of a man, with black hair down to his shoulders and an American baseball cap on his head, carried a tire iron in one enormous hand. They leered and guffawed, their eyes opaque as cats' eyes in the firelight, but no one paid them any heed tonight. Even the children ignored them.

Most of the villagers clustered around Pinuccia, a toothless old woman, virtually bald, who was reputed to possess the gift of the third eye. She spoke in a rasping tone, with the facial expressions and grandiloquent manner of a classic tragedian. Pinuccia had the story: ". . . And then, at last, he laid his hands upon her naked belly and said a prayer, or a blessing, or an incantation!"

"How do you know?"

The ancient tapped the middle of her forehead with her index finger three times, indicating the invisible eye. "Besides, Anna herself told me everything! She came to old Pinuccia to learn whether the blessing was a true one, whether the grace was good. I said it was. I could feel it, see it! I could observe her baby through the wall of her flesh, through the thickness of her womb, and he was perfect in every way. Normal. Healed, even handsome. Saved! His *pene* is already grown as big as *this,*" she said, holding one thumb aloft for everyone to see. "I could see it quite clearly. He will make many women very happy. . . . The priest has driven the devil right out of Anna—and out of the child. That makes two so far!"

"Two *what* so far?" a voice yelled from deep within the crowd. "Give me some room here, I can't catch a word."

"Two miracles! Two miracles that the priest has performed."

"Tell us the other miracle."

"He cured the mute, Isabella, after a fall that would have been fatal. He turned her back from the gates of death. She is awake now and almost recovered. Soon, I am convinced, she will hear, for the first time in her life. Then she will speak, astounding us all. Pinuccia knows: two miracles. This man is a *saint!*"

A gasp went up, spreading from those near the clairvoyant to those at the farthest reaches of the throng. "A saint!" Her pronouncement passed from ear to ear, from mother to daughter, from father to son, from sister to brother, from cousin to cousin, so that the sibilant syllables, endlessly repeated, sounded like air escaping from a gigantic rubber balloon. The gypsy Caterina and Carlo the Awful, uncomprehending of Pinuccia's words, but aware that they were participants in an event of magnitude, began to imitate what they heard on the fringes of the gathering, hissing through their teeth like a pair of snakes.

"*Sì!* Everyone, hear me! The signs point to it. I pricked a duck's egg and the yolk ran red. I milked my goat and the milk turned green in the pail! I cut off the head of a chicken . . . and it talked back to me! 'Pinuccia,' it cried, 'the time for killing is ended!' . . . This man has not only been revealed to us as a priest of Holy

Mother Church but, in my unmistaken belief, as a *saint!* . . . And if this is so, then he was sent to our village by God. He may even be," she caught her breath, "the Son Himself, returned to earth as promised!"

Another communal intake of air echoed up and down the street. "But wait! I am not finished."

"Now she is going to tell us about those who dropped from the sky," a woman with a wispy white beard predicted.

A hush descended. The children, running and playing, stopped in their tracks. Somewhere a baby cried, then fell silent. Caterina and Carlo tried to get closer to Pinuccia, and a few people in the back made way to let them through the crowd. Flames from the fiercely burning torches rushed, crackling, into the cold air. There was no other sound.

"The men who tumbled out of heaven tonight: You know, of course, that it was no accident either. It was not without divine significance. They are angels, almost surely."

At this, the collective gasp became a shrilling, as if the entire multitude might keel over at once, together.

"It seems likely . . . very likely," the old woman rasped, "that these men were sent here to aid the saint in his mission."

"What is his mission, Pinuccia?" the goateed woman coaxed.

Pinuccia's watery eyes glittered in the fire's glow. "Have the Last Days finally arrived? Is the Day of Judgment truly upon us?" She threw her hands open to the people. "Here my signals are cloudy. This has not yet been fully revealed. Perhaps he himself does not know and awaits his instructions. I have told you what I see."

"*È impossibile!*" a young man with slicked-back hair scoffed. "All of it. A good ghost story—but angels do not come crashing down to earth in flying machines."

"Who gave you the habits of angels to report to us?" Pinuccia inquired haughtily. "You are still a boy, silly and blind. Our Savior Himself may arrive aboard an ocean liner, or on a train, or a bicycle . . . or driving a truck! So why shouldn't His angels visit the earth in flying machines?" She paused to scratch her lower regions. "If Alphonse Fedelio could fly—"

The angel, Tuttobene, reached out to the table by his bed, retrieved the gun, and slipped it under his pillow.

"No sense," he said to himself, "in taking chances. With these hotheaded provincials, one never knows . . ."

. . .

In *il Papa's* dream, the monks with their spears chase him into Donna Lucia's arms. He is not surprised to be there. She shoves away his tormentors like a mother shooing so many naughty children, and then kisses him on the mouth. She touches his lips again and again with her own. She kisses his eyes, his cheeks, his high, moist forehead. She takes his earlobe into her mouth. She presses her lips to his shoulder, the crook of his neck. Her hands find the bare flesh underneath his garments; slowly, slowly, they traverse his hard forearms, his chest. She disrobes him, kissing his nipples, the palms of his hands. He does not protest. He catches her long hair in his hands. Still he utters not a word. "It is a dream," he tells himself, within his dream. "Therefore there is no reason to stop or to speak. A man cannot dictate his own dreams."

Donna Lucia thrusts the tip of her tongue inside his mouth, then lowers her head to kiss his stomach, his navel, the inside of his thigh.

"No reason to stop?" His mind whirls. "But to be faithful," he remembers, "means to remain true in the darkness to all that we accept in the light."

It does not bring the dream to a close. And when, finally, it ends, is so cataclysmic that it causes him pain, as if the forces of the iverse are pressing in on him . . . squeezing, tugging . . . wrenching out of him . . . the buried secret of his life.

)OOOOOO!" He purses his lips in amazement and some- e within him a window flies open.

"Alphonse who?"

The witch glared scornfully at the young man. "You were not even born on that glorious night when Donna Lucia's husband took off into the sky wearing nothing but his wings and her *sottovesti*."

"Her *sottovesti*? What was he doing in his wife's underwear?"

"How else would you have him dress for such a voyage? He said that it would bring him luck. Besides, another ounce of clothing and he might have plunged into the lake . . ."

"The man was crazy! We all knew it," another voice, farther back in the crowd, called out.

"But that Fedelio was a genius of his kind," Pinuccia objected. "A visionary!"

"Yes," an old man shouted. "Alphonse was my friend. I even helped him to undress for the flight and strap on his wings. Modern times demand modern miracles, he said to me. Perhaps he is angel now too."

A heated argument ensued with everyone babbling at once.

"Angels fly on wings!"

"Angels can travel however they please, even with cars ers!"

"Angels sleep in the clouds!"

"Angels sleep wherever they want!"

"Angels go naked!"

"Angels grow hair like spaghetti!"

"Or no hair at all. They can take any form th

"Angels!"

"Angels!"

"*Angeli e santi!*"

It was midnight.

· · ·

The renegade Pope slept deeply, una
elevated, somewhat.

XII

"WE HAVE NEW GUESTS," Donna Lucia repeated.

Leo had not heard her the first time, nor could he bring himself to look at her now. She opened the curtain a little. A shaft of morning sunlight shot across the floor.

"Guests?" He spoke with his head in the pillow. His bedclothes were damp. Leo felt light, as if filled with helium. He stole a glance at the woman and was startled, as well as perturbed, to discover that shame did not overwhelm him.

Donna Lucia came to the bed and placed her hand on his forehead. Warmth spread through his body. He tried to regret it, but could not.

"Your temperature is down," she said.

"*Una febbre?* Me?"

"You don't remember? You have been sick."

Relief washed over him. *Ah, the sickness must account for it: these unholy impulses, these dreams.*

"You are much better today." Leo watched her as she went around the room, straightening his shirt and trousers which hung over the back of a chair, wiping a table top, closing a bureau drawer.

Do not delude yourself, Bellini. It is not wholly the sickness. "Who are our new guests?" he said aloud, speaking as though having lived out the intimacy of illness here, he had acquired a proprietor's interest in the place.

She suppressed a gurgle of delight. "Last night, two angels fell out of the heavens from a helicopter and they are now asleep in the next room."

Leo raised himself in bed. "A helicopter? From heaven? What are you talking about?"

"*Sì.* One of the angels carries a gun, a long pistol. . . ."

He looked at her suspiciously. "I still must be delirious."

Donna Lucia sat down on the edge of the bed and put her small hand over his large one.

"I wish you wouldn't do that," *il Papa* said.

"This?" she asked, lifting her hand and smiling. He nodded. Suddenly her smile broadened. "I don't believe you with your wishes," she said, clamping his hand tightly. "Anyway, you are not delirious. But the angels are only the beginning. You have been declared a saint in your own lifetime! Last night there was such a commotion! The parlor is alive with them—"

He did not try to move his hand again. "Alive with angels? Donna Lucia, please . . ."

"Alive with people who want to see you. The two angels are down the hall—"

"Have you lost your mind or have I?"

"—with their broken bones," Donna Lucia continued, ignoring his remark. "Yes, and with firearms. So, as you can imagine, I am doubly glad to see you getting well. I need some protection."

She related the entire story.

The cloak of sickness was lifting. As his temperature dropped, sounds lost their sharp edges. Leo's head, which had felt like a ripe melon, shrank to its normal size and shape. His beard scraped the pillow. His bedsheets were gray with perspiration.

He was able to stay out of bed for longer periods of time. Now he sat for part of the morning and part of the afternoon in a chair by the window, listening to the life of the house. The atmosphere was charged. Leo's former peace was broken. He discerned new voices outside his door, through the walls. The "angels" at the end of the corridor whined for Donna Lucia, ceaselessly clanging a large bell that she had made the mistake of giving them. He saw the house as an insect mound, carved out of the earth, containing all their lives. He imagined other mounds the world over, containing millions more lives: the scurrying, building, destroying and building again, loving, trying and failing to love, and, against every obstacle, trying again. Amid the comfortable sounds of clanking pots, hurried footsteps, voices raised in talk, and the good smells of cooking, he drifted off in his chair to explore one last pocket of dreamless sleep.

Donna Lucia was producing immense, expensive quantities of food: sausages, preserves, cakes and cookies; dried fruits and nuts; greens, braised in broth; thick, fragrant slices of veal; rich soups in which floated fresh vegetables—onions, celery, tomatoes, and mushrooms. She set before him steaming plates of pasta: spaghetti, lasagne, tortellini, white noodles and green. In one day, Leo had linguine in a light butter sauce for breakfast, fettuccine with cream and onions and salad for lunch, and eggplant with mozzarella cheese and fresh tomatoes for dinner.

But rather than relishing this bounty, Leo was embarrassed by his convalescent's appetite and uneasy in the face of the sumptuous meals.

"Where does it all come from?" he asked Donna Lucia, as she removed a weighty tray of empty dishes from his lap. She shrugged. He persisted. *"Where?"*

"Pasta comes from flour, tomatoes from the vine, cheese from the milk of cows and—"

"You are teasing me again." No one had ever teased him this way, not since Cecilia was seven.

Donna Lucia set the tray down and turned to him. "You will howl when I say it, but I'll say it anyway. It's a miracle."

He stifled his exasperation. "I thought—I was sure—I thought I could count on your common sense, Donna Lucia."

"You don't believe in miracles, Padre, under any circumstances?"

"Yes, but—I mean—well, call it *buona fortuna,* call it unexpected graces—but I must maintain that there have been no miracles here! At least as far as my dinners go." He laughed ruefully, for he was less and less certain of his certainty, even in the matter of the food.

Cautiously, Leo got up from his chair and found that something—some inhibiting, interior membrane—had fallen away from him. He felt almost springy as he walked around the room, a human receptor through which unfamiliar signals coursed, the impulses faint at first, but growing stronger. He felt cleaner too, refreshed, as if he had sweated off internal poisons. He observed small details of his surroundings for the first time, signs of domestic neglect that had previously escaped his eyes: a bubbling and blistering of paint in one corner of the bedroom where the ceiling joined the wall; a hole at the base of another wall; a rip in the curtain.

With an unexpected twinge, *il Papa* noticed a cigarette burn on top of the bureau. Who had occupied these premises before him? He knew. Alphonse Fedelio, of course. Was this the room in which Donna Lucia's husband had constructed his flying gear? Had he set down his cigarette on the bureau, forgetting it for a moment too long while he pored over the fine geometry of his master plan? Alphonse Fedelio, Alphonse Fedelio. . . . How many wings did you discard before developing your perfect model? Was your workroom *filled* with wings? hanging from the ceiling? stacked in piles against the walls? propped against the window in layers so deep that the light of the world was shut off even from you, a dreamer?

"I am telling you the truth, as always." Donna Lucia spoke in her own defense, interrupting Leo's fantasy. "You, who tell the truth only once in a great while, cannot always recognize it when you hear it." She explained how the feasts came to pass. "A few days ago, while you were so ill, friends began to appear at my door with offerings. Now, since the 'angels' came, they are arriving with mountains of food such as I have not seen since my wedding day! If you knew my neighbors and their circumstances, you would have no doubt that it's a miracle."

He averted his face from her vituperation.

"I don't ask so many questions as you. 'Where did you get the cheese? What's in the soup?' I am simply grateful for the food. Perhaps 'good luck,' as you so cordially put it, is often the work of a greater power; therefore wondrous." She gave him a rather disapproving look. "How else could I feed a household of hungry men—not to mention offering refreshments to those people who wait in my living room downstairs?"

Alarm inched up Leo's spine. "Now that I am so much recovered, will you kindly explain who is waiting downstairs?"

"Practically the entire village."

"Why are they waiting?" he asked, although he knew the answer.

Her sigh was long and grave. "They want you to help them, naturally."

"No, this is unnatural," he said, surprised at the sounds of his own voice. He had not expected such a burst of fervor in his frail condition. "To purchase such food, they must have sold all their possessions . . ."

"They have no possessions," Donna Lucia said.

"Furniture, clothing, jewelry . . ."

"Jewelry? It is you who have gone mad."

"Lucia! These good people will believe whatever they want. When two fools on an outing crash their plane in the middle of town, it doesn't mean that we have angels in our midst. When one girl wakes up from a mild concussion and another from a nightmare, it doesn't make me a saint." Panicked by the recognition of what might lie before him, Leo's tongue ran wild. "Why, they even believe . . . your own husband! . . . abandoned you! . . . on *wings!*"

"Well, Padre, he did," Lucia Fedelio said quietly. "I too believe . . . that he did."

For a moment, *il Papa* was stunned by her conviction.

"Whatever you have to say to my neighbors downstairs, you will have to say it yourself," she went on. "But perhaps you should consider helping us, rather than rebuking us."

Leo withered before her suggestion. "Please understand. I am touched, I am moved beyond words, by the quality of your faith. But your faith in me . . . in *me*, you see—is misplaced. I cannot give all of you the earthly miracles that you, in fact, deserve. The jobs, roads, doctors . . . that only Rome's true miracle men," he said with unaccustomed irony, "can dispense."

"Much more may be within your power than you find convenient to believe," the innkeeper said huskily, as though her throat was choked with dust. "I will leave it to you. I trust that you will know what is best."

Il Papa washed and dressed studiously, drawing each activity out for as long as he could, washing his hands twice before he realized what he had done. As he regarded himself in the bathroom mirror, he decided on impulse not to shave. His beard had grown in thickly, several shades greyer than the hair on his head. Leo was pleased, but taken aback by his new appearance. He did not wholly recognize himself. Normally, priests were not permitted beards, but he determined, at least for the present, to maintain his masquerade.

Measuring the length of his tread, swaying ever so slightly, Leo left his room. Sickness had transformed him or, as it passed through his body and spirit, a process of unfolding had occurred. He saw that the door of the room next to his was ajar. Leo hesitated only for a moment, then walked in.

"What do you want?" Federico Ottaviani whispered, drawing the blankets closer to his chin in a protective gesture. In the adjacent bed, his back to them, Ugo Tuttobene snored spasmodically.

Il Papa approached Ottaviani's bedside, a smile playing at the corners of his eyes. "Just to see how you are getting on." His smile vanished almost instantly. Hanging from hooks, on the wall that faced him, he spied the tattered remains of their *carabinieri* uniforms.

Ottoviani's expression brightened. Had he finally found a friend? "We're better, thank you, but not too well." He glanced at Tuttobene, who stirred in his sleep. "Speak softly, please. My boss will be furious if he is disturbed."

"You had an accident, I hear," Leo prodded the young man.

"We did indeed!" Ottaviani tried to raise himself a little. Leo slipped one arm under the patient and helped him to sit. "*Grazie.* Yes, we were in an awful crash. How could you have missed it?"

"I haven't been very well myself."

"It was quite a landing—smoke and flames!—the ship was smashed to pieces. My boss blames me. He's very annoyed."

"Hasn't anyone come looking for you?"

"Not yet, sir, not yet. But I expect them before long." Federico Ottaviani stole another glance at his superior. Dare he say more? "I'll tell you," he went on, his whispers now barely audible, "it's *government property.* Pretty soon they'll notice it is gone, an expensive machine like that, and then they'll start searching."

Leo edged toward the door, having found out what he wanted to know. "The wheels of bureaucracy turn exceedingly slow," Leo whispered. "It might be weeks before your colleagues realize something's amiss."

"Sir?"

"I mean before they process all the papers, take an inventory of their aircraft . . . By then you may have figured out a good excuse for the theft."

"Sir?" Ottaviani stopped him. "My boss is a mean and nervous type. He'd have, excuse me, my *testicoli* for talking to a stranger."

Leo turned, startled.

"Oh, yes," Ottaviani nodded, "he's threatened more than once."

"Not a word. I won't breathe a word," Leo promised, closing the door securely behind him. So these were the angels—civil servants, policemen!

Il Papa walked to the end of the corridor and began to descend the stairs. "God help me," he implored as, taking three steps down, he bent over to survey, from this concealed position, his flock.

The sight that greeted Leo seized his heart. The small parlor, like himself, had been transformed; it pulsed with the life of a permanent campground. The front door was open and people spilled in from the road. Many of them had listened to Pinuccia the night before. Dogs and cats and even two piglets picked their way through the parlor. The smell of food and sweat was strong; human and animal voices swelled and ebbed. The expectation and the excitement were palpable, as though another larger presence—besides Leo and besides the throng—was hidden among them. The air outside was brisk, yet the sheer numbers within kept the house warm.

Leo could see each face clearly, as he was unable to do when crowds congested in huge St. Peter's Square: victims of poverty, accident, neglect, and centuries of inbreeding . . . club-footed, legless, armless, dwarfed, blind. He could not catalogue all the misery. Two Mongoloid children maneuvered their pudgy frames across the room, smiling benignly, hugging the adults indiscriminately, begging for sweets.

Through the open windows Leo saw that some of the sick had been carried into the street on beds and couches and homemade conveyances of many kinds. They waited there, patient in their suffering, to be delivered of their infirmities.

"Like an army," he whispered to himself, "a defeated army, they have surrounded me. If it is my destiny, I cannot escape it . . ."

. . .

The roadside *osteria* was empty, except for some old men who sipped from a bottle of cheap wine, and *il Papa's* pursuers—Ghezzi, Rocca, Pio, and Biondi.

Their clothing was dirty, stiff with sweat. Pio lit one cigarette with the glowing end of another. Rocca propped his chin on the heels of his hands, whistling tunelessly. Biondi worried an angry red pimple with a yellow center that had erupted in the fold between his cheek and nose. Ghezzi, restless, tipped his fork on its prongs and let it fall to the table with a clank, again and again.

He gazed at his companions and pondered their collectively regressed condition. "It is entirely possible," he thought, "that in our furious pursuit of him, the original motive of our mission has gotten lost, and we have finally come to this: pursued ourselves only by the notion of pursuit . . ." His thought slipped away, swept into the stream of his mind, from which he was unable to retrieve it. The priest put down his fork, picked up a knife from his place setting and ran the blade lightly over his fingers.

For a long time no one spoke—mired as they were in filth, exhaustion, and wonderment that deepened every day at the turn their lives had taken. Speculations overwhelmed and nearly destroyed them—deductions, hypotheses, theories, plans, formulations, solutions, arguments, and counter-arguments. Yet now, in silence, at the end of another day, set apart and bound together at once, the men loosed their separate imaginations on *il Papa*. But they shared an image, ghostly, of their prize: always obscured, in natural shadow, never seen quite clearly anymore by any of them: His features were blurred, without definition, as if submerged under water, but his face remained somehow illuminated from within.

All his pursuers held this vision in some form, unable to rout it from their brains. But it was not so strange, for what else mattered more at this moment? Whose light shone more brightly than his? And they followed his light, each in his own fashion . . . in rage, sorrow, puzzlement, frustration, in pity, and in self-pity, in hope, in faith. The priests, the bishop, and the brother-in-law moved inexorably, inevitably, in the direction of his light. . . .

Nevertheless, the feeling was upon all of them this evening, as common as the round table beneath which their legs met, that they had reached a desperate impasse. They would never find him. The Holy Father was gone forever—prey to some weird compulsion—to them, unfathomable, capricious, morbid.

Earlier in the day, Pio had suggested that there was no tenable way to proceed. "Notwithstanding our best intentions," he stated, "we have come to the end of the road."

"No, we have *not* come to the end of the road. An act of God will help us now," Biondi insisted.

But the others took no heart from his prediction. Wherever they went, whomever they asked, their questions remained unanswered. People stared at them blankly and shook their heads when presented with a description of Leo and his truck. Or the quirky little band was laughed at, ridiculed: Many villages had not seen an unfamiliar face, had welcomed no outsider except for the tax collector or the undertaker, in a decade. Some women nodded eagerly when presented with the details of Leo's appearance, but not because they had set eyes on him. "Oh, then he's good-looking! Is he married?" they wanted to know. "A little limp is no great defect. Is he in the market for a wife? A mistress? I have a daughter, a sister, an aunt, a cousin. My husband is dead . . .disappeared . . . decrepit . . . disinterested."

Ghezzi puckered his lips in revulsion before these recent memories. There seemed no sense of modesty, of dignity, of privacy, of moral order anywhere. As he traveled through the towns, Ghezzi held a handkerchief over his vulnerable nostrils against the stench of backed-up sewers or, worse, no sewers at all. He recalled a dwelling they had visited that morning, furnished with one cot and one stool with three legs. A shovel, an ax, and a hoe leaned against the far wall of the tiny room. A horse's harness was thrown over an empty sack that once held feed. Chickens roosted on a roof beam, staring down at Ghezzi. Four people lived there, on a dirt floor. A woman offered them coffee from a pot on a two-ring burner. She explained with pride that it was their new stove.

For no special reason, Ghezzi focused his attention on Pio Cavagna's right hand as it moved a cigarette in agitation from his mouth to an ashtray on the table, and back again. He waited, half-consciously, for the ash to fall and the cigarette to rest, so that he could examine the dirt under Pio's nails. They ignored hygiene these days, barely bothering to bathe. It seemed to Ghezzi that Pio

pointed chin. The second had ears that were long and straight like a rabbit's. The third was missing most of his teeth; his lips curled in over the void.

"... and so, as I heard it, once the man was revealed to be a priest, the angels fell to earth!" the man with no teeth exclaimed.

"They came in a bucket, the two together!" added the man with the hooked nose and sharp chin.

"What do you mean 'bucket'?" asked the one whose ears resembled a rabbit's. "Angels do not travel in tin cans."

"How do you know the way angels go around?" replied Hooked Nose. "Who are you anyway, *il Papa*? The story that I got from my nephew, who arrived here this morning from the village, is that a shining *silver* bucket came tumbling end over end out of the clouds and it landed—plop! plop!—" he slapped the palm of his hand on the table twice "—like that! In a ball of flame and bursts of white light, carrying two angels."

"And what about this so-called priest?" asked Rabbit Ears, who appeared to be the skeptic among them.

"He is not a so-called priest—he is a saint!" lisped Toothless, grandly. His listeners, including the table of eavesdroppers, murmured exclamations of disbelief.

"One becomes a saint only after an act of the cardinals confirms ... or some such ... Anyway, in my view, your whole tale, including the plop-plop and the ball of flame—"

"Don't quarrel about fine points and foolish definitions! Whatever you wish to call him—priest or saint or not—he is a holy man, someone very unusual. Already he has performed remarkable miracles," Toothless interjected.

"What kind of miracles, Carmine?" Rabbit Ears interrupted, ears twitching.

"The real kind. He saved the life of a girl who had been in an accident and given up for dead. He drove Satan from the womb of a pregnant woman. He cured a man's goiter and a child's warts by merely touching them. He can cause a chair," Carmine rattled on wildly, "or a bag of flour, or a two-hundred-year-old tree to disap-

spoke almost exclusively in profanities and blasphemies now, unmindful or uncaring or forgetful of the company he kept. Ghezzi watched, nauseated, as the bishop tugged and squeezed at his revolting blemish. Each of them was haggard, deteriorating in his own fashion: Biondi was bloated; the scar that divided Alfredo Rocca's face in half was discolored an ugly greenish-blue, and bits of grime had become embedded in the skin there. Pio's eyes were red, inflamed, as though infected, and he had developed an ominous, hacking cough from too much smoking. Francesco Ghezzi silently thanked God that he was not able to see himself, and assiduously avoided mirrors when he passed them, also panes of glass. He even sidestepped puddles of water for fear of catching a glimpse of his own wasted visage.

"We will return to Rome," Ghezzi said to himself, forming the phrase with his lips, kneading it like dough, examining its texture, its tenor, and timbre, its very substance. Although it was less than a fortnight since Leo had left the Vatican, the days stretched out in the monsignor's mind like a century of time. "For the sake of everyone, even for the sake of our church, we must return, return . . . return . . ." The word echoed in his head, chasing its own tail. He measured his companions one after the other, with an unreasonable quiver of anger. The anger sickened him physically.

"Shhh!" Biondi cautioned suddenly.

The others looked at him, empty-eyed.

"Shhh! Listen!" The bishop put a finger to his lips and cocked his head backwards, in the direction of the old men at a nearby table. Their conversation had suddenly increased in intensity and volume.

"What the hell?" Pio said, lighting yet another cigarette. He wheezed, coughed, and spat on the floor.

"Will you *kindly*? . . ." Ghezzi began, through clenched teeth. The thick little pool of phlegm glistened up at him like the eye of a blind man.

"*Per piacere!*" Biondi asked a second time. "*Listen.* Listen to what they are saying."

There were three men at the table. One had a hooked nose and

pear with just a glance of his eyes. He produces food from his sleeves, like a conjurer."

"That is exactly what he sounds like: a very good conjurer," Rabbit Ears ventured softly. "A fraud, perhaps a fiend, a circus performer." He reviewed the terms of the story. "First, from nowhere and for no earthly reason, a priest comes in the night. Then suddenly the whole village hails him as a saint. He heals the sick, makes the lame to walk, drives away demons, runs a kitchen out of his sleeves and pockets. For goodness sake! What does he bake up there, if I may be so bold as to ask? Did your nephew tell you that? *Amaretti? Biscotti? Ciambelle? Baba? Sfogliatelle* for all the little children? Eh?" The man was enjoying his monologue, the more so because his friends did not interrupt him. "Angels falling from burning cans? They cannot keep their balance, these angels? They cannot keep their seats? Answer me if you can, otherwise admit that either it is a mass delusion or simply that your nephew has gone berserk. Unless this sorcerer brings his act over here, we will have to die without knowing the truth. What do you say to that, Carmine?"

He raised a gnarled finger. "I say: *Remember Alphonse Fedelio!*"

That put an end to it.

Alfredo Rocca drove fast, taking the dangerous curves at a speed that made the tires of the small car squeal, and forcing the hearts of its occupants into their throats. They climbed into the hills.

"What dire fate have you in store for us, Alfredo?" Francesco Ghezzi inquired of Rocca.

"Another chance!" the bishop exulted silently in the automobile's back seat. "I knew it would come. We will see *il Papa* again! Thank you, Father!"

"I grant that He works in marvelous and terrible ways," Ghezzi continued, "but I cannot believe that He has brought us so far only to hurl us off a cliff. Can *you?* Alfredo! Can you believe that this is His plan?"

Rocca stepped sharply on the brakes, throwing everyone forward with a rocking motion.

. . .

Leo appeared on the stairs. When he descended far enough so that all could see him, a clamor went up and, just as suddenly, ceased. The crowd caught its breath: Here was the man for whom they had waited. Leo held his own breath, as if engaged in some sort of instructive, wordless dialogue with them. They were suspended in time, in this tiny parlor—all part of the greater world, so it seemed to him, yet each one separately distinct, unique. Anything was possible. He felt as though his limbs had no weight.

"My dear brothers and sisters, I greet you with love, from the fullness of my heart," he began, in the mellifluous tones of an orator, the tones in which he had been trained for so long. "I very willingly impart my Blessing to you, to your neighbors and to members of your families, and, above all, to the sick and to those who are suffering." The phrases were familiar; they had come from his lips in various constructions a thousand times before, and he too was comforted.

"The saint! Mama, will he float for us? Will he do the tricks now?" a little girl cried. She stood at the foot of the stairs. "Look at him, Mama. He is just like the picture of *il Papa* we have at home, except for the hair on his face."

Leo blanched, certain that the whole room must have heard the child. But nobody took up her remark.

"No, he will not float and there will be no sleight of hand," Leo said. A hubbub of protest grew. He bent his lips in a tentative smile, and raised his arms. "Now, all of you. Please, brothers and sisters!" He kept his arms raised until the people were still again. "I am a priest, not an illusionist! These are ill-conceived notions." He closed his eyes for a moment. "Let us not wait for the truth to find us. That will waste time. Let us go and fetch the truth ourselves. It must not be kept waiting another minute.

"I am no saint! The miracles of which you have heard, the miracles in which you want to believe . . . they did not occur." There was more stirring and whispered imprecations. "First of all, to be declared a saint, endless legal proceedings must establish beyond all reasonable doubt that at least *four* miracles are the direct result of intercession on the part of the person in question. So you see, you cannot all by yourselves declare—"

"Rules, rules, rules!" an outraged old voice cried. It was Pinuccia, so crumpled up within herself that she was practically invisible in the crowd. "Isabella—one! Anna—two! Angels—three! So?" she flailed her arms in disdain. "You need only one more. It will come. *Sì, sì!*" She pointed a bony finger at Leo, as though daring him to deny his divinity—on the basis of only one missing miracle—before all the assembled. "You hide behind law books, but you can't hide from me. *Pinuccia knows a saint when she sees one!*"

Leo did not really attempt to answer her twisted argument. "I am a simple priest, dear lady, and through the sacraments, empowered by Christ to administer in His name. I am only—" he hesitated, "—the agent." Leo halted again to allow his meaning to burrow into the crowd. "The agent," he repeated. "It is in this capacity that I have decided . . . decided to celebrate Mass for all those who wish it; to baptize those who wish it; and to anoint the sick." There was a smattering of applause that threatened to swell. "This does not mean—please do not misunderstand!—this does not mean that I have the power to cure." *Il Papa* offered a careful, catechetical explanation of the anointing of the sick, knowing in advance it would fall on deaf ears. "It is a sacrament of the New Law instituted by Christ to give spiritual aid and strength and perfect spiritual health—including, if need be, the remission of sins. . . . It is what I can do. All I can do."

A man's voice rang through one of the open windows. "But wait! But wait! We need explanations." He had dark, troubled eyes hooded by heavy eyebrows that grew over the bridge of his nose. His beefy arms, covered with carpets of silky black hair, held a frail child whose head lolled listlessly on his shoulder. "Tell us who are you and where have you come from. And for what reason? Tell us about the angels who came after you. . . ."

Leo's heart beat fast now, expanding inside his chest until it seemed to him to displace his lungs. "At some future time—some near future time—I shall try to deal with all your questions." But this was not enough; somehow he had to address himself more directly to their concerns. "I . . . I can assure you of this much: those men who . . . *fell* . . . into this village are mortals, I have satisfied myself of this. Not cherubim, not seraphim, but men. As I am, too, a man."

Leo waited for his audience to quiet down. "Enough, for now. Night is coming swiftly, and I want to offer Mass tomorrow morning. I shall hear your confessions at dawn. Meanwhile your church is a shambles, a ruin, unfit to welcome Him. We have to spend this night making it, and ourselves, ready." The word buzzed, like one more ascending question, around the room.

Donna Lucia was standing close to him. "Ready?" she echoed, "What can we do? What can these people do? Look at them, will you? In one night?"

Leo's eyes wandered over the gathering. It was true, they were, by and large, a sickly, unkempt, bedraggled bunch; yet the sight quickened his heart.

"Nevertheless! Donna Lucia! We must always demand of ourselves the unattainable, because however hard we try, we are still His unprofitable servants. No standard is acceptable, except the highest. Little has been asked of these fine people; so little has been achieved."

Deploying his forces, Leo became a whirlwind of dispatch. Not since leaving Rome had he moved with such decision. "Now you, Donna Lucia, you will bake the bread for the Host. Gather a team, bake the bread—it need not be leavened—and have it ready by morning." He scanned the swarming room. "Signor Pisticci, where are you? Are you here?"

"Here, Padre!" the café owner replied, waving a hand from the center of the crowd.

"Can you provide us with the wine?"

"Yes certainly, Padre."

"Good. As for the rest of you, all men and women able to work should return to their homes and bring with them to the church every hammer, every rusty nail, every scrap of lumber that they can reasonably spare." Leo's face flushed as he weighed the prospect of what he proposed, the grandeur of reconstruction. "Nuts and bolts, wrenches, saws, pliers, paint! Soaps and mops and buckets and brooms! We will work through the night and by daylight your church will be fit as a house of worship."

"With every hammer and saw and able-bodied man in the village—we still won't be able to do the job in a single night," the burly man at the window objected. "Forgive me, Father, but yours is the vision of a person who never turned a screwdriver."

"It will be imperfect," Leo said, his voice rising in challenge, "but it will reflect our intention. It will be good."

"It will be a failure," Leo's adversary continued. "One hundred men laboring night and day for a week could not shore up that wreck of a place."

"Set your mind and your heart on it and the rest will come. We must attempt. Follow me," he enjoined his flock.

"If we succeed, Father, then truly you will have worked the fourth miracle," Pinuccia pointed out. Her observation ended in a cackle and her eyes met *il Papa*'s with a mixture of reproach and affection.

He came down the stairs and was among the people. The throng stirred. "Now I must go to Guglielmo," Leo said to Donna Lucia, who stood beside him.

"Guglielmo's a drunkard and a slob," someone who had overheard protested. "He disgraces himself and will disgrace our effort too."

"If the commandments are to be taken seriously, we must acknowledge that all men are the children of a common father," Leo said, "Aldo Guglielmo is no exception. He should have the chance to help us."

Il Papa spoke to all of them now. "The gifts of divine grace are meant to be enjoyed without distinction. None should be denied their heavenly inheritance, except those who disinherit themselves."

"Aldo Guglielmo will only delay us by dragging his feet," another voice snapped. "The man we need now is that Fedelio fellow. Not much of a navigator, and as strange as a fish with feet, but a master craftsman if ever I saw one!"

Leo kept his eyes lowered as he began to make his slow passage toward the door.

Upstairs, Ugo Tuttobene and Federico Ottaviani lay in twin beds, side by side. "I still think it is incumbent upon us to reveal who we are and the nature of our search," Ottaviani ventured to his superior.

Tuttobene, his face contorted with pain, perspiration coating his upper lip, raised himself on one elbow and reached for the pistol, which lay under his pillow. "If you say it again I will take this gun and shoot you in your one good leg, *il mio amico*! Things could not be much worse."

"My mama says, 'Things could *always* get worse,'" Ottaviani said, optimistically, as he settled into his pillows.

. . .

"Guglielmo! Aldo Guglielmo! Open this door at once, or I will push it in!" The violence of his threat reassured Leo that he meant what he said. His shoulder throbbed with the imagined contact of flesh against wood.

In another minute, the door opened reluctantly. Guglielmo, clad in a threadbare shirt and baggy trousers, appeared even more sodden than the last time Leo had seen him, like a man just rescued from drowning. His complexion was grey, his lips cracked and pulpy, his cheeks sunken, his nose red, his hair stood up in greasy stalks.

"What can I do for you, Signor Ghezzi? What's the new emergency down there now?"

Leo pushed past him into the darkened room.

"You do live like a swine, do you know that?"

Guglielmo looked at his visitor uncomprehending, as though

trying to fight his way through fog. "Why—for God's sake— should it concern you how I live?"

"That's just it: For God's sake! The village needs you and you give nothing. All these years, *nothing!*" Leo paced the room, throwing aside Guglielmo's dirty bedclothes, opening and closing drawers, tossing their contents on the floor in a fury. He came upon a bottle of whiskey and a mug sitting on Guglielmo's rickety table. With one motion of his arm he swept them off. They fell with a crash.

"*Alt! Alt!*" Guglielmo cried. "What business is it of yours? How do you know, *uno-due-tre,* what the 'village' needs?" Guglielmo moved closer to Leo, seeming about to strike him, but then abruptly drew away. His thin chest heaved. "I am no worse a swine than most of them!"

"More is expected of you. More *was* expected of you upon your ordination. When the bishop pronounced the words, 'Receive the Holy Spirit,' there was a conferral of divine gifts, as you well know. It is no rite of mere human invention. Holy Orders is a sacrament administered by Christ our Lord. It is not a mantle that one takes up and puts down at will!"

"Who the devil are you to be telling me about Holy Orders? What gives you the right to break in here and throw your stuffy pieties in my face like confetti?"

Leo stopped in his tracks and faced him. "I too am a priest, Padre. A priest, your brother. This gives me the right."

Guglielmo took in the other man's words slowly. "You are a liar," he decided finally, but with less than absolute assurance. "What about those religious novelty items you mentioned not long ago? Pictures of the Vicar of Christ on watch faces, plastic relics . . ."

"I am a liar. I am also a priest. You, of all people, should realize that they are not mutually exclusive. And I am guilty of more than just mendacity. I know that too. Meanwhile, there is something else at stake—the faith of these people in themselves—and, to restore that, I need your help. I need the altar cloths, your vestments, if they have not rotted away. . . . Everything, anything."

Aldo Guglielmo drew back a step. "For what purpose?" He controlled his excitement. Scratching his arms and yawning boldly, he feigned boredom.

"Tomorrow I will celebrate Mass."

Guglielmo's lips parted. "I do not believe you. You're an imposter."

"Believe me. I will celebrate Mass in the morning. I will hear confession. I will baptize. But first, tonight, with your help and with the help of the people of the village, we shall transform that place into a church worthy of the celebration." Leo drew himself up. He looked down on Guglielmo. "Will you supply me with what I need?"

Guglielmo gazed at Leo for a long time. *Il Papa* returned Guglielmo's curious glance unopened, like a sealed envelope. Finally the spoiled priest disappeared into the blackest corner of the room. Leo remained still, afraid to stir or make a sound. A match was struck; Guglielmo lit a stubby candle on a shelf. He hovered near a cumbersome shape, as tall as the room, pushed against the wall.

"Come here," he commanded Leo.

The floor creaked under *il Papa's* feet. He examined the shape in the gloom. It was an old-fashioned wardrobe, secured with a brass clasp.

"Open it. Go ahead."

Leo did so, undoing the clasp with hands that shook.

Inside, the chest was lined with cedar. The vestments, shining gently like forgotten treasures, hung neatly on their hangers. Although in places the silk had worn, the colors had faded, they were remarkably intact. Leo sought for green, the color of spring and renewal, but found as well white, for purity; violet, for penance; red, the color of fire and blood; and black, for mourning. Draped over other hangers were the white linen amice, the alb, the cincture, the stole, the humeral veil—the whole priestly wardrobe.

At last *il Papa* closed the chest, with care, as though anything but the most soft touch would insult its contents. "It is all better, so much better, than I could have hoped," he said, chastened.

"It's better than *I* could have hoped." Aldo Guglielmo took a deep breath. "They were at the church when I arrived. I checked over and over on the inventory that had been left for me, but nowhere did these magnificent vestments appear." Guglielmo bowed his head. "I was never really worthy of my vocation, even before I came here. . . ." He cast his eyes at the wardrobe. "But I have taken care of everything, as best as I could. I think now that, after all, you may be the one for whom I was waiting."

"You were waiting?"

Guglielmo did not reply. "Let me take you to the church now," he said. "The tabernacle, the chalice and paten—everything else is there."

XIII

"THEN WHERE IS EVERYONE?" Francesco Ghezzi demanded of Franco Pisticci.

"I told you. At this late hour, people are asleep," Pisticci lied. "Permit me to observe that this is a rather curious time of night to come into a town, looking for some friend or other you claim to have lost—or misplaced."

"It is not so late. The village is virtually deserted," Ghezzi said, his eyes narrow slits. "What has happened here?"

"Nothing, nothing at all, Signore," Pisticci averted his eyes from Ghezzi's steady glare. "These tales that you have heard are the innocent inventions of old men. I cannot imagine how such quaint rumors start. Saints, angels—it's all no more than a joke to me."

"Can it," Pio advised him bluntly.

Biondi and Rocca studied the café owner as if he were a regional artifact or a face torn from an old book of drawings. "We do not mean to be intimidating," the bishop apologized.

"You're not," Pisticci replied, affably. "I myself am from the city originally, as you gentlemen must be. Beneath these rough garments, beats the heart of a civilized man. I love my neighbors dearly, but I pay no attention to their nonsense. I accept *none* of their peculiar visions, not for a moment, not a word. As I say, this place is as quiet as a cemetery. As usual. Perhaps you have the wrong address?"

Leo XIV's pursuers and Franco Pisticci sat at a table in his café. It was close to midnight. They had been haggling for nearly an hour.

"Let us return once more to the person in question," Ghezzi went on between his teeth. He wiped his brow with a red checkered napkin. "The man we wish to locate."

"And I must ask you again: Who is he? Who is this man? I cannot even begin to search my brain until you give me some decent clue."

The monsignor spoke irritably. "What do you mean 'Search your brain'? 'Decent clue'? How many strangers do you see here each day? This region is not quite a . . . a resort colony, after all."

"It might have been," Pisticci replied, offended. "If luck had gone our way. And we do get our fair share of visitors. The views, you know, the climate. You would be surprised."

"I would be, indeed."

"So then, who is this fellow you're after, and why?"

Ghezzi, Biondi, Cavagna, and Rocca exchanged agitated glances.

"He is a man quite important . . . high up . . . very high up . . ." Ghezzi cast about feebly.

"High up as an angel?" Pisticci teased, stalling for time. "Does he practice incantations, abracadabra?" His mind raced up the mountain toward the church. How could he keep these men at bay long enough to get word to the priest that he was being hunted?

"Signor Pisticci, do not toy with us. We are all exhausted," Ghezzi was saying.

Pisticci's mind switched directions and raced down the street toward Lucia Fedelio's inn. The priest would not return at least until after Mass tomorrow morning; meanwhile, Donna Lucia herself, when she came back from the church, could be trusted to keep her own counsel. Besides, what else was there to do? "Let me show you to some rooms in a clean house down the road," he suggested to the men. "What you need is a good night's sleep."

None of them denied it.

The unmistakable odor of freshly baked bread perfumed the air, but the house was obviously empty. Only a single light burned in an upstairs window.

"You see?" Francesco Ghezzi whispered as they entered, "There is no one here either."

"It is odd, I'll admit," Pisticci mumbled, bumping around against doorframes and walls in a half-hearted attempt to find a candle or a lamp. The longer he kept them in the dark, both figuratively and literally, the better.

Ghezzi sniffed like a bloodhound, wiggling his great nose. "Your neighbor seems to have baked bread enough for a regiment and then disappeared from the house," he said.

Rocca watched Pisticci light a lamp. "In view of all the unsavory rumors circulating, are you perhaps not uneasy?" he asked.

"Someone must have taken ill," Pisticci said. "Donna Lucia Fedelio, who runs the inn, is a ministering angel to this little town."

"Ah ha, another angel," Pio muttered, returning from the kitchen. "She ministers apparently to those who have become ill from starvation."

Pisticci wheeled about.

"The whole town has to be starving, I mean to say." Pio continued. "There's not a scrap of bread in there, just piles of crumbs. She must have taken it all with her, in gunny sacks."

"Well, yes . . . yes. Not starving, but . . . well, they look forward to it. Donna Lucia gives gifts of bread to the people from time to time. It's her lifelong tradition. . . . She never disappoints them. You see, she is even out now, after midnight, still making her

rounds. Let me show you to your rooms," he added, before anyone could respond.

"*Per piacere,*" Biondi replied. He had collapsed in a chair.

Ghezzi was peering into all the nooks and crannies, as if he might find *il Papa* hiding in the shadows. "But you are not the proprietor of this place," he said to Pisticci over his shoulder, closing the door on a cabinet that contained some dishes and cups. "What makes you so at home?"

"We don't stand on ceremony around here. Donna Lucia will welcome some paying guests for a change."

"An angel indeed," Pio ventured. "Who else accommodates guests that don't pay? And delivers bread before sun-up."

Pisticci mounted the stairs from which, hours earlier, the Primate of Italy had addressed the villagers. "Princes and beggars are the same to Donna Lucia," the fat man called down, lumbering up the steps ahead of them, his voice a hollow echo in the stairwell. "Popes and paupers . . ."

Federico Ottaviani crawled back into his bed. With one hand he held his broken arm crooked to his chest.

"So?" Ugo Tuttobene demanded, fingering the pistol that now rested beside him on the blanket. "So what did you find out? What was all that commotion earlier? Whose voices did I hear downstairs?"

"I don't know what happened earlier. But there are some men here now, sir, and one of them is your friend, the priest, Monsignor Ghezzi."

"*Ghezzi?* No, it is impossible."

"I saw him right in the middle of the parlor, sir, quarreling with that fat man who helped carry us up here after the accident."

"Are you absolutely positive?" The senior officer's tone grew weaker. "From where did you observe him?"

"From the top of the stairs," Ottaviani responded, gazing at his superior. "I did exactly as you instructed. I went to the top of the stairs and looked down. Those *were* your instructions, weren't they? And there was Monsignor Ghezzi."

Tuttobene closed his eyes and folded his hands across his chest. "This is the end," he murmured. "He cannot find us here. Under cover of darkness, as soon as they go, *we* go. We must escape."

"I can't run, sir. I'm in too much pain."

"Then I will go myself. How much worse luck could I have alone than with you?"

Ottaviani drew a long breath. "Sir, I think you ought to know: They are not leaving the house. They're on their way upstairs right now. I think they plan to stay here for a while."

. . .

"Be careful, up there," Leo cautioned from the ground. He and two other men steadied a tall ladder at its base while another scaled it to the top, swiftly, like a fireman. They labored by the light of several torches that were planted in the hard earth. The ladder was old—as precarious to negotiate, it seemed to Leo, as a wire stretched not quite taut. It sagged visibly as the climber made his way along the rungs.

Leo had organized everyone into work crews, and he went from group to group offering advice, support, assistance, and encouragement. When the first man arrived on the roof, his team cheered. Leo smiled, tested the ladder to see that it would not slide, and walked inside, satisfied.

The interior of the church blazed with hundreds of candles: long tapers and short, sputtering stubs. He saw them as hundreds of industrious fingers, filling the sanctuary with a new, natural radiance. The stone altar gleamed in the candlelight. Leo limped slowly down the center aisle to the transept, his leg responding to the damp night air. All around him he heard the mumble of voices, the steady rasp of saws, the banging of hammers against wood, the slap of paintbrushes, the chipping of knives into brittle plaster.

—

What had begun for him as a night of hard labor and—once more—a crazy reach into the impossible, had now taken on the quality of mirage: His clothes were covered with mud and grime; plaster, sawdust, and flecks of white paint dusted his hair and face. Earlier, he had slipped from simple weariness to insupportable fatigue; but now, well after midnight, buoyed on a wave of fresh energy that surprised him, he felt as though he could go on forever.

Il Papa got down on his hands and knees holding a big, prickly pad of steel wool. With rapt attention, he examined the floor for bad spots. The steel hairs cut his fingers but he applied himself mightily to erase the damage and the dirt of years. His idea—rather his single-minded intention—was to shellac the floor; but first he prepared it to receive the gloss, stroking the wood hard with the round, bristly wire puff. Then someone handed him a scraper. The sight of the thick, gracefully curled shavings he raised with it gave him physical pleasure. Leo gathered a handful of the pink, moist, sweet-smelling ribbons and held them to his nose, inhaling the fragrance that had lain, buried for so long, just beneath the rot.

. . .

"*Idiota!*" Francesco Ghezzi hissed. He was clad in a demure costume: his thin cotton vest, long blue blanket wrapped about his middle, mud-caked black shoes that poked out below the blanket's hem.

Ugo Tuttobene tried to submerge his head in the pillow, but, immobilized by his bruises, he succeeded in hiding only a cheek and an ear. The other cheek was ashen. The deputy commissioner seemed to have lost the power of speech.

"So you are the good angels! Hmm! Why should I be surprised?"

"What did we do good?" Federico Ottaviani asked hopefully.

"*Idiota!*" Ghezzi roared again, this time at the younger man. "In the last day, news of your—words *escape* me!—news of your miraculous arrival on this planet has spread out in a radius of at least fifty kilometers." He waited for the import of that to explode in their weak minds. "Who stole your halos, gentlemen?"

Tuttobene and Ottaviani exchanged frightened looks. It dawned on both of them at once that the little monsignor wound in the blue blanket had retreated into a world of his own devising.

"And angels of the lowest order!" Ghezzi went on. "Oh, how disappointing! After such a fuss, such a storm, such an upheaval of the general population, I was certain that at least archangels would await us here."

Ottaviani shook his head glumly at Tuttobene. Tuttobene delivered an obscene gesture to Ottaviani.

"Tut-to-*be*-ne here. He is Ot-ta-vi-*a*-ni," the deputy commissioner said to the priest, enunciating each syllable as if talking through a tube.

"And I am the Queen of England and this is Buckingham Palace! *Idiota!* Pio Cavagna was right, as much as I hate to admit it. I should never have placed that telephone call. It was wishful thinking, incorrigible optimist that I am . . ."

Tuttobene's voice shook—a compound of anger and anxiety. "We have sustained an accident, Francesco, unfortunate, and unforeseen. We have been confined to this room for days." He sought a way to dramatize the enormity of their plight. "We have been reduced to *urinating in saucepans.*"

"I am not conducting a confession! I do not want to hear every disgusting detail!" Ghezzi stormed. "Go no further, I warn you."

Tuttobene rolled around his bed, in a frenzy of self-justification. "I beg you, Francesco, to extend to us simple pity. We are in great distress. Our bones and our spirits are shattered. Sweet Mother of God, we may die here. . . ."

"What makes you think so?" Ottaviani asked him, appalled. "I only have a broken arm!"

"You both deserve no better," Ghezzi thundered. "To die and be buried here, on the side of an unnamed mountain, with a rock for your coffin pillow. It would befit your rank imbecility." He took a deep breath. "The worst of it is the helicopter. What were my very last words to you, Ugo? Who gave you permission to help yourself to a helicopter?"

"Permission?" the police captain shrieked louder than the monsignor. "How could I request permission? Did you yourself not swear me to secrecy?"

"After all, with *il Papa* kidnapped . . ." Ottaviani interjected in impulsive support of Tuttobene.

Ghezzi hitched and tightened his long blue skirt. "Nothing of the kind. *Il Papa* was not kidnapped," he said.

Ottaviani began to wheeze and pointed at the deputy commissioner. Tuttobene surveyed the ceiling. "But he *told* me! . . . Mary and Joseph and the saints in heaven! . . . He told me!"

"I cannot help what he told you," Ghezzi replied, almost casual. "It was only a white lie—"

"A lie is a lie. O God! Who cares about the color?" Tuttobene wailed.

"If every person who told a lie, my young friend, were to gain ten pounds," Ghezzi went on in Ottaviani's direction, "the streets of the world would cave in and all of humanity would plunge into the center of the earth."

"Was he killed?" Ottaviani whispered. "Has *il Papa* been taken from us?"

"Only God knows that," Ghezzi responded.

This time it was Tuttobene's turn to spring to Ottaviani's support. "The boy is beating down death's door—to say nothing of myself—and you tell him, 'Only God knows that'? We have both been presented with engraved invitations to the gates of heaven— we who were ready to give our very lives in service to the Church, *your* Church—and you have the callousness to stand there and proclaim 'Only God knows that'?"

"All right, all right," Ghezzi waved a naked, skinny arm irritably. "He has been here for days."

"Here? For days?" Ottaviani choked. "Oh no, Padre, that is in error, for *we* have been here for days."

"For days, *sì!* Locked in a room, pissing in soup bowls!"

"Francesco, you *are* insane," said Tuttobene somberly. "And extremely insulting to boot."

"Not insane, no. *Il Papa* is here—somewhere—I am sure of it. The Holy Father has been living in this village—perhaps in this very house—right under your noses! *Idiote!* Defectives! Were you born without a sense of smell?"

A wan smile broke out on Federico Ottaviani's face. He raised his head off the pillow. "Well, as my dear mama often says, 'In life, it seems that, in the end, everyone winds up in the same place.' " Then, all of a sudden, the young man's face went grey. "Oh no," he announced in a high, strangled whisper. "You don't think . . . could he . . . could *il Papa* have grown . . . a *beard?*"

. . .

The almost narcotic aroma of the shellac rose, shimmering, from the church floor. Most of the townspeople had returned to their homes for a few hours' rest, dispersing in quiet groups of twos and threes. Some of the stronger men remained. It had been their plan, and they had promised Leo, that they would work with him throughout the night. But finally even they succumbed to the combined effects of the fumes and their own weariness, and lay fast asleep in twisted positions on the pews.

Il Papa, on his knees, applied himself to his task with a vigor and urgency that increased the more he abused his body. His neck, arms, and back were cramped in knots. Shall I ever walk upright again? he wondered, almost amused. Shall I always slump, turned inward on myself, a question-mark of a man? Will I have to stand on a box tomorrow to be visible above the altar?

In the pure quiet of the church his paintbrush made a steady swish against the wood, like a sleeper breathing, dreaming. He advanced across the floor by inches. Some of the candles began to flicker, then dim.

Leo's lungs burned, as if seared by fire. Stripes of white-hot pain ran lengthwise in his chest. His mouth and nose were raw. In his temples and the back of his head, it felt like guns were going off. Fatigue stenciled fine lines around his lips and under his eyes.

He moved his arm in wide, sweeping arcs over the floor, pausing every now and then to examine his progress. But as he worked, his strokes became shorter, until eventually they were no more than mere flicks of the wrist. At last Leo grew perplexed by this fore-shortening; he picked up his head and turned around.

"Ahhhh," he murmured as he realized the nature of his predicament: He had, quite literally, painted himself into a corner. He was trapped on a little island at the edge of a shining shellac sea. He turned the can of varnish so that he could read the instructions on the wrapper. The stuff required at least four hours to dry thoroughly. "I see," he sighed, awed rather than dismayed by his miscalculation. It was only a trial of limited duration.

Leo stood up. Little by little he became aware of sounds within the silence. He perceived the shifting of wood deep in the bowels of the church as a sort of contented groan that rose to envelop the room and its occupants. Overhead, he heard the scraping of sharp claws on the roof, moving hurriedly—some nocturnal creature off on an urgent errand. Outside the wind blew, stirring up a leafy rustle of the trees. A bird cackled, assaulted in its perch by the strong breeze, then just as suddenly, was still. One of the men in the pews called out in his sleep, thickly, as if his tongue were a wet rag: *Mi è stato rubato il denaro!* Another man, his head thrown over the back of a bench, made sucking noises like an infant.

Trapped in his corner, Leo began to feel pins and needles attacking his legs. He transferred his weight from one foot to the other, shut his eyes, and took leave of time as he drifted off, semi-conscious, half-asleep. Like a sailboat moving on the water, its prow bumping and slicing through small waves, he encountered stray images.... Cecilia approaches, begging him to return to the farm.... Monsignor Ghezzi, in Leo's bed at the Vatican, devours a pile of pancakes made of chestnut flour, pine-nuts, and currants, *il Papa's* favorite delicacy. He sees only Ghezzi's back; the plate rests on his pillow as though it were a tray.... Leo swings the censer over an altar in an unfamiliar church; without warning, it bursts into flames and the sleeve of his robe catches fire....

He opened his eyes again. The lids were leaden. He could no longer support the strain of standing. With extreme care he lowered himself and sat down, crosslegged, in his tiny space. He manipulated his brush in a circle, tidying the shoreline of his isolation. When satisfied that he had done all he could, *il Papa* closed his eyes again, his head resting awkwardly on his shoulder, with the can of shellac beside him, its bittersweet vapors mingling with his sleep.

In the grey, frigid dawn, a voice that called him from a distance roused Leo. He peered, blinking, into the early morning light. A figure at the door to the church beckoned him, repeating the name by which he had become known among the townspeople in a high, frantic whisper.

"Father Ghezzi! Father Ghezzi! Come quick, I have a message!"

Leo got to his feet with difficulty. His joints seemed frozen in place, either from the cold or overwork. His toes inside his shoes were like ten stones. He wiggled them in an attempt to restore the circulation. His bladder was full and hard and painful.

"Padre, hurry. I have an important message."

Leo was about to take a step, when he remembered the reason for his confinement. He hesitated, surveying the scene from his peculiar mooring. The floor's high gloss did not reveal whether it was wet or dry, and he had no idea how much time had elapsed since he had fallen asleep. "I can simply walk on my toes," he said to himself, "and later return to touch up the marks." Yet he was loath to make a move.

He crouched, knees cracking, and felt the floor. But his fingers were still too tacky with shellac to convey any certain information. "Ah well," he breathed, "so be it." Taking the can and brush, he made his way with a gentle tread over the freshly varnished surface that shone like a still lake under the moon.

The young messenger handed the priest his morsel of paper.

Leo leaned against the closed door of the church, reading the message it contained. The air, although biting, invigorated him, cooled the parched membranes of his lungs. His breath issued from his mouth in a whitish fog.

Il Papa pondered the note that Pisticci had scrawled. His chilled fingers curled around it like pink claws. ". . . wears heavy glasses . . . scar across his face . . . one is fat . . . another lean . . . a chain-smoker . . ." The words danced before his eyes, jumbled. He stared at the paper that fluttered in his hands in the haze of dawn, like a dying butterfly.

Leo composed a terse reply of his own. The boy carried it off in his head: *Distract the men as long as possible. Keep them away from this church until I have fulfilled the promises I made. I can tolerate no inter-ference.*

Even as he spoke the words Leo suspected that they would not satisfy Pisticci. Questions of identity would nag him: Who are the hunters and whom, really, do they hunt? But he could not tell Pisticci more without telling him all.

"And I have come too far," he remarked, "to surrender myself to them now. Not yet. I have come too far for that."

· · ·

"He was in this room? You *spoke* to him?" Ugo Tuttobene shrieked.

"Lower your voice," Francesco Ghezzi commanded. "It isn't six o'clock yet. You'll wake the others."

"Where was *I?*" Tuttobene cried, in a whisper now.

"You?" Ottaviani asked, trembling. "You were *sleeping.*" He shrank into the pillows. "He seemed . . . he seemed such a nice fellow . . . so friendly. . . . O God! My mama always told me that flesh-and-blood was not fated to enjoy a moment's peace on this earth. I wish I was dead!"

"If only you had not lost your gun, *idiota,* I would make you kill yourself." Tuttobene lifted his gun in both hands. "But as God's avenging angel, I will gladly do it for you!"

· · ·

The confessional, a small wooden booth inside the church, was drafty. Leo shivered, blowing on his hands surreptitiously. So far, he had heard only the usual roster of unremarkable sins—yet to those who confessed them, they seemed grand enough to inspire guilt and the need for absolution.

"My name is Fredo. . . ."

"You must not tell me your name."

"No? These are the new rules?"

Although unable to see the speaker, Leo recognized from his cracked, quavering speech that he was no longer a boy.

"These have always been the rules. When was your last good confession?"

"I don't remember. Maybe ten years ago. Frankly, Padre, I can hardly recall what I did yesterday. My memory is not what it used to be. Thoughts slip through my brain these days like *lire* through the fingers of the rich."

Il Papa was growing edgy. For well over an hour he had been listening to penitents, several of whom wanted to recite the whole history of their lives. Many more waited outside for their turns.

"Suppose, then, you begin by telling me why you have stayed away from confession for such a long time?"

"Eh? I can't hear you."

Il Papa raised his voice. "Is that better?"

"No, I just can't hear you! If you don't believe me, then let's change places and see for yourself. Otherwise, speak up!"

Leo raised his tone still more, forming each syllable with emphasis. "Please tell me why you have stayed away from confession for such a long time."

"No confessor. No church. That *donnola* Guglielmo—"

"We are not concerned here with Aldo Guglielmo's alleged shortcomings, but only with our own."

"Mi scusi." A short silence followed. "I am starting to remember what I wish to say."

"Yes?"

"I broke the Sixth Commandment. I'm a married man."

Il Papa yawned in spite of himself, feeling the toll of the long night's work overtake him again. Sometimes, it seemed to him, the Sixth Commandment had been given by God for the express purpose of sending men quietly to confession.

"Would you like to tell me exactly how?"

"No. But I will anyway. I broke it with the wolves."

Leo's interest was somewhat rekindled, but his tone remained even. Decades spent in the confessional had prepared him for the most bizarre of tales. "Did I understand you to say . . . with animals?"

"Not just any old animals, Padre. Not with bitches, or goats. With the wolves—real beauties, hard to resist! You can't really blame me, now can you?"

"We do not assign blame here." Leo paused. "Are wolves actually found in these hills?" he inquired almost innocently.

"I don't know, Padre," Fredo answered, irritable. "Maybe they're porcupines. So what? My eyesight's not much better than my hearing. Just let me explain. You see, I myself turn into a wolf every once in a while. I run with the pack in the hills, at night, under the stars."

"You feel that you become one . . . with the wolves?"

"I'm sure of it." Fredo's thin voice shook with indignation. "It runs through my family like a streak. My father was this way and his father before him and his father before him, and so on. I'm Fredo Ippolito, and it's an old Ippolito custom."

"No names, please." Leo waited for the old man to go further. He did not.

"After ten years, you have nothing more to confess?"

"Isn't it *enough*? What else do you want? I have run with the wolves perhaps five hundred times. I am not a young man, you know." He lapsed into a long, evaluating silence. "But other than this . . . Yes, I would say, in all honesty, other than the wolves, I am spotless."

"Spotless? For ten years?" Leo rearranged himself on the bench and shrugged somewhere between amusement and astonishment. It did not appear to puzzle Fredo that he could be a man and an animal at once. This duality seemed almost as natural to him as the sun rising and setting, as angels falling from the heavens, as a saint driving into town in a pickup truck. He was governed, ultimately, by nature, not religion. Capricious, hostile, often incomprehensible, nature was nevertheless, for him, divinity.

"Quite spotless? You are certain?" Leo inquired a second time, when the man did not speak.

"*Sì.* A good father to twelve children, a good husband, aside from the wolves, a good lover to my wife—at my age!"

"It is all commendable. But nothing else troubles you—nothing that you may find painful to tell me?"

"You think I am hiding something, Padre?" Fredo asked testily.

"Not at all. However, I want you to be satisfied with your confession, to be able to go in peace."

"To rest in peace? I'm not dead *yet,* my friend!"

"To *go* in peace," Leo called.

"Oh, I see. Well, I tell you I have made only one little sin. Doesn't this interest you enough to absolve me?"

"Listen to me. It is not only *one* sin that you describe—"

"The Sixth Commandment, that is all," Fredo said stubbornly. "The other nine—never."

"But a commandment broken again and again: Each time you violate the law of God." There was no response from the other side of the grate. "Promise me something . . ."

"Speak up, you're fading out again!"

"Promise me that you won't run with the wolves anymore!" Leo shouted.

"*Non capisco.*"

"If the wolves—or the porcupines—offer an occasion that, for you, is ripe with temptation, then remove the temptation," *il Papa* enjoined him loudly, "and you will no longer have reason to break the commandment."

"*Non capisco,*" Fredo repeated, sullen now.

"It is what is called 'an occasion of sin'—"

"Ah, *sì*," the old man said. "*Sì.* I will tell my girlfriends what you say, but they will not be happy with it. May I have my penance now, Padre? My knees are sore. I am not used to this position."

"How long has it been since your last confession?" Leo inquired of the next penitent, a woman with a gruff voice.

"Never been at all," the woman said.

"Never?"

"No sir, this is my first time out."

"Why have you never been?"

"I'm Jewish: Luria's my name. We go back to the fifteenth century."

Leo sighed. "Then what are you doing here?"

"They say you're a holy man. I don't sneeze on that. Besides, the way I look at it, sir, it all goes into the same pot, no?"

. . .

"No, I disagree," Alfredo Rocca remarked, patting his mouth with a napkin. "Drink is not the worst." He stifled a belch, folding his chin into his neck. "There are three ways that a man can *totally* ruin himself: Gambling, women, and farming. I'm certain of this, because my father chose the most boring way—but he spoke affectionately of the other two."

"Would you object, Capovilla, if we turned our attention to more pressing matters?" Monsignor Ghezzi asked his colleague.

The band of four men and Franco Pisticci, gathered around a table in Pisticci's café, had just consumed a meal of spaghetti and wine, although it was still early morning. To detain them, Pisticci had hit on the diversion of some hot food—and spaghetti was the only dish he knew how to prepare with style. Wine, another inspiration on his part, while at first resisted, was soon imbibed. Only Ghezzi fought against its soporific effects. He gripped the table as an alcohol stupor spread throughout his brain. Succumbing to Pisticci's hospitality—which he now perceived as the plot it was—had made him furious with himself. "Where is he?" Ghezzi demanded, as nausea threatened to unleash itself on his stomach. "Don't force me to plow the same damn field all over again!"

"Ah, yes," Pisticci replied, as relaxed as Ghezzi was enraged. "You refer, I take it, to our theoretical miracle man."

"*Theory* has no place in our discussions. We have already discovered your angels, so there is no way to continue to conceal your 'miracle man.' I happen to know he's here. One of these 'angels' had words with him."

The café owner did not blink an eye. He poured more wine for everyone, the perfect facsimile of a courteous host. "Two things stand out in my mind: Whoever you may be, you are *not* the police. And whatever he may be, he is *not* a criminal."

"He is a moral criminal," Rocca broke in, encouraged by drink to extravagant statement. He wagged an index finger in the air. "A betrayer of his own . . . !"

"Why should I believe you?" Pisticci asked, interrupting Rocca's outburst. "As far as I know, this man has hurt no one, perhaps he has even helped many."

"Ah-hah! '*This man.*' Which man?" Rocca stormed, swilling wine and breathing into Pisticci's face.

Pisticci put out his hands in a gesture of ignorance. "Only you know who you're looking for. You persist in not confiding in me. If this man is a murderer, even wicked in some lesser way, I might then appreciate your plight. However, all you have told me is that he is 'up, high up' and that you believe he may have lost his mind. But how can I be sure? And what crime is it to step down out of one's mind? How can I be sure of anything? It could be you who wish to injure *him*."

. . .

In the stretcher, the grandmother's eyes were closed, her mouth pinched into a shriveled "O," her breathing punctuated by low, moaning whistles. Her white pate reminded Leo of a skull.

Kneeling, he placed a vial of oil on the ground beside her. Two candles in glass cups rested near her head, their flames whipped by the breeze. The front doors of the church hung open and some of the congregants watched from the threshold.

Il Papa touched a small crucifix to the lips of the dying woman. She did not have enough strength to kiss it. Then he took a piece of cotton soaked in oil and administered the unction on the woman's forehead and hands. *"Per istam Sanctam Unctionem et suam piissimam misericordiam adiuvet te Dominus gratia Spiritus Sancti, ut a peccatis liberatum te salvet atque propitius allevet."*

. . .

"Everybody up! We must get organized," Francesco Ghezzi admonished the men. Their response was disheartening to the priest. Biondi gazed at him with bloodshot, uncomprehending eyes. Pio Cavagna lit another cigarette. Frustrated, Ghezzi swept his arm over the table, upsetting a wine glass and, inadvertently, hitting Alfredo Rocca in the face. Rocca looked up, startled, having fallen into a doze.

"Gentlemen! Let us pull ourselves together. The time has come—for action!" Nobody moved.

But Franco Pisticci had trouble preventing the muscles around his lips from relaxing into a broad, satisfied grin.

. . .

With the fluid movement that came from a lifetime of genuflecting Leo bowed before the altar. He turned, facing the assembled congregation. There were no empty seats. To his delight he spotted Aldo Guglielmo, standing, by the door.

"In the name of the Father, and of the Son, and of the Holy Spirit."

"Amen."

"The grace of our Lord Jesus Christ and the love of God and the fellowship of the Holy Spirit be with you all."

"And also with you."

. . .

"*Caffè!* Pisticci! Hurry now. *Caffè* all around," Ghezzi called to the fat man, who lounged at the door of the tavern, his back to the four of them. The priest was not sure what their next move ought to be; only that he himself somehow would have to devise it.

"Hmmm?" Pisticci murmured, his eyes upon a distant point. The town was still.

. . .

". . . Blessed are You, Lord, God of all creation. Through Your goodness we have this bread to offer, which earth has given and human hands have made—" Against his will, Leo stole a glance at Lucia Fedelio, who sat in the front row. Her eyes glistened—with tears, he thought. ". . . It will become for us the bread of life."

"Blessed be God forever."

. . .

"Drink, Capovilla, all of it. There, that's a good fellow." Ghezzi propped a mug of steaming coffee and milk against the priest's lips. Rocca sipped twice, winced, sipped again; a thin stream of brownish liquid dribbled out the corner of his mouth and down his chin.

"You're getting it all over him," Pio Cavagna pointed out, unnecessarily, as he rose to join Franco Pisticci at the threshold of the café.

"I can *see* that," Monsignor Ghezzi murmured. "Anyway, mind your own business. I'm not getting it all over you."

Looking away, Ghezzi observed the bishop, hands in his lap, staring blindly into his own cup of coffee. "Try a little, Lo Bianco," he coaxed, in a tone coated with honey and venom, humiliated before Pisticci that he was obliged to wheedle his companions like nursery-school children. "You'll feel ever so much better." He put the coffee cup into Biondi's hands.

"No, I can't. I'm much too ill, Fran—Della Chiesa," the bishop grimaced. "It'll come right back on me."

"Drink it, you elephant. Just *swallow!*"

. . .

Leo poured the wine and a little water into the chalice, saying quietly: "By the mystery of this water and wine, may we come to share in the divinity of Christ, who humbled Himself to share in our humanity. Blessed are You, Lord, God of all creation. Through Your goodness we have this wine to offer, fruit of the vine and work of human hands. It will be our spiritual drink."

"Blessed be God forever."

"Lord God," Leo continued quietly, "we ask You to receive us and be pleased with the sacrifice we offer You with humble and contrite hearts." He washed his hands, saying, "Lord, wash away my iniquity; cleanse me from my sin.

"Pray, brethren, that our sacrifice may be acceptable to God, the almighty Father."

The congregation responded, valiantly if raggedly, passing the few Missals along the rows.

Carlo the Awful and Caterina sat to one side, hoarding a Missal between them. Carlo held it upside down. Caterina's dog, seated on her lap, nibbled at one corner of the book. Leo looked up and, seeing the dog, said to himself, "Human beings are not the only ones here who are hungry."

"May the Lord accept the sacrifice at your hands for the praise and glory of His name, for our good, and the good of all His Church."

. . .

The five men stood on the sunny street before the café. All at once, the sky turned leaden and fierce. In Biondi and Rocca—both shaken, dizzy with drink—the abrupt change from light to dark produced a primitive foreboding.

"What shall we do now?" Pio asked wryly, his question echoing in the quiet road. "Shall we search every house in the village from top to bottom?"

"If it comes to that, yes," Ghezzi said, face burning, head bursting, limbs twitching restlessly as a racehorse.

Pio's eyes wandered down the road, his gaze saw everything, absorbed nothing. "Look, we're pretty certain he is here. So why not just wait? He will appear sooner or—" A familiar sight snapped his sentence in two.

At first, familiar as it was, he could not place or name the apparition. Shock gave way to surprise, then awe, at last supplanted by a curious dread. *"Santo cielo! . . ."* he breathed. There, not twenty yards away from Pisticci's café, protruding from behind a clump of chest-high, scrubby brush, was the front end of Pio's truck. No mistaking it: the dangling headlight, cracked windshield, missing license plate. About to cry out his recognition, he thought better of it, and held his tongue.

But Cavagna might just as well have screamed, or sang. For his sudden silence spoke louder than any sound, and Francesco Ghezzi, alerted, followed Pio's line of sight. The coffee had only mildly improved his state of being. The landscape wavered before his eyes.

"My God. My *God.* Cavagna! Is that it?"

Pio nodded, said nothing, somber, grim.

"Cavagna? *Speak to me.*"

. . .

Leo raised his arms, hands cupped. "Let us proclaim the mystery of faith."

"Christ has died, Christ is risen, Christ will come again . . ."

. . .

"No!" Franco Pisticci roared, his voice bouncing off the faces of the buildings. "No!"

Ghezzi sprinted toward the vehicle, the haze and distress that had enveloped him minutes earlier now lifted.

Pisticci cursed himself wholeheartedly for neglecting this one most crucial detail: He could so easily have steered the truck to a safer hiding place. "Get back! Get back!" he bellowed, feeling foolish.

"There it is!" Ghezzi whooped, his voice breaking register like a boy's. "Mary, Mother of God! We have found him at last!"

"Alt! Alt!" Pisticci yelled, barreling after the priest. "That truck does not belong to you!"

"Maybe not," Ghezzi called back, pointing at Pio as he ran, "but it does belong to *him*." He reached the vehicle ahead of the fat man and rushed his way past the dry, scratchy brush. Laying his hands with sacramental tenderness upon the hood, Francesco Ghezzi prayed. But it came out crudely, ill-conceived, impaled as he was—skewered, in fact—on the sharp tip of glee: "O God! ... We have the holy *bastardo* now!"

. . .

"The Lord be with you."

"And also with you," the people responded.

"May almighty God bless you the Father, and the Son," he made the sign of the cross over them, "and the Holy Spirit."

"Amen."

"The Mass is ended, go in peace."

"Thanks be to God."

Lowering his head, Leo relaxed, his mind free of thought. He felt calm, cleansed, relieved.

Donna Lucia watched him. His complexion was waxen. His hands, with their long, elegant, sensitive fingers, trembled upon the altar. They recalled to her Michelangelo's famous sculpture, well-known from picture postcards, in which the Virgin cradles her son in her arms, his fingers caught eloquently in the folds of her dress. Her thought shamed her in the context of the service, but she was not able to banish it from her mind: She longed for this man at the altar to touch her that way, while she cradled his fine head against her breast. A flush began in her chest and rose until it engulfed her cheeks, setting them afire.

It was *il Papa's* intention to rest for a while in Aldo Guglielmo's shack, but to get there he had somehow to paddle through the river of worshippers. They were not through with him yet. Men and women sought to touch him, to ask for his blessing on the small religious trinkets they carried. Someone waved a medallion on a chain in front of his face. He recognized, with a start, that the poorly executed profile adorning the cheap metal was his own.

Trailing the saint they themselves had proclaimed down the center aisle of the church and then along the rocky path leading to Aldo Guglielmo's, the people called out their gratitude and sang hymns. A teenage girl fell to her knees, weeping, crossing herself with astonishing energy. Leo broke from the throng, brought the girl to her feet, and bade her walk by his side.

"*Santo!*" Children ran ahead, a tattered advance guard. "Watch out! Make way for the *santo!*"

Alone in the church, Guglielmo snuffed out the tall altar candle with a small metal cap affixed to the end of a long rod. He folded the altar clothes, and closed the Gospel Book. Raising the empty chalice, the priest stole a furtive glance about the sanctuary. "*Cincin!*" he whispered to the sky.

Leo sat for a while in Guglielmo's shack. The train of his followers had at last disbanded. They moved down the mountain in small groups, according to the instructions of their new savior, who asked them not to arouse the suspicions of the men waiting in the village below.

> "*Hail Mary, full of Grace!*
> *The Lord is with thee;*
> *Blessed are thou among women,*
> *And blessed is the fruit*
> *Of thy womb, Jesus.*
> *Holy Mary, Mother of God,*
> *Pray for us sinners,*
> *Now and at the hour of our death.*
> *Amen.*"

He said a decade of the beads, wrapping them around his thumb as he went.

Now the little room—gloomy save for a solitary candle burning in a corner—was cold. *Il Papa* opened his eyes and discovered Guglielmo's pitcher at his elbow. He put down the beads, helping himself to a quick, hot draught, then another. It revived his strength. Outside the window, the heavens were overcast, but a stream of sunlight poked its way through the clouds, fanning out over the ground. Next to the window, Guglielmo had strung an old round mirror on a length of twine. Leo looked at himself—the flesh of his face pearly, the beard grey, his eyes bottomless. He heard the echo of his heart.

There was a knock on the door, frantic.

XIV

"THANK GOD!"

"Always."

"*Mi scusi?*" She did not wait for an explanation. "I was afraid you would not be here."

"Where else would I be?"

"I brought you something." She produced a prosciutto sandwich on a hard roll and a bottle of red Gragnano. "Not exactly breakfast, but all that I could manage. I hope you're hungry."

"Ravenous. *Grazie.*" He bit gratefully into the bread, scattering crumbs. "The sacraments have a new effect on me. They make me want to eat." He removed the cork from the wine, found two mugs, and filled each one to the rim. "I feel like filling my belly." *Il Papa* sipped the wine. "Who knows but that I have always had a little hedonism in my heart?"

Donna Lucia nodded, then asked, "What is this 'hedonism'?"

"Oh, it's a . . . philosophy of pleasure, that pleasure is the first good of life. A hedonist is a person who enjoys food and drink— all the earthbound pleasures—perhaps too much for his own good."

Donna Lucia shrugged. "How much is too much?" she asked.

Leo smiled as he chewed another mouthful of sandwich. "So tell me, why is it that you could 'manage' only this fine prosciutto for my breakfast?"

Donna Lucia sat down on a low stool. "You seem tired." She chose to ignore his query.

"A man ought to be tired as much of the time as he can stand," Leo said. "Evil thoughts and acts are like weeds: They find fertile soil in untilled fields."

"I am to blame for your exhaustion. I should not have permitted you to leave your bed so soon." The sound of Leo's chewing came to Donna Lucia's ears as the crunching of dry leaves in a forest. "It's bedlam back there!" she blurted out, unable to defer the bad news any longer. The innkeeper did not pretend to understand why a posse of angry men had arrived at her house in the middle of the night, or the meaning of their hot pursuit of the defenseless priest, but neither did she care. Her only concern was that they did not catch him.

"You should go away for a day or two, at least," she beseeched Leo. "Franco Pisticci and I have devised a plan. One of his friends is on his way here, by a back road, with a car. He will drive you to another place, where he has a cousin. You can hide there."

"Why must I run?" Leo asked, although of course he knew why. "What's happened?"

"The men—those chasing you—have taken over the whole town. They've dragged the angels from their beds. One angel is sitting in the middle of the main street with a gun in his hand. Another man is guarding my house, with a *fucile* that he took from a neighbor. They are fully armed. No one is to enter and no one is to leave. . . . They lie in wait for you. They are interrogating everyone."

"They have no right!"

"Well, who will argue with pistols or rifles?"

"I cannot allow it to continue. Unless I put a stop to this lunacy, I could be responsible for . . ."

Lucia Fedelio was determined to detain him. "They are hurting no one, actually; just making a lot of noise," she said hastily. "In a day or so, maybe they'll grow bored with their games and go home. Above all, you must not surrender to them."

"I have neglected certain . . . trusts," Leo said.

"What's past is past. Your errors, such as they may be, are forgiven. The people venerate their saint."

Il Papa's eyes clouded. "The past is forever with us, Lucia. And how many times must I tell you? I don't want veneration. I regret being thought of as a saint."

"Perhaps it is out of your hands. What one wants and what one receives, they are not always the same. Love comes . . . or not, unbidden. Besides, those others hate you, whoever they are."

"They don't hate me. They bear me less ill will than I bear myself. Look, there is no further point in dissembling. I know who they are, and they know that I must return."

"Return?" Her black eyes burned with intensity that he could feel even in the gloom of Don Aldo's shack. "Did you escape from prison? I have often wondered."

"It was a jail without bars," he responded. "Although I see now, less confining than I made it."

"I do not understand."

"Nor do I—altogether." His voice trailed off and when he spoke again his tone was heavy. "I lived with it poorly, my confinement. But there is no creature on earth who moves without constraint. Who is not, in his own place, confined? Who, on this earth, has freedom? 'Free as a bird' we say. But even the birds fly in formation and obey the laws of gravity."

"You are needed here," Lucia Fedelio pleaded. "We accomplished more in a day and a night with you as our inspiration and our guide than we accomplished before in ten years."

"It was all of you who were my inspiration and my guide. For that, I am happy, and thankful. But now I must fulfill a prior obligation. I am needed elsewhere."

She grasped one of his hands in both of hers. "No. Nowhere more than here! Don Aldo himself came to the Mass. You may have delivered even him from his torment."

"If that is so, then I am grateful indeed." He spoke quietly. "But I have been given a cross, you see, that for a long time I was disinclined to carry. In these last few days, I have learned that my cross belongs to me and no one else—and that this destiny has a certain joy."

Her breath rose and fell rapidly. "You'll come back . . . soon?"

"Who can tell what twists and turns the future holds?" he said, moved by the gentle pressure of her fingers on his skin. "I will give you this promise: You and your neighbors won't be cheated of a true priest, whatever Guglielmo does or does not do, and you will have a church of which you can be proud."

Donna Lucia's eyes narrowed. "You are a friend of the wealthy and the powerful," she said, almost as an accusation. "Otherwise, how . . . ?"

"I have . . . connections," Leo admitted, "important connections . . . in Rome. I shall speak out in your behalf, in behalf of this town. You need a school and a doctor as well as an able priest. For these reasons alone, I must . . . go home."

"Let me go with you, at least for a little while, as your housekeeper," she said. "I will take Isabella . . . and we will look after you."

Leo shook his head. "This I cannot do . . ."

"I love you," Donna Lucia told him. There was urgency in her voice, but no desperation.

"I love you too." Leo did not hesitate to speak the words. For if he failed to say them now, he knew that he would have no second chance. They rolled off his tongue fluently, and he was amazed.

At his admission, her final reservation dropped away. She drew so close to him that their bodies touched. "Then why . . . ?"

"Sometimes people must leave each other *because* they love each other. Yet this love continues to exist—beyond the dailiness of our lives, beyond everything . . ."

"How can that be?" Donna Lucia asked, wishing to be persuaded.

"Only God knows. Just as only He knows what transpired in the church last night. And what happened in Isabella's sick room . . ."

She put her arms around Leo. He shook his head hard, as if to deny the power of his need.

"Padre?" A rapping came at the door. "Are you ready? We haven't much time." A car engine, tinny and rattling, could be heard in the distance.

"It's the driver. Pisticci's friend," Donna Lucia whispered. "He's here."

"Nothing ends," Leo promised her. "Life itself is an unfinished moment."

. . .

The crowd milled about in front of Lucia Fedelio's house, thinning out in places and bulging elsewhere, like a snake that has swallowed rats.

"Single file, please!" Alfredo Rocca instructed the townspeople. He stood at the door to the inn. Under one arm he cradled a shotgun.

"*Give* me that," Pio Cavagna said, approaching Rocca. "It could go off by accident. Then they'll scatter to the winds. We'll never keep them here."

Rocca clutched the weapon closer. "Monsignor Ghezzi told me it was mine to hold. I've got to maintain order. I may not hand it over without his permission."

"Since when do we observe formalities? You run a serious danger of shooting an innocent bystander . . . or shooting yourself in the foot."

"Don't worry. It's not loaded," Rocca confided under his breath. "Francesco took out all the bullets. . . ."

"He what?"

"They're in his pocket."

Pio started to laugh. "What's he going to do? Throw them?"

"All right, folks," Rocca called again, ignoring Pio's remarks. "Let's straighten this out a little! Single file, I say. And please try to collect your thoughts. Prepare to answer two simple questions: When was the last time you saw the magician and where was he bound?"

A soft mumble of protest went up from the crowd.

"He heals."

"He mends."

"He does not practice witchcraft!"

"To hell with all that!" Pio shouted. "Just try to remember: Which way did the stranger go?"

But the people's eyes were hard and their lips were sealed.

Ugo Tuttobene sat at the side of the road, legs splayed, in an armchair that had been dragged from Donna Lucia's parlor. His pistol rested, unattended, on its right arm. Stuffing from the cushion spilled onto the ground at his feet. "I'm freezing to death," he complained loudly to no one in particular.

"Freeze to death later!" Francesco Ghezzi emerged from the inn in time to catch the deputy commissioner's whining. "Get that chair into the middle of the street, Ugo! I told you twice already— in the *middle*. Don't you speak Italian?"

"I can't push the thing any further. It weighs a ton."

"Then kick it or drag it by your teeth, but get it out there!" Ghezzi ordered. "I don't want anyone walking away."

"What difference does it make? They won't talk anyhow," Tuttobene said. A faint smile tickled the corners of his mouth. "They're more loyal to their new saint than Catholics to the Pope."

The veins in Ghezzi's neck turned purple. "They'll talk, all right. Three of them are in there, talking already."

· · ·

Leo's fingers closed over the fisherman's ring, warm and weighty in his trouser pocket.

"Where does this path lead?" The car went slowly, creeping over the mounds and ruts.

"To the main road, the long way around."

"Take me there and leave me, *per favore*."

"Pardon me, Padre, but that is not the idea," the driver replied, discomforted by the request. "My orders are to take you directly to my cousin. No stops along the way."

"I am forced to change your orders."

"But I cannot leave you. Franco Pisticci would kill me." His eyes bulged at the thought of the big man's hands circling his throat. "Let you go off alone? Our saint? I refuse to do that, sir."

"Then if you truly want to help me, drive me into Rome."

As they drove away from the town and its people, from the church, from the woman, Leo weighed the presence of suffering in his heart. He was inspirited. Departing, he felt, too, the imminence of arrival.

And then Leo laughed. Laughter welled up from the depths of his soul in a rush, spilling out with a vigor he had once almost forgotten he possessed.

. . .

"Padre, stop!" *il Papa's* driver screamed. "Come back!"

They were halted in traffic on the outskirts of the city. The walls on both sides of the narrow two-lane road were perhaps eight or nine feet high. Grass and weeds choked the cracks in the crumbling, rough-hewn brick. This was the old Appian Way—the place where, according to tradition, Christ appeared to St. Peter as he was escaping Rome during Nero's persecution. But now, vehicles of every size and vintage sped in both directions.

Leo had bolted from the car and was bounding toward a bus a few yards ahead of them.

"*Grazie,* my friend," he called back, as the rear doors closed behind him."However, from here I will have to go on alone!" Belching smoke, the dirty green bus rolled off.

. . .

Carlo the Awful grunted affably, shifting from buttock to buttock on the small stool provided for his inquisition. Caterina stood beside him in Lucia Fedelio's parlor. Her little dog cowered under her cloak of rags, whimpering in fear.

The parlor was a symphony for the nose—sweat, animal urine, tobacco. Even Biondi had finally resumed his old habit, smoking. Billows of fumes issued from where he stood. He was questioning an old man dressed in the frayed vestiges of fashion: cracked leather shoes, threadbare black suit, soiled grey-white shirt. He was so thin that his wrists did not half fill the cuffs.

Federico Ottaviani had positioned himself at the door, arms folded across his chest.

"Perhaps they're deaf and dumb," Alfredo Rocca suggested to Francesco Ghezzi, turning away in disgust from the two gypsies.

"Just dumb. Leave them alone," Pio advised, grinding out a cigarette beneath his heel. "They're useless to us, they know nothing."

"Who says?" Carlo the Awful cried, offended. Spittle had hardened on his lower lip into a little white ball. Pio thought he would gag at the sight of it. "I'm ugly, not stupid. And I know what's what." His tone was wounded.

"So you admit, at last, to living in this town?" Monsignor Ghezzi came around to confront him, a wild light in his eye.

"We live nearby. In a cave," Caterina volunteered. She approached Ghezzi, her three-legged mongrel nipping at her heels.

"In a *cave* . . . ?"

"It's not bad. Warm in the winter, cool in the summer, easy to care for." She hesitated, thinking. "We know of this man you want."

"You have seen him?" Pio asked. Perhaps, finally, they had found two informers; and perhaps they shared with informers everywhere that quality of eagerness, of zeal, that would cause them to take on this pursuit as their own. In any event the gypsies were the first people to respond earnestly to their mission.

"This man has been living in the village for a while," Carlo said.

"So you *have* seen him then?"

"No," Caterina lied, recalling the Mass just ended. "We have not. We heard Pinuccia speak of him."

She and Carlo gazed around the room, dazzled by all the eyes upon them. Until now regarded by the townspeople as little more than animals, they had suddenly become repositories of vital information. They had no real intention of exposing the saint; nevertheless, they basked in their fleeting importance.

"Who is Pinuccia?" Ghezzi turned to Rocca. "Get that name!" he ordered.

At that moment, Biondi broke away from the faded old man he was cross-examining and summoned his companions. "This one says he is a man of medicine whose specialty is, ah, restoring the virginity of young women." Puzzled silence ensued. "The service is, as you might expect, costly, and since few in this region can afford it, he starves." When nobody spoke, Biondi went on. "He guarantees his work for seven days and seven nights."

"Better than the real thing, probably," Pio allowed, "if you have the pocketbook for it."

"We have not convened to gather peasant folklore, gentlemen," Ghezzi reminded them sternly. "What else does the old fellow know?"

"Not a blessed thing," Biondi sighed. "He says he has so little to eat that he spends most of his days in bed."

Ghezzi returned to Carlo, who had lifted Caterina's dog onto his lap and was contentedly picking at a horny scab on its back. "This Pinuccia . . ." the monsignor began.

"Pinuccia's a witch and a prophetess. She sees with three eyes. She claims to have seen the man you want," Caterina spoke for her mate.

Ghezzi fingered his nose, reflecting. It was impossible to know whether these people were to be trusted with their outlandish stories. "How did she describe him? What did she say?"

Caterina stuck out her tongue. Carlo screwed up his face. The mask of dirt cracked and brown dust fell from his cheeks. "*Sì*, I can tell you. I can tell you—everything. But what's in it for me if I do?"

Pio, who had vanished into the kitchen, reappeared. A long salami dangled from his hand. "This," he said solemnly.

Carlo's eyes bulged. Caterina kicked him in the shins.

. . .

Il Papa fished in his pocket for some change. He found two coins and fed them to the fare box. The collection machine whirred, hummed, clicked busily, and finally, with prodigious effort, spit out a little cream-colored ticket. The aisle was not crowded and Leo took a seat near the middle on the left.

Across from him, two American girls in blue jeans and sneakers chattered amiably. Earlier in the day, apparently, they had visited the Capuchin cemetery where the bones and skulls of four thousand monks decorated the walls and ceilings of five chapels. "Fantastic!" Leo heard one of them say of the baroque display. A young man farther back in the bus bit into an apple, making satisfied, wet sounds. A woman with a triple chin and a plastic bag of groceries, slept. On the seat in front of him Leo discovered a copy of *Il Tempo*. Scooping it up, he buried his face in its pages: A guerrilla war was being fought in an African nation; a general strike of postal workers and bank tellers throughout Italy was called for the following day; a famous movie star was dead; prices continued to rise all over the world. On the third page, a box caught his eye:

POPE IMPROVES

Rome—The Vatican announced today that Pope Leo XIV will not offer his traditional Sunday blessing in St. Peter's Square. He is still suffering from the effects of influenza, although his condition has improved considerably.

Leo gazed out the window of the bus. Night was falling. In the distance, the Arch of Constantine came into view and, looming beyond that, the high, ragged edges of the Colosseum, the "gladiator's bloody circus."

Il Papa descended from the bus, obliged to transfer to another.

"Dove l'autobus per il Vaticano?"

"Right here, sir. Just stand behind me, on this line. It's the Number Seventy-seven. It'll take you right there."

"Grazie," Leo said to the boy.

The Piazza del Risorgimento, ringed mostly by banks—Banca Commerciale Italiana, Banca Nazionale del Lavoro, Banco di Santo Spirito—was lit as if for a festival. At this terminal stop for city buses, the scent of diesel fuel lay in the air like soup in a dish. Leo hurried across the piazza—his head down—and along the outside of the great Vatican walls. Passing St. Anne's Gate he looked up briefly, nodding to the young Swiss Guard in blue cape, beret, and ankle-high black shoes. Directly across the street a store selling "Souvenirs Religiosi" was already shuttered. A light rain had begun. He moved through the human wave—the priests, the nuns, the seminary students, the tourists—that poured out from between Bernini's columns. In the middle of St. Peter's Square, he paused to glance up at his windows in the Apostolic Palace. A light glowed in his bedroom window, beckoning.

"Are you sure you want to go up?" the ticket seller in St. Peter's basilica asked, scratching his scalp as he totted up some figures on a scrap of paper. "The roof closes in fifteen minutes."

"Fifteen minutes is more than enough." Leo tugged at the brim of Pio's hat, bringing it low over his eyes. He ran a hand lightly over his cheeks and chin as if to touch his beard for the last time.

The man in the ticket booth took Leo's money. "Very well. Wait around the corner. The last elevator will be down shortly."

A steep stairway spiraled upward between the inner and outer domes. The passage was so tortured, so tight, that the walls curled like the inside of a tube. There was space only for a single man.

Winding his way up the narrow, circuitous steps, Leo could feel the walls closing in on him—yellowed walls, illuminated by bare bulbs, etched with ancient and modern graffiti in all the tongues of the world. His footfalls clanked on the iron steps, echoing up and down the empty chamber.

At last, perspiring and short of breath, he arrived on the circular balcony outside the lantern on the top of St. Peter's. The city shone at his feet, refreshed by the shower. A full moon, partly obscured by clouds, bathed the sky in a milky light. Leo removed the fisherman's ring from his pocket and slipped it on his finger. Out of another pocket, he brought the rosary. "Hail Mary, full of grace, the Lord is with Thee . . ." Full of grace. Full of grace. The idea rang within him again and again, pealing like a bell. What heavenly grace overflowed into the world!

· · ·

Somewhere in the night, over Procida—the wildest island in the Bay of Naples—Alphonse Fedelio ascended lightly and swept over the clouds, his wings describing wide, sloping arcs as he tested the winds, the prevailing currents and, satisfied that they were good, marked his course. Then, at last, after his long and mysterious passage, he nosed his craft in the general direction of the tiny village of T———.

A NOTE ABOUT THE AUTHOR

Celia Gittelson was born in New York City, where she
now lives. She was educated at Bennington and
Sarah Lawrence.

A NOTE ON THE TYPE

The text of this book was set in a computer version of
Garamond, a modern rendering of the type first cut in
the sixteenth century by Claude Garamond (1510–1561).
Garamond was a pupil of Geoffrey Troy and is believed
to have based his letters on the Venetian models, although he introduced a number of important differences.
It is to him we owe the letter which we know as old
style. He gave to his letters a certain elegance and a feeling of movement which won for himself an immediate
reputation and the patronage of King Francis I of France.

Composed (CRT) by American–Stratford Graphic
Services, Inc., Brattleboro, Vermont.
Printed and bound by The Haddon Craftsmen, Inc.,
Scranton, Pennsylvania.

Designed by Judith Henry